AND THEY WERE NEIGHBORS

ALSO BY BRENNA BAILEY

Juniper Creek Golden Years Series
"I Want to Hold Your Hand" (short story)
A Tale of Two Florists
Of Love and Libraries
Wishing on Winter
Forever in Flowers

AND THEY WERE NEIGHBORS

JUNIPER CREEK ROMANCES
BOOK ONE

BRENNA BAILEY

BOOKMARTEN PRESS

Published by Bookmarten Press

And They Were Neighbors

Published by Bookmarten Press
PO Box 27033
Calgary RPO Tuscany, AB
T3L 2Y1
contact@brennabailey.com

ISBN (eBook): 978-1-7382941-3-8
ISBN (paperback): 978-1-7382941-4-5
ISBN (large print paperback): 978-1-7382941-5-2

Manufacturer details:
Copytech (UK) Ltd, Trading as Printondemand-worldwide.com
15 Culley Ct, Bakewell Rd, Orton Southgate, Peterborough
PE2 6XD
United Kingdom
gpsr@podww.com
01733 237867

EU GPSR Authorised Representative:
Easy Access System Europe Oü, 16879218
Mustamäe tee 50, 10621, Tallinn, Estonia
gpsr.requests@easproject.com
+358 40 500 3575

Cover design by Yummy Book Covers
Edited by Jessica Renwick

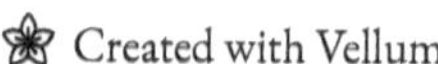
Created with Vellum

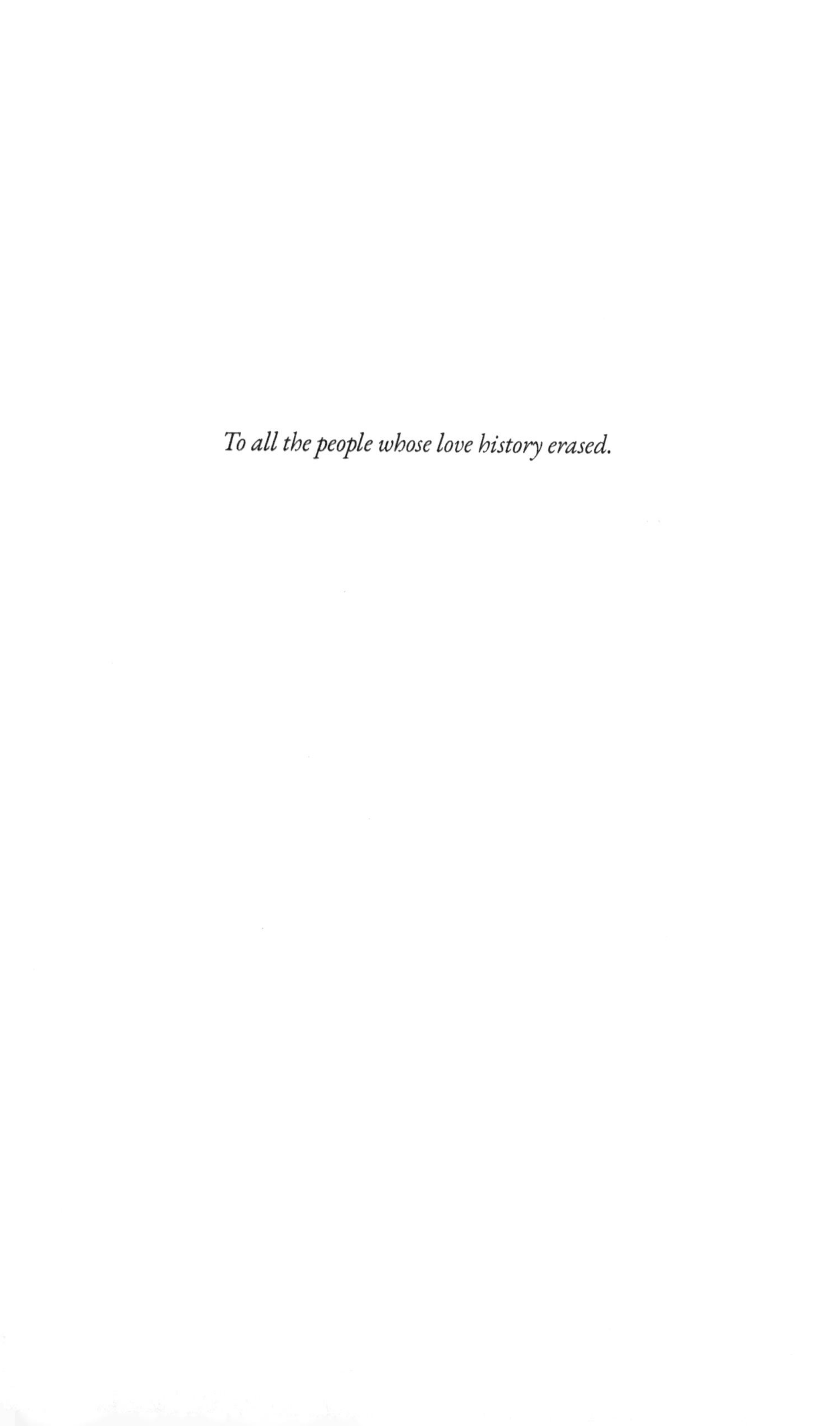

To all the people whose love history erased.

ONE

MINA

Mina Hasanza hefted the comfort basket in her arms, feeling slightly ridiculous. "You want me to take all of this?" she asked Vera, her employer and self-appointed mother figure.

They stood by Vera's car in front of the grocery store where they worked. Mina had just finished her shift for the day.

"Yes," Vera said firmly. "I know you won't tell me how upset you are, so I pulled together enough to cover all the bases. I hope. And if you need anything else, all you need to do is ask."

"Okay. Thank you." Mina was grateful her arms were full so she didn't have to awkwardly hug Vera. Not that she didn't appreciate the gesture. She did, more than Vera probably knew. But Mina didn't feel the need to sulk or eat tubs of ice cream or watch cheesy movies or whatever else people did when they got broken up with. She didn't know how to tell Vera that although she was upset Christian had left her—especially the *way* he had left her, discarding her as if she were common loot in a video game—her greatest emotion regarding the breakup was relief.

Pure, unadulterated relief.

The feeling confused her, and she hadn't known what to do

with herself since her boyfriend of nine years walked out their front door three days ago.

She'd gone about her life as usual since then, going to her shifts at Juniper Foods during the day then going home to make herself dinner and play *Elden Ring* online with Declan, her best friend back in Ontario.

It didn't even feel out of the ordinary for her to be by herself since Christian hadn't been home for two-thirds of the year anyway. And when he had been home, he'd been locked in his office in meetings, or he had to drive to work in Vancouver.

The breakup hadn't changed much at all, and yet it had changed everything.

"Why don't I give you a ride home?" Vera asked. "Then you don't have to walk the whole way with that thing."

Mina's instinct was to say no, but she knew it would hurt Vera to deny her help. Vera's child had recently left for university, and it had seemingly thrown Vera into *extra care* mode. "Sure. Thanks."

She inspected the contents of the basket as she sat in Vera's passenger seat on the short drive back to her townhouse. Chocolate bars, cookies, face masks, a couple of books that looked like romcoms, a journal and a pen, a pack of positive affirmation cards, a cozy blanket, a box of tea. Vera truly had covered all the bases. Mina's eye fell on one more thing she'd initially missed since it was tucked behind the blanket.

A candle. The label read A Cozy Library Nook and it was from Bell Lights, Mina's neighbor's small business. For some reason, out of all the items in the basket, the candle cheered up Mina the most.

"Thanks again," Mina said as she exited Vera's car once they had parked in front of her townhouse. "For the ride and the basket."

"Of course. I care about you, Mina."

Mina didn't know what to do with that, and she turned away before Vera could see the tears welling in her eyes. She waved and walked up her front steps, and her throat grew thicker as Vera stayed in front of the house until she got safely inside.

She hugged the basket to her chest for a moment then set it on the floor at the bottom of the stairs. Zelda, her black cat, approached to sniff it. "This is mine," Mina said, running her hand down Zelda's silky back. "Don't chew on anything, please."

She went upstairs to change into her gray sweatpants and a hoodie—the one that said "Ew, David" that Declan had got her for her birthday last year.

Work had tired her, so she went downstairs and pulled out one of the frozen lentil stews she had prepped and put it on the stove to heat for dinner.

She leaned against the counter to wait, and her phone vibrated. Her family text thread popped up to show a photo of both her sisters and their spouses smiling at the camera, a table in front of them overflowing with what looked like expensive food. Farrah and Yasmin both wore perfect makeup, as always, and their long dark hair hung around their shoulders.

YASMIN

Hope you all are having a good dinner too!

BABA

Look at my beautiful girls!

Mina tried not to roll her eyes. Of course her sisters would need to share a photo of their fancy dinner with everyone. They regularly filled the family chat with gorgeous selfies and news of their accomplishments, while Mina stayed quiet. She didn't have much to share.

And she knew her father didn't mean to exclude her with his comment, but something twinged in her chest, nonetheless. *My beautiful girls.* Mina was one of them too, technically, but she hadn't lived with or even near her family for so long that she didn't feel like she belonged in the same way anymore. Even when she did visit, a gulf had opened between them that seemed impossible to cross.

That gulf had been part of the reason she'd left in the first place, attending university all the way across the country to escape the relentless pressure from her parents.

FARRAH

Wish you were here, Mina! We miss you! Hope you're having a good day.

Mina raised an eyebrow. At least Farrah made the effort to include her. She'd always been closer to Mina than any of her other family members, maybe because she was nearer to Mina in age than Yasmin, and because Mina had often been dragged to Farrah's swim practices—with their nanny, of course. Their parents had been too busy doing whatever they did as lawyers to chauffeur their children around.

The next text made any sense of belonging Farrah had given her fly out the window.

MAMAN

Mina, have you and Christian booked time off yet to come for Christmas?

MINA

Not yet

MAMAN

We can pay for the flight out for both of you.

MINA

I know, I'll ask soon

Mina sighed heavily. In general, she didn't enjoy family gatherings. They were opportunities for her mother to compare her to her sisters and tell her everything she'd done wrong or hadn't yet done right. And if she went for Christmas this year, things would be even worse.

She hadn't told her family that Christian had left. Once she shared the news, she'd be the target of even more scrutiny because her parents loved Christian. He was well dressed, he had high ideals, he was financially stable. He worked as a management consultant for a renewable energy business and was trying to save the world, for fuck's sake. What parents wouldn't like him?

But he'd left Mina, not even giving her a solid reason for it. *I got promoted,* he'd written in the letter he'd left her. *They're moving me to Texas.*

He'd packed his stuff and gone while Mina was at work. She'd arrived home that evening to find a note on the kitchen table, half of their closet empty, Christian's office cleared out, and most of his knickknacks gone from their shelves. He must have taken the whole day to do it, which meant it'd been planned.

And he hadn't asked Mina to join him. He hadn't mentioned their nine years together. He'd just left.

She didn't know how to tell her family that, so she hadn't. And she planned to keep it that way for as long as humanly possible. Probably until her mom called and gave her a stern talking-to because Ava Hasanza did not yell.

Mina tried not to think about her family or Christian anymore as she ate dinner. Once she was done, she pulled out the samovar her maternal grandparents had sent her from Iran. They'd sent each of her sisters one as well—a beautiful set of three.

She scooped her favorite fragrant tea leaves straight into the strainer and added two freshly crushed cardamom pods, a few dried rosebuds, and two threads of saffron.

After setting the samovar to boil, she grabbed her plate to put it in the dishwasher, and movement outside her window caught her eye. Zoey, her neighbor, was cleaning up her dinner in her own kitchen. Their townhouses faced each other with only a narrow strip of grass between them.

Zoey looked over for a second, loose strands of brown hair framing her face from where they'd escaped her ponytail, and Mina waved. Zoey's answering smile filled her with warmth.

Without fail, every time Mina and Zoey made eye contact through their kitchen window, Zoey would smile at her. Such a small thing made her oddly happy and eased the tension in her body. Zoey had always had that effect on her, even though they barely knew each other.

The image of Zoey's smile lingered in her mind as she finished the dishes, poured her tea into a clear mug, then settled on the couch, her legs pulled beneath her. Hints of rose, cardamom, and saffron wafted over her, and she closed her eyes to revel in the scents.

When she opened her eyes, the first thing she saw was the box on the table in front of her. She frowned.

Yesterday, she'd gone around the house and collected everything that reminded her of Christian: framed photos of the two of them, papers he'd left lying around, a pair of pajama pants she'd stolen from him, the bear he'd won for her at the fair on their third date, the scrapbook filled with their memories she'd gifted him. She didn't need his stuff anymore, but she didn't know what to do with it, so it sat here in a box.

She'd probably throw it out eventually.

Now, she threw her phone across the couch then went upstairs to her desktop and opened Discord. Even though Declan still lived in Toronto, and Ontario was three hours ahead of British Columbia, he was online playing *Helldivers 2*. Somehow, he managed to thrive on four or five hours of sleep, and Mina was grateful for that today. She didn't usually play shooter games by herself, but she enjoyed playing them with Declan.

And tonight, she would love to shoot alien bugs and robots.

TWO

ZOEY

Zoey Bell stood in the middle of the flower shop, fairy lights twinkling on the walls, and raised her glass of champagne in a toast. "I'll be honest, when Adi started working here, I had doubts. But he proved himself talented at working with plants, and he's got a brain for business."

Adi, the lanky dark-haired Indian boy—*man*, now that he was eighteen—standing by the front desk ducked his head and looked at his shoes. His girlfriend, a pale redhead named Aisling, nudged him and grinned.

Zoey continued, "He's also funny, and he filled many of my days here with laughter. I'm sad to see him go, but I know he's got great things ahead of him. He just better come back and visit us."

Eleanor, Zoey's septuagenarian employer at Thistles and Stems, nodded. Zoey lifted her glass further. "To Adi!"

The small crowd in the store echoed her and clinked their glasses together. Zoey touched hers to Eleanor's and the two of them sipped their fizzy drinks, which bubbled across Zoey's tongue. She'd never been a huge fan of champagne, but she'd made an exception for Adi's farewell party.

Zoey walked over to Adi and gave him a hug.

"Thanks, Zoey," he said, his long lashes brushing his cheeks.

He'd never been able to take compliments well, and he kept looking at the ground until Aisling linked her arm with his. "I'll miss this place."

"Well, like I said, you'll have to come back and visit us."

"I think that'll be pretty easy, since my parents own the bakery." His gaze flicked outside to the Dawood Bakery, which stood across Main Street. The wooden flower boxes along the sidewalks burst with color, flourishing in the summer heat.

"Good." Zoey nodded. "I look forward to hearing about your university adventures."

A group of Adi's friends swarmed him, so Zoey went to stand with Eleanor by the side wall where they displayed their succulents in quirky pots—a llama one, a jellyfish one, one painted white with black splotches like a cow, and even one with a vulva and a gold-encrusted clit on it.

"That was a lovely speech, dearie," Eleanor said in her delightful Scottish brogue. She shifted her weight from one foot to the other, and her long yellow dress swished around her legs. "I'm going to miss that boy too. You know, when I hired him initially, it was more to spite Minnie than anything. It worked out better than I had hoped." Eleanor had married her wife, Minnie, the previous summer, but the two of them had started out as rival florists, not thinking that Juniper Creek had space for both of their flower shops. Each shop turned out to have its own character, though, since Minnie focused on flowers and Eleanor on greenery.

"It did work out well," Zoey replied. "And we still need to find someone to replace him."

The end of summer was not a great time to be left high and dry as a flower shop, but Zoey and Eleanor hadn't been able to find anyone well-suited to taking Adi's job. Minnie had offered them use of her employees until they could find someone else, but Eleanor didn't want to overtax her wife's business longer than she needed to.

The search for a new employee had put Zoey's own plans for

the flower shop on pause. She wanted to approach Eleanor about selling her candles at the store, but it wasn't a current priority.

Eleanor clutched her amethyst necklace. "We'll find someone soon enough. The universe has a way of giving us things right when we need them."

Zoey didn't quite share Eleanor's optimism, but she nodded anyway. She checked the time on her phone and frowned.

"Need to get going?" Eleanor asked. "It's call night with your mother, isn't it?"

"Yeah." Zoey had a love/hate relationship with her weekly calls with her mother. Knowing how her mother was doing helped ease Zoey's worries, but the woman could get on her nerves at times. "Her friend's daughter has started dating so she's probably going to say something, yet again, about how I'm still single."

"I'm sorry," Eleanor said, rubbing Zoey's arm.

Zoey waved her off. "It's fine. I'm used to it. Is it alright if I take off early?"

Eleanor raised her eyebrows and looked at the crowd. "I think there are more than enough people here to help with closing."

"Okay." Zoey side-hugged Eleanor then went to the back room to grab her bag.

The warm evening August air brushed her cheeks as she went outside, and the sun bathed the sky in gold. Popping in an earbud and turning on a true crime podcast, Zoey put one sandal-clad foot in front of the other and walked home.

She was just finishing the pasta she'd made for dinner when her mother phoned. Zoey wiped her mouth on a napkin and propped her phone against her glass of water. She took a fortified breath, pasted on a smile, and answered the video call.

"Hey, honey!" Mom chirped. "How are you?"

"I'm good, Mom. How are you?"

"Oh, you know. Same old, same old." Her eyes crinkled as she smiled and pushed back a lock of brown hair peppered with gray. "We're sorting everything out in preparation for the new year.

We've got two new teachers this time, and I've heard that one of them can be difficult to work with. But she seems nice enough. She brought me coffee today while I was working."

Zoey's mom worked as an administrator at the elementary school in Vancouver where Zoey and her best friend Wren used to go. Hearing about her mom's daily activities locked Zoey in a perpetual state of nostalgia for when she and Wren first met and spent all those days hunkered in the school library together.

"That's nice of her."

"Yes. So, what's new in my favorite daughter's life?"

Zoey resisted the urge to roll her eyes. She was her mother's *only* daughter.

"Same old, same old for me too. We had a farewell party for Adi tonight since he's leaving for university. He's taking engineering, and I do not envy him."

"Oh, good for him! His parents own the bakery, right?"

"Yep."

"I need to come to town again for their cheese buns. I can't find anything as good here. And how's Wren? Have you talked to her lately?"

"She's good, as far as I know." Wren had texted her earlier that day about work drama, which seemed to never end at the hair salon. Either one of her coworkers would do something ridiculous, or a client would come in with an outrageous story, usually about a relationship.

"Is she still living alone? No boys on the horizon? Or girls?"

There it was. Mom was going for Wren first, but she'd start in on Zoey soon enough. "Mom, Wren doesn't want to date anyone. You know that." It wasn't entirely true. Wren was open to dating if she found the right person, but she'd had enough dates gone wrong that she was taking what she called an "extended break."

Mom frowned. "Yes, well. I just worry about her, all alone and away from home. Doesn't she get lonely?"

"She has lots of friends, and it's not like she's that far from home. Bellingham is only a couple hours away."

"Hmm." Mom didn't look convinced. "Well, what about you then? You aren't lonely, are you?" The concern in her eyes softened Zoey's annoyance.

"I'm not lonely, Mom. I have friends here too. You don't need to worry about me." She rose to put on the kettle, taking the phone with her.

Mom scoffed. "I'm your mother. I'm always going to worry about you. Speaking of, Janice was telling me the other day that her daughter went on a date with a girl she met on one of those dating apps. I was skeptical, you know, when those things came out, but maybe they're not as bad as I thought!"

"Oh wow." Zoey's attempt to infuse her voice with enthusiasm failed miserably, but Mom didn't seem to notice.

"Yes, the date went well apparently. They've got a second date planned!" Mom beamed at her expectantly.

"Good for her. I hope it goes well."

As Zoey turned back to the table, she caught a glimpse of movement out her kitchen window that made heat rush to her cheeks. It was Mina Hasanza, moving around in her own kitchen next door. That was two days in a row now that they'd seen each other through their windows. Mina's dark hair obscured part of her face as she turned to grab something from the sink.

"Me too. I was thinking, honey, what if you tried the app? I'm sure there are lovely girls in Juniper Creek you haven't met yet."

"While that's probably true, I'm not really interested."

Mina gave her a small wave, and Zoey realized she'd been staring. She waved back, a smile lifting the corners of her lips, then turned to grab a mug from the cupboard.

"You won't even give it a try? You're thirty-one and in your prime, hon. You never know what you could be missing out on!"

Zoey's annoyance increased exponentially, and she let out a long breath through her nose as she looked at her phone screen. "Mom, I'm really okay. I don't need an app to find someone."

Little did her mother know, she'd used apps many times

already to find hookups. And hookups were all she was looking for.

"Okay, well, the option is there if you want it."

Mom would let it go for now, but Zoey knew she'd bring up the topic again the next time they spoke. And probably the next, and the next. She supposed she should be thankful that it had taken so long for Mom to start pushing dating apps.

The rest of the conversation was fine, but Zoey couldn't enjoy it. She didn't understand her mother's obsession with her love life.

When Mom finally hung up, Zoey leaned her head back and groaned. Without thinking, she turned to look through her kitchen window again. Mina wasn't there anymore.

Zoey made herself tea and put on her true crime podcast, then she grabbed her melting pot. Potential murder and the familiar actions of pouring wax and trimming wicks would help calm her before bed. She needed to sleep well so she could get up early for her shift at Thistles and Stems, but Mom's fixation on romance had her keyed up.

It had always bothered her, but lately she'd found it increasingly annoying.

As she finally drifted to sleep, her mind put together a blurry image of Mina standing in her kitchen, Zoey helping her with the dishes.

THREE

MINA

For a few weeks after Christian left, Mina avoided looking at her finances, but she couldn't put it off any longer. Rent was coming due, and the numbers scared her.

Christian had always overseen paying their bills, but he'd graciously left all the information with his letter for Mina the day he'd walked out. When they first rented the place, Christian had insisted that Mina didn't need to pay for anything since his job more than covered their rent. His job had been the reason they'd moved to this town in the first place; he'd been working with a nearby wind farm. The shift from city life in Vancouver to small town life in Juniper Creek had been a lot for Mina, and she'd insisted on paying her share of the rent to assert some semblance of control.

Now, looking at her bank account, part of her wished she had accepted his offer. Her income and savings wouldn't last long. Not living here; not at this rate. Juniper Creek might be small, but it was touristy and popular for its festivals and markets, and it wasn't exactly cheap. Mina's job at Juniper Foods paid above minimum wage and gave her decent benefits, but it wasn't going to be enough.

Mina needed another job.

She sat at her desktop, gnawing on her bottom lip as she scrolled through job postings online. She needed something part time, preferably in town so she could go there straight from her shifts at Juniper Foods. Something familiar would help too, since her anxiety could get bad if she tried to tackle something she wasn't comfortable with. Those factors narrowed her search a lot.

Mina opened Discord, and Declan was already streaming in their chat. She gave him a quick hello to see if he could keep her company and prevent her from freaking out too much.

"Why don't you look for a 3D modelling job?" he asked. "Isn't that why you took classes, anyway? Oh shit, one sec." He was likely playing yet another shooter game and needed to focus.

"It is, but I don't know if I'm really qualified yet." Mina had finished her last online 3D modelling course two weeks before, and she only had three models in her portfolio that she felt confident about. With Christian gone, she'd considered letting her software subscriptions lapse since they were expensive, and she wouldn't be able to finish any more models without that software.

Declan replied a few seconds later. "Sorry, a stalker came at me. You are totally qualified. Some of your professors were big names in the industry, right? And you aren't going to get any more experience unless you put yourself out there."

Mina hummed halfheartedly in agreement. Declan wasn't wrong, but the idea of trying to get a job as a 3D artist made her want to throw up. "Maybe I'll look later. I think I'm going to go for a walk." She needed to get away from her computer to clear her head.

"Okay. Don't die out there," Declan said—his classic parting words.

Mina logged off and went outside. The fresh summer air calmed her racing pulse. She walked around the pond beside the park where the town held its outdoor events, letting the musical sounds of birds and rustling leaves ground her.

By the time she got home, she had an idea. She'd look for a job in town while she added to her portfolio, and once she had a few more models ready to go, she'd start applying for the 3D modelling gigs she'd always dreamed of. Another local job could at least tide her over until she found what she truly wanted.

She returned to her desktop and pulled up the resume she'd used to apply for 3D modelling classes, made a few updates, then pressed PRINT. The printer window informed her she was out of paper.

She groaned. Everything seemed to be against her these days.

After twenty minutes of scouring her house from top to bottom for extra paper, she just about gave up. She took a deep breath. "This isn't a big deal," she said to herself. "All you have to do is walk downtown and buy more."

Except her feet stayed rooted to the floor, and she couldn't bring herself to move. The fifteen-minute walk suddenly stretched, seeming much longer and somehow daunting even though she'd just gone for an hour-long stroll. Mina considered taking her extra anxiety medication, the one she took on top of her Celexa for situations like this, but she told herself she could manage without it.

"Just put your shoes on. Put your shoes on and go outside." She focused on those two tasks, which were easier and less formidable.

When she got outside, a more appealing idea occurred to her. She didn't need to walk all the way to Main Street, not when she had nice neighbors. So instead of heading straight down the street, she turned up the path to Zoey's front door. Zoey had to be home because her car, a silver Honda Civic, was parked out front beside Mina's red Mini Cooper. Mina's car had been a gift from her parents when she'd moved across the country, and she got mixed feelings whenever she drove it. When she got it, the first thing she did was stick a pansexual flag sticker to the bumper to make it more hers.

Zoey's place looked almost identical to Mina's since both belonged to a row of gray townhouses with white trim. Zoey had a pale orange free library box on her lawn with a little flower garden at the bottom that she filled every spring, but Mina's side was just grass.

Mina rolled her shoulders and knocked on Zoey's front door. She heard Zoey's muffled footsteps from inside, then the door opened. Zoey wore a burgundy knee-length dress, her tanned legs bare with yellow moccasin-style slippers on her feet. Her brown hair was pulled back in a ponytail, as usual. Mina didn't think she'd ever seen Zoey's hair down, and she pushed aside the spark of curiosity about what Zoey would look like with those waves framing her face.

Zoey smiled, and her blue eyes seemed to brighten. "Hey, what's up?"

Feeling a bit out of her depth now that she was standing on Zoey's front step, Mina rubbed the back of her neck. "Hey. Um, do you have any printer paper I can borrow?"

Zoey pushed her lips to the side as she thought. "I think so. Come in, and I'll go look."

She stepped aside so Mina could enter. Mina hadn't been in Zoey's house since Zoey first moved in three years ago, but the shape of the space mirrored Mina's. The biggest difference was Zoey's choice of décor. Zoey's furniture was orange and white, whereas Mina's was mostly gray. Christian had insisted that gray would calm Mina's anxiety, but instead it bored her and made their house feel like it had no personality. *Her* house now, not Christian's.

"If I have any, it'll be in my office," Zoey said. "One sec." She ran up the stairs, giving Mina a chance to look around more.

A can of Bubly sat on the living room table beside a laptop. Zoey must have been sitting on the low white couch only moments before. A crime show played on the TV against the far wall and a tall shelf packed full of brightly colored books stood beside it.

"Here we go!" Zoey said, coming down the stairs holding a stack of paper. She handed it to Mina.

"Thanks. I just need to print my resume. Thought I'd hand it out at the shops on Main Street, see if anything is available."

Zoey's brows drew together. "Why do you need a new job? Did you quit Juniper Foods?"

"No." Mina shook her head. She hadn't intended to explain this to Zoey, but she supposed it was inevitable now. "Christian kind of . . . left me. A few weeks ago."

Zoey gasped and covered her mouth. "He did?"

"Yeah," Mina said with a half shrug.

"Are you okay?" Zoey moved toward Mina, her arms held out as if she was going for a hug, but then she stepped back.

"I'm fine. Strangely okay, actually. But now I need another job to cover rent. So, there's that."

"Eesh." Zoey shook her head. "I thought he was just gone for work again or something."

"Yeah, seems that way, doesn't it?"

Zoey's lips turned down, and Mina tried not to stare at them. When Zoey had first moved in next door, her lips were one of the first things Mina had noticed. They were so full. So pink.

Zoey's expression shifted, her eyes narrowing as she pulled at her bottom lip with her teeth. She crossed her arms, giving Mina a once-over that made Mina's entire body flush with heat.

"What about Thistles and Stems?" Zoey asked.

"What?"

"For a job. What if you worked at Thistles and Stems with me and Eleanor? Adi left, and we've been looking for someone to take his position. It's part time, mostly evening and weekend shifts, sometimes an event or two. Since I know you already, you'd be a shoo-in for the job."

"But I know nothing about flowers."

"That's totally fine!" Zoey's voice was bright. "We work with greenery more than flowers, and Adi didn't know anything either when he started working with us. You can learn on the job."

Mina swallowed her instinct to say no. She'd never considered working at a flower shop before. She didn't have any experience with plants, but she'd worked customer service jobs back in Toronto as a teen, and she had her experience at Juniper Foods.

Plus, if she took this job, she'd get to work with Zoey.

"Are you sure? I don't want to take the job from someone else just because you know me."

Zoey raised one eyebrow. Mina had always been jealous of people who could do that. "It's not *just* because I know you, Mina. I think you'd be good for the job. I've seen you work at Juniper Foods, and you're good with people."

Mina licked her lips. "Okay. Sure, why not?"

"Yes!" Zoey clapped. "Why don't you email me your resume, and I can give it to Eleanor tomorrow? You'll have to do an interview with her, of course, but it'll be chill."

"Okay."

"Sweet. It'll be cool if we end up working together." Zoey's smile was so genuine, it made Mina's heart ache.

"Yeah, totally."

If Mina got this position, it would be the easiest job search of her life.

FOUR

ZOEY

"This is it," Zoey said, pulling up to the address Aunt Shannon had given her. Her new home was one of the townhouses her aunt owned in Juniper Creek. Apparently, there was a garage around back along with a small backyard that mirrored the quaint green lawn out front.

"It's not as small as I thought," Wren said as she opened the passenger-side door to get out. "At least, on the outside."

Zoey agreed. She hadn't seen the inside in person yet, but it had looked spacious enough in her aunt's photos. She wasn't going to turn it down regardless of how small it was, not when Aunt Shannon was charging her half of what anyone else would charge for rent. She didn't love the special treatment, but it was either accept her aunt's offer, continue living with her mother, or find a cheaper place that likely wouldn't be as nice.

Zoey accepted the offer. Once she grew her business, she'd be able to pay her aunt the full rent and then some to thank her.

The moving truck her mom had hired pulled up behind them. Zoey had protested, saying she could figure it out on her own, but her mom had insisted. "It's not every day your only daughter moves out," she said. "Let me do this for you, please." The sheen of tears in her mother's eyes had won.

Zoey got out to open the front door with Wren on her heels. "Not bad at all," Wren said as they stepped inside.

"I can't believe my aunt is renting me this place." Zoey shook her head. She stepped farther in, turning around, already loving how the front window let in so much natural light and how the beige walls created a sense of warmth. The house smelled like lemons and a tang of chemicals, likely from the cleaners her aunt had brought in the week before.

Zoey and Wren briefly toured the rest of the townhouse so they could direct the movers with Zoey's meager belongings. The living room and kitchen were attached, a decent-sized island breaking up the space. A small bathroom sat on the main floor across from the back door, and a door off the living room/kitchen led downstairs to an unfinished basement. Its cement floor was cold on Zoey's feet, and she shivered at the chill in the air. She'd never loved unfinished basements—they creeped her out, possibly because she listened to so much true crime—but her aunt had left her a washer and dryer down there, which Zoey was grateful for.

"Let's go upstairs," she said, keeping her voice soft as if she'd startle something unsettling out of the shadows.

"Yes please." Wren shuddered dramatically then grabbed Zoey's wrist, practically pulling her up the wooden steps.

The stairs to the second floor stood across from the front door, carpeted and soft against Zoey's toes. Three bedrooms and a bathroom took up the top floor. She didn't need that much space, but she supposed she could convert one room to an office for her candle business. The other would be a guest room.

"Basement aside, this is a really nice space," Wren said, her dark eyebrows raised. "I'm impressed."

Zoey nodded, feeling slightly dazed. "Me too."

"Miss Bell, are you ready for us to start moving furniture?" a voice called from downstairs. It must have been one of the movers.

"Yeah, sure!" Zoey puffed out her cheeks. She was really doing this. She was going to live by herself in a town she'd only been to a few times when she'd visited Aunt Shannon.

"I'll stay up here," Wren said. "You direct downstairs." Thank goodness one of them could think straight.

Before Zoey knew it, the movers had brought in her things, and she was left sitting on an orange velvet chair she'd found at a thrift store while Wren sat on one of the two chairs for her small dining table. "I'm going to need more furniture," she said, looking around at the space. The emptiness felt sad, absent of life. "But this'll do for now."

Wren kicked one of the boxes lightly. "Can we unpack these tomorrow? We still need to get everything out of the car, and I'm tired."

"Definitely. I'll just unpack stuff we can use for dinner."

"Good idea." Wren went outside to start bringing in the rest of Zoey's things while Zoey opened a box labeled "Kitchen" and pulled out the small kitchenware set she'd bought. The orange plates and bowls matched the orange mugs, four of each in the set along with four glasses and four sets of cutlery.

She opened one of the cupboards, running her finger over the shelf inside. No dust. Her aunt had been thorough. Or the cleaners had been, at least. Zoey put the plates, bowls, mugs, and glasses in the cupboard for now; she could rearrange them later if she needed to. As she closed the cupboard, her gaze shifted to the kitchen window beside it.

Why the builders had put the kitchen window facing the other townhouse rather than facing the backyard baffled Zoey. She had a perfect view into her neighbor's kitchen—a mirror of hers, but clearly lived in. Looking into someone else's home made her feel intrusive, even more so when her neighbor walked into view.

A woman with wavy short dark hair pulled something out of the oven. She wore black jeans and a button-up T-shirt with a pattern on it, and Zoey guessed she was roughly her own age—in her late twenties—if not younger. The woman put the casserole dish she'd pulled out of the oven onto her kitchen table, which evidently sat directly in front of the window. Then she looked up.

Right at Zoey.

Zoey's lips parted in surprise. But the woman smiled at her, her face all soft angles, her skin brown with warm undertones. A small gold ring glinted from the side of her nose. Zoey's stomach flipped. She hadn't felt *that* since she'd had a baby queer crush on her high school English teacher.

A smile grew on her own face as she waved and felt a bit foolish. She'd have to introduce herself soon in case this happened again. It wouldn't be as awkward if she at least knew her neighbor's name. Her very attractive neighbor's name.

The woman turned her head, and a broad-shouldered man entered Zoey's view as if she were watching a new character enter a movie screen. He wore a blue shirt and had black glasses perched on his pale nose. When the woman said something to him, he ran a hand through his sandy blond hair. He looked at Zoey and gave a curt nod—a nod that was barely an acknowledgment—then he sat at the table while the woman went to get something from a cupboard.

Zoey bit her lip and turned away. Leave it to her to immediately crush on her neighbor who was clearly already in a relationship. Possibly married even. She groaned.

"What's the *ughhhh* noise for?" Wren asked, coming into the kitchen with a cardboard box full of food.

"I have a view straight into my neighbor's kitchen," Zoey said, gesturing to the window.

"Oh. That's awkward." Wren looked through it with her hands on her hips, then she shrugged. "Maybe you can put up blinds or something."

"Yeah, maybe."

They made gluten-free macaroni and cheese with hot dogs for dinner, then Wren convinced her to go out for ice cream right before the shops on Main Street closed. Juniper Creek was adorably small, and Zoey couldn't wait to explore more of the town. She'd been to most of the shops already with her aunt, but now the town was home rather than a cute location for a day trip.

When they got back to her new place, they put Zoey's bedroom together—the bare minimum, at least—so they'd have somewhere to sleep.

"What am I going to do without you here to keep me company?" Zoey asked Wren as they both stood in their pajamas in her new bathroom. Wren's had alpacas on them, and Zoey's had sloths. They'd seen them in a store in Bellingham, and they couldn't resist buying them.

"Suffer," Wren said around a mouthful of toothpaste, white foam on her lips. She finished brushing her teeth and wiped her mouth on a towel. "You'll be fine." She bumped Zoey's hip with her own.

"I know. It'll just be weird, living by myself." Weird, but exciting. She'd never had so much freedom in her life. She scooched past Wren to grab her own toothbrush.

"You'll get used to it. I love it, and I don't even have this much space." Wren had moved into her apartment in Bellingham a year prior when one of her friends offered her a job at their salon.

"I hope you're right."

Zoey had always enjoyed being alone. She liked interacting with people for short stretches, but she needed quiet time on her own to recharge. After her father left when she was thirteen, it had been only her and her mother. And Wren whenever she came over, which was often. Having a small circle suited Zoey, which was part of why she'd moved to Juniper Creek. She also thought her candle business would do well here since the town was known for its markets and events.

Despite Zoey's nerves and excitement at being in a new house in a new town, at the prospect of being the most independent she had ever been, the warmth of Wren beside her, and the familiar smell of Wren's cocoa butter face cream soothed her. Zoey fell asleep quickly.

THE NEXT MORNING, NEITHER ZOEY NOR WREN bothered to shower. They planned to spend the day unpacking, and they'd both be sweaty by the end of it.

They'd just gotten through putting away the rest of the kitchen supplies when the doorbell rang. Wren looked up from where she was folding an empty box, but Zoey waved her off and went to answer it.

It was the woman from next door—the neighbor she'd seen through her kitchen window. She held a casserole dish full of steaming cinnamon buns.

"Hi," the woman said, her voice as warm as her expression. Wings of black eyeliner made her brown eyes stand out, and a brush of matte red lip gloss drew Zoey's gaze to her mouth. The stomach flip Zoey had experienced the night before happened again. "I hope you haven't eaten breakfast yet. I'm Mina."

FIVE

MINA

THREE YEARS AGO

The heat from the dish of cinnamon buns in Mina's hands was making her sweat, and she was grateful when her new neighbor, Zoey, invited her inside to put them on the kitchen counter. "Wren!" she called. "Can you find the hot mats?"

A tall woman with curly hair, a couple shades darker than Zoey's, rummaged through drawers in the kitchen. She wore black yoga pants that matched Zoey's, but her tank top was purple whereas Zoey wore a plain orange T-shirt. "Who's this?" the woman asked.

"Mina," Mina said. "I live next door." She nodded toward the window, which looked straight into her own kitchen.

"This is Wren," Zoey said. "My best friend. She's helping me get settled."

"Found them!" Wren pulled a set of woven hot mats out of a drawer and plopped them on the counter.

Mina placed the cinnamon buns on top and shook out her hands. "I brought breakfast. Or brunch, I guess. I hope you like cinnamon buns." She felt self-conscious, standing in her new neighbor's kitchen. She'd asked Christian to come with her to welcome Zoey to town, but he'd had too much work to do.

Nothing new there.

"I love cinnamon buns," Zoey said. She leaned over and smelled them, her eyes closing as her face took on an expression of bliss. Her cheeks and neck were flushed, the rest of her skin softly golden. Mina smiled.

"Me too, except I have celiac," Wren said with an apologetic shrug. "They look delicious, though."

"Shit, I'm sorry! If you want, I can run to the bakery and get you a gluten-free one. They make really good gluten-free stuff."

Mina turned around to head out again, but Wren said, "No, it's okay, really. I brought a bunch of breakfast cookies I made. I'll just have those."

"Are you sure?" Mina really didn't mind running to the bakery. She felt bad that she hadn't considered making something without gluten in it.

Wren nodded.

"I can't eat all of these by myself, though," Zoey said, eyeing the twelve cinnamon buns. "Why don't you stay and have some?"

Mina blinked, taken aback. She hadn't expected to be invited to breakfast. "Um, sure."

Zoey gestured to one of the chairs at the small kitchen table. "Can I make you tea? I don't have any coffee, unfortunately. I don't drink it."

"It's a travesty," Wren added, grabbing three orange plates from a cupboard.

The situation made Mina uncomfortable. She'd brought over breakfast to welcome her new neighbor to town, and now Zoey was making *her* feel at home. That wasn't how this was supposed to go, but Mina guessed she couldn't do anything about it.

"Tea is fine." Preferable, really. Mina only drank coffee when she was in the zone working on her 3D models and needed the caffeine boost.

A few minutes later, all three of them sat at the table. Well,

Mina and Zoey sat on the only two dining chairs at the table with their cinnamon buns while Wren sat in the burnt-orange velvet chair she'd pulled up. She munched on her breakfast cookies.

"So, what brings you to town?" Mina asked, trying to talk to both Zoey and Wren even though her eyes constantly found their way back to Zoey. When Zoey licked icing off her thumb, Mina snapped her eyes to her plate and hoped her ears hadn't just turned red. A gesture that casual had no right being sensual.

"I'm renting this place from my aunt. Wren and I grew up in Vancouver, but I think it'll be nice to live somewhere quieter. And I can sell my candles here at the markets."

"Candles?"

"I have a small candle business called Bell Lights," Zoey explained. She sipped her tea then continued, "I make coconut wax candles with pithy names like *Fall Leaves Under Your Feet*." The way she said it made it sound like she was partially making fun of herself, but she seemed proud all the same.

Wren made a noise, finishing her bite. "Lemon Zest in the Spring is the best one, in my humble opinion." She wiped a crumb off her chin. "It makes the entire room smell like lemons."

"That's awesome. Are you thinking of opening a storefront?"

Zoey laughed and shared a look with Wren. Mina had the feeling they'd talked about that idea before. "Maybe one day," Zoey said. "What about you? What do you do?"

"I work at Juniper Foods, the grocery store on Main Street. I enjoy it, although I'll probably only stay there until I get a job in my field."

"What field is that?" Zoey asked. She took another cinnamon bun, and Mina fought a satisfied smile.

"I have a degree in business, but I'm not sure what I'll do with it yet." The business degree had been her parents' idea. She'd gone through with it to make them happy, but she had no idea where to go from there. All she knew was that she refused to work in the corporate world, no matter what her family suggested. Her anxiety was hard enough to deal with as is, and even the thought of going into business with capitalist higher-ups was enough to send her spiraling. "Ideally, I'd work in video games."

Wren sat up straighter. "Video games? Dude, that's so cool! Do you code or something?"

"I can code, but I like the art side better. I like making character models."

"Like 3D modelling? I saw a video about that once somewhere. Do you have any models you can show us?" Zoey asked.

"I might." As Mina scrolled through her phone for screenshots of her latest model, she tried to decipher the restless feeling in her chest. It felt like anxiety but not as uncomfortable. Excitement, maybe? She couldn't remember the last time someone had shown interest in her art. She didn't talk about it often with anyone other than Declan because she didn't think anyone would care. Christian certainly didn't.

The few times she'd tried to talk to him about the process, he zoned out or had to leave mid-conversation for a work call. And the few times she'd shown him her models, he'd nit-picked what he didn't like about them in a way that made her impostor syndrome flare up. It was better for her to keep her art to herself these days.

And yet here she was, showing it to her new neighbor.

"This is a plant dragon I've been working on," she said, setting her phone on the table so both Zoey and Wren could see it. She held her breath as they leaned over to look at it. "It's not done yet, and that's not a great angle."

"That's rad," Wren said. "Those wings are so detailed! How long did this take?"

"This one took me a long time because I was trying out new things. Probably over a hundred hours so far."

Zoey's jaw dropped. "Holy shit." She looked at Mina with wide eyes. "And this will be in a video game?"

"Not this one. I've just been working on it for fun." She almost cringed at her own words. Christian always referred to her art as a hobby, as if all it was good for was *fun.*

"I don't play many video games, but I feel like you'll have no problem getting a job with work like that," Zoey said. Her praise washed over Mina like a wave of sunshine.

"I *do* play many video games," Wren said, "and I agree. This is fantastic. The style reminds me of *Skyrim*, but like . . . more whimsical somehow."

"Thanks." Mina's ears were burning now.

They chatted for a few more minutes, then Mina offered to help them unpack. They waved her off, saying she'd done enough already by bringing breakfast. "I wouldn't turn down more cinnamon buns, though, if you wanted to bring them over again someday." Zoey winked at her.

Mina pressed her lips together, pleased. "Noted. Let me know if you need anything else. You know where to find me."

Back in her own house, she poked her head into Christian's office to see if he was free. She wanted to tell him how breakfast went—how they'd lucked out and gotten a wonderful new neighbor. Unsurprisingly, though, he was on a video call.

Oh well. She'd tell him all about it later, after her shift at Juniper Foods. She sat at her computer to work on her art until then, feeling a renewed sense of confidence.

SIX

MINA

Declan's voice held an air of pompous importance. "What's the most embarrassing moment you've experienced at work, and how did you deal with it?"

Mina rolled her eyes and leaned back in her gaming chair. It had only taken two days for Eleanor to contact her for an interview for the job at Thistles and Stems, and Mina needed to prepare. "Declan, I don't think Eleanor will ask about my most embarrassing moment."

"Why not? She might."

"Maybe a moment when a customer disagreed with me or something. But I doubt she'll care about the time I bent over and ripped my pants then slipped on a wet floor."

Declan cackled. "I remember that. You were *mortified*."

"Yes, thank you for your sympathy. Can you please ask me something actually useful?"

"Hey, you asked for my help and I'm doing it. As the interviewer, I get to pick the questions."

Mina sighed. She probably should have asked Zoey for help instead of Declan, but Zoey had already taken in Mina's resume and put in a good word for her. Mina didn't want to bother her even more about this job.

"Fine, go ahead."

Declan cleared his throat. "So, your most embarrassing moment was ripping your pants and proceeding to fall on a wet floor. How did you survive the rest of your shift?"

Mina flopped forward on her desk with her head on her forearms as Declan's cackle burst once more through her headphones.

THE NEXT DAY, WHILE ON SHIFT AT JUNIPER FOODS, Mina ran through the questions Declan had asked her—once he'd gotten his jokes out of his system and shifted to genuinely helping her. She didn't want to script her answers because that had always gone badly in the past, but she also needed to be as prepared as possible.

Part of her wished she'd had today off so she could continue preparing, but it was probably better that she needed to work. It distracted her somewhat, so there was less chance of her throwing up.

Except now she was on her break with nothing to do but eat her sandwich, and she couldn't eat it because her stomach was rebelling. Instead, she paced from one end of the break room to the other, reminding herself to breathe as she tried to envision what the interview setup might look like. They were meeting in the bakery, which was familiar at least. She pressed her fist into her sternum, trying to quell the tight feeling there.

Vera came in and turned on the coffee maker, and she frowned at Mina. "Everything okay?"

"Yeah," Mina said, shaking out her hands. Her fingers felt numb. "I have a job interview after work." At the look on Vera's face, she added, "For a part-time job in addition to this one."

Vera's shoulders, which had moved toward her ears, relaxed. "Oh. What's the interview for?"

Mina stared at Vera for a second as she realized the irony of where she was applying. Eleanor was Vera's mom. "I'm applying at Thistles and Stems, actually."

"Oh!" Vera's face lit up. "Mum didn't tell me she was interviewing you today. You'll do great. Mum is a very casual employer, and I know she'll like you. You'll get along well, I'm sure."

"I hope so." Mina tried to smile, but it felt more like a grimace.

The sound of the coffee maker spitting out Vera's drink interrupted their conversation. It grumbled then hissed, and Mina wondered when it had been cleaned last. It sounded like it was struggling.

"Do you want me to run through practice questions with you?" Vera asked as she poured cream into her coffee.

The offer was tempting, but Mina shook her head. "I think I just need to do the interview and get it over with. I practiced last night."

"Okay. Well, say hi to Mum for me when you get there."

"I will."

Vera lifted her coffee in acknowledgment then left the room.

Mina scowled at herself for not remembering that Eleanor was Vera's mom. Now if she got the job, she wouldn't know if Eleanor hired her for *her* or because both Zoey and Vera liked her. It wasn't the worst thing to start ahead of the game, but she wanted to get the job on her own merit. Then again, if Eleanor was anything like Vera, she wouldn't put too much stock in other people's opinions and she would focus more on Mina herself.

This situation felt messier by the minute. Mina couldn't wait until the interview was over. She'd been planning to wait until the end of her shift to take her extra anxiety medication, but she took it now instead then donned her navy Juniper Foods vest again and clocked in.

The rest of her shift crawled by as if time had been steeped in glue, and Mina's chest felt tight as she restocked the cereal. She tried to focus on the color of each box, and she counted them as she placed each one on the shelf. Anything to ground her and pull her out of her head. She made a rule that she wasn't allowed to look at the time until she cleared an entire pallet of boxes, and that helped a bit.

Finally, it was time to go. She ran to the break room to clock out and grab her stuff, then she changed in the bathroom and ran a hand through her hair, hoping it didn't look too messy. Her hair was never truly *neat*, but she didn't want to be unprofessional. She fixed her eyeliner where it had smudged, and she reapplied her red lipstick. She wore it like armor, ready to face the world as long as her lips made her appear confident.

Now there was nothing left to do but the interview itself.

She walked out the door toward the bakery, grateful for the balmy September weather and the lack of a breeze. Fall décor adorned the black lampposts, and many of the shops had leaf decals stuck to their windows. A few advertised upcoming deals for the Pumpkin Days festival, which took place on the weekends in October. As she passed Thistles and Stems across the street, she considered peeking in to say hi to Zoey, but she was on a mission. That mission did not leave time for pleasantries, even if seeing Zoey might make her feel better.

She slowed her steps right before the bakery so she didn't look like she was rushing. Taking a deep breath, she smoothed her black button-up shirt dotted with tiny white flowers, then she opened the bakery door.

The scents of cinnamon, freshly baked bread, and coffee enveloped her, but today even that wasn't enough to make her shoulders relax. Eleanor was already there, sitting at a table against the wall with a mug in front of her. She looked up and waved when Mina entered, and Mina waved back. "Hello," she said, smiling.

Mina approached and hung her backpack off the wooden chair opposite Eleanor, then she sat, keeping her back so straight that it wasn't even touching the chair.

"What can I get you?" Eleanor asked, gesturing to the front counter. "A tea, or a coffee? I want you to be comfortable."

Mina hadn't expected this question, and it threw her off. Eleanor smiled, waiting for her answer.

"Coffee would be great, thank you," Mina said, thankful she'd managed to get out words. She had no idea why she'd asked for a coffee, though. It would likely make her more anxious.

She tapped her foot as Eleanor stood and headed to the counter. She wore a long pastel pink dress with yellow flowers today, and she looked like she belonged in a flower shop. Which was probably why she owned one.

Mina looked around the bakery, focusing on specific details to calm her nerves. A picture of the Fraser Valley hung askew on the wall above their table. The table beside theirs was empty but hadn't been cleaned yet, a few crumbs lying forlorn on the black tabletop. Aaliyah and Kamran, the bakery's owners, moved in tandem behind the counter as they served Eleanor and two other customers, and Aaliyah's white hijab glowed brightly under the pot lights.

Mina was focusing on the smooth hiss of the coffee machine —much smoother than the one from work—when Eleanor returned with a mug of coffee in hand. "Here you are," she said, setting it down so gently that it barely made a sound.

"Thank you."

Mina wrapped her hands around it, not even caring that it was almost hot enough to burn her. The heat kept her in her body. She looked at Eleanor and assumed what she thought of as her customer-service smile. She wore it often enough at work that she was confident it looked alright.

"So," Eleanor began, "I don't think we need to make this difficult. I know you have customer service experience already from working at Juniper Foods, and both Zoey and my daughter have said good things about you."

Mina tried not to wince. She didn't want this job handed to her on a silver platter, but she couldn't exactly act upset at Eleanor's words.

"That doesn't mean you'll be good for Thistles and Stems,

though," Eleanor said, nudging her green horn-rimmed glasses farther up her nose. "So, tell me what you think you'd bring to our team."

That was much better. Mina had a chance to prove herself, and this was what she'd been preparing for.

SEVEN

ZOEY

Zoey worked the closing shift that night, and all evening she wondered how Mina's interview had gone. She had no doubt Mina would get the job, but she still wanted to hear about it, and Eleanor hadn't come by the shop to spill any details.

So instead of heading straight home after work, Zoey went past her own door to Mina's.

When Mina opened it, she was clearly in lounge mode. Her short, shaggy mullet-esque hairstyle was on point, as always, but she rocked gray sweatpants and a boygenius T-shirt instead of her usual dark jeans and patterned top, and she wasn't wearing makeup. Mina's style was usually edgy in a way Zoey could think of only as Kristen Stewart meets Noel Fielding. Mina's current outfit might have been a muted version of that, but it still made Zoey's heart race.

"Hey," Mina said.

"Hi. I thought I'd come over and see how the interview went."

Mina shrugged. She crossed her arms and leaned against her doorframe in a move so effortlessly nonchalant it was almost infuriating. "I think it went okay. I hope it did, anyway. Eleanor didn't say anything?"

"She didn't come back to work after the interview. I'm sure it went well, though. Eleanor's super nice."

"Yeah, I got that vibe."

"Did she tell you when she'd let you know?"

"She just said soon." Mina inhaled shakily, and Zoey suspected she was more nervous about the interview than she looked.

"Alright, well, maybe I'll find out tomorrow. But I'll let her tell you, obviously. It's not my place." Although it would be fun if Zoey got to tell Mina she got the job. She wanted to see the look on Mina's face at the news.

"Okay."

They stood awkwardly for another few moments until Zoey realized the ball was in her court to get this interaction moving. "I should probably go home. I hope you have a good evening!"

"Thanks, you too." The look Mina gave her when she closed the door was puzzled, but not in a bad way. Zoey was sure she saw a spark of curiosity there, and she liked it.

At home, she changed into her pajamas and wiped her face clear of makeup, then she sat down with her laptop. She had intended to work on her business proposal this evening, now that they had probably hired someone to replace Adi. But, as had always happened in the past few weeks when she tried to work on her proposal, she stared at her screen and had no idea what to do.

She'd built her business from the ground up, and she had no experience or education when it came to business planning. She'd acted on instinct and learned as she went, and it had worked for her because she'd never had to pitch any of her ideas to an employer. She was her own employer, and that's the way she liked it.

Now, though, she wanted to get her candles into other shops. She'd thought about opening her own storefront, but the more she thought about it, the less it appealed to her. She'd have to find new products to sell, hire employees, and buy or rent a building. Getting her candles into other shops was a more attainable goal that didn't tie her to one place, and that sounded better.

But it meant she had to pitch her business to other business owners. She had to put together a proposal to show that Bell Lights was viable and successful, that people liked her stuff. She had social proof from markets and her online shop, but she wasn't sure how to showcase that.

The idea had been swirling in her mind for the past year, but she hadn't had the courage or the knowledge to put it into motion yet. Oddly, it scared her more than starting the business in the first place, and she didn't understand why. Maybe because expanding meant involving other people, and she struggled to trust other people with the things that mattered to her.

In her experience, if you wanted something done properly, you had to do it yourself.

She sighed and shut her laptop, shaking her head. This was a problem for another day, yet again.

EIGHT

ZOEY

Zoey had been in love with Juniper Creek before she moved there, and she loved it even more every time she went out to explore the town. Each shop had its own character, most of them old enough to give Main Street an aura of nostalgia. She yearned to get more acquainted with the nooks and crannies of the shopping area, but she also wanted to mingle with the townsfolk since she planned to sell her candles at the local markets.

Although she didn't have much money, she made a point of buying something small in every single shop: a set of strawberry-shaped salt and pepper shakers from Mabel's Antiques, a board game from Tabletop Time, a mug from The June Bug diner. She chatted up the owners and other employees, being friendly and refraining from mentioning Bell Lights. She had enough experience with networking to know that selling yourself right out the gate wasn't the way to do things. And she wanted to make genuine connections, in any case.

So far, her go-to businesses were Cedar Logs art gallery, Yellow Brick Books, and Sugar & Spice. The art gallery because it sold works from local artists she admired, the bookstore because it smelled like paper and ink and had enough romance books to last her a lifetime, and Sugar & Spice because of the charmingly patterned tea towels.

It was a bonus that all the shops in Juniper Creek were close together, so she could pop into the grocery store on her rounds. Since living on her own, she found herself going downtown almost daily for groceries rather than following the weekly grocery run her mother had instilled in her growing up.

One Wednesday afternoon when Zoey popped into Juniper Foods, Mina grinned at her from behind the till. Her matte lipstick was a deep red that reminded Zoey of velvet and cherries.

"Are you stalking me or something?" Mina asked.

Zoey frowned. "Stalking you? Why would I do that?"

Mina shrugged. "You tell me. New girl in town, lives next door to me, always seems to show up here when I'm on shift . . ."

Zoey froze in place, then saw the smirk on Mina's face and relaxed. "You got me. I am, unfortunately, stalking you. It's the only way to make sure you're not the one behind the disappearing packages."

Mina laughed wryly. "Yours got stolen too? We should really get doorbell cameras."

"Probably." Zoey shifted from foot to foot, still freaking out at the stalking accusation but trying not to let it show.

"Other than your stolen mail, how are you settling in?" Mina asked.

"Great so far. This town seems really sweet, package thieves excluded."

Mina nodded. "It is, mostly. Until you do something the entire town starts gossiping about. Then you see the darker side of Juniper Creek."

That piqued Zoey's interest. "Do you know this from experience? Am I missing any juicy secrets?"

Mina's eyes crinkled at the corners as she smirked, her eyeliner wings disappearing briefly. "No, thank god. I've seen it happen to other people, though. The latest was a rumor about one of the high school teachers having an affair with the janitor's daughter." She shrugged. "I try not to get too invested."

"That's fair." Zoey was disappointed. Small towns in books and movies always had a dark past to unearth, but so far Juniper Creek had come up empty.

As Zoey walked home with her bag of groceries, Mina's question replayed in her mind. *Are you stalking me or something?* Now that Zoey thought about it, she *was* always visiting Juniper Foods when Mina was working. And the fact that Zoey knew roughly when Mina worked definitely cast suspicion on her motives for being there. It's not like she really needed to get groceries that often, but she enjoyed deciding what to eat for dinner based on her mood.

Plus, it made sense that she knew when Mina worked because they lived next to each other. Since Zoey worked from home, she knew when Mina was out because her car wasn't parked out front. That car was bright enough to be conspicuous when it wasn't in its spot on their street.

Not to mention that Zoey had spent a lot of time on Main Street lately, and she'd still been buying bits and bobs to make her house feel like a home. That was all. It was purely coincidence.

She bit her lip, trying to get Mina's words out of her head. She was *not* stalking her neighbor. To prove it to herself, she cut her shopping to twice a week for the next month.

WREN DROVE TO TOWN FOR ZOEY'S BIRTHDAY IN September so they could marathon *BuzzFeed Unsolved*. "This is how much I love you," Wren said as they drove to Juniper Foods to pick up snacks. "I'm going to have nightmares for the next three weeks."

"We don't have to watch true crime stuff," Zoey said for the third time in the past hour. "We can watch something that won't freak you out so much."

"Nope." Wren shook her head. "No way. You always watch teen drama movies for me even though you hate them. I can be brave." She tilted her chin and assumed a stoic expression. "I've got this."

Zoey laughed. "Sure you do."

The sliding doors of the grocery store opened. They walked inside, and Zoey grabbed a basket. "So chips, ice cream, chocolate, anything else?"

"Let's see what they've got for gluten-free stuff." Wren turned to a navy-vested employee mopping the floor. "Excuse me, where can we find gluten-free snacks?"

Zoey realized a split second before the employee looked up that it was Mina, and she felt suddenly flustered.

Mina wore her usual dark jeans, but a gray button-up shirt had replaced her normal patterned one under the Juniper Foods vest. Her hair was messily pulled back in a clip, and she didn't have any eyeliner on today, but her lips were as red as ever as she smiled at them.

"Hey, Zoey," she said. "And Wren, right?"

"Yeah, good memory," Wren replied, looking impressed.

"Gluten-free snacks are this way." Mina put the mop in its yellow bucket and pushed it aside, then led them through the store until they reached the correct aisle. "Let me know if you need anything else," she said, giving them a wave as she headed back to the bucket.

Zoey tightened her ponytail and directed her attention to the shelves of chips and cookies, ignoring how her heartbeat had quickened.

"Why's your face so red?" Wren asked, her voice amused.

"Hm?" Zoey didn't look at her friend, instead grabbing a box of Oreos and trying her best to focus on the words on the back.

"Your cheeks. You've turned into a lobster."

Wren's words made Zoey flush even more, and she cursed her body for betraying her. "I'm fine, it's just warm in here."

"Uh-huh."

Zoey could tell Wren was still looking at her. When she didn't respond to her best friend's attention, Wren sidled closer and put her chin on Zoey's shoulder, her face right in Zoey's so she couldn't be ignored.

"You sure it's not your cute neighbor who just happens to work here?"

Zoey rolled her eyes and shrugged Wren off. "Yes, Mina's cute. What about it? I thought we were here for snacks."

"Oh, we are." Wren snatched a pack of chips from the shelf. "But I'm not letting this go so easily, missy. What's going on with you two?"

"Nothing." When Wren made a noise of disbelief, Zoey turned to glare at her friend. "I'm serious. She's still dating that guy, Christian or whatever his name is. And even if she wasn't, it wouldn't matter."

"Why? You don't think you'd hook up with her?"

Zoey crinkled her nose. "No, I wouldn't." No matter how attractive she found Mina, no matter that she knew Mina was pansexual because of the sticker on her car, she never let her thoughts go further than that. Mina had a partner.

"Why? If I lived here, I probably would."

"Well, I don't share that interest." Zoey didn't want to talk about this anymore. "Can we get the snacks, please?"

She was grateful when a different employee checked out their goods and Mina was nowhere to be seen as they left. She knew Wren wouldn't make another comment about it, but Zoey didn't want to look at Mina again and feel that ache in her chest.

The ache that said she wished Mina was single. That Mina would see her as more than just her neighbor.

No one she knew had ever seen her as more than a friend, as more than the sweet, friendly, responsible girl who had weird hobbies like making candles. And her hookups never saw her as more than a night of sweaty, satisfying sex. And that was perfectly fine with her. Being single was easy when she didn't have to turn anyone down.

There was no chance of her life being thrown off course like it had been when her father had left her and her mother.

MINA

Every time Mina had seen Zoey through the window for the past couple days, Zoey had looked at her with wide eyes then run from the kitchen. It was definitely weird and un-Zoey-like, and Mina suspected it had something to do with her interview. Zoey must know something.

Mina's suspicions were confirmed when Eleanor phoned the next day. "I'd like to officially offer you the position at Thistles and Stems," she said, her voice bright.

The corners of Mina's mouth lifted. Waiting for a response always kicked her nerves into high gear, and now she could relax. "And I would like to officially accept."

"Perfect. How soon can you start?"

"How soon would you like me there?"

"Would tomorrow afternoon work? You can do a short shift with Zoey, and she can show you the ropes."

Mina didn't have a shift at Juniper Foods the next day, which was lucky. She could focus on her new job and settle into it before she had to manage both in the same day. "That's perfect. I'll be there."

"Lovely. See you then!"

Mina wasn't sure why, but her first thought was to tell Zoey she got the job. There was no chance Zoey didn't know, but Mina wanted to tell her anyway, especially since her neighbor had clearly been struggling to keep the lid on the news.

Not bothering with a jacket, Mina slid her bare feet into her purple flipflops and walked over to Zoey's.

"I got the job," she said as soon as Zoey opened the door.

Zoey squealed. "Yes, you did!" She flung her arms around Mina and squeezed, just for a second. But that second was enough for Mina to smell her vanilla perfume and her coconut shampoo, to feel her chest pressed against Mina's own, and she sucked in a sharp breath. "When do you start?"

"Tomorrow. I guess you're on trainer duty."

"Awesome. I look forward to it." Zoey's smile was wide. "What are you doing to celebrate?"

Mina frowned. She hadn't really considered celebrating, aside from telling Zoey. "I don't know."

"Oh my god, you have to do something! This is a big win, isn't it?" Zoey pulled out her phone to check the time. "Why don't we go get ice cream or something?"

The suggestion made Mina's heartbeat pick up. She knew Zoey would be happy for her, but she hadn't expected this. It wasn't a bad idea, though, and she didn't want to turn Zoey down.

"Sure. Let me grab my wallet."

She felt lighter as she walked home. She'd been happy when Eleanor told her she'd got the job, but that happiness had expanded at Zoey's reaction. And now they were going to get ice cream.

Mina snatched her wallet off the counter and quickly checked her makeup in the bathroom mirror. Eyeliner sharp. Lips red. Perfect.

When Mina returned outside, Zoey was bouncing on the balls of her feet on the sidewalk. She had changed out of the black yoga pants and olive-green tank top she'd had on when she'd opened the door. Now she wore a cream dress with a lacey T-shirt top, the hem brushing her thighs just above her knees. Mina ached to trail her fingers along the golden skin there, to see if Zoey was as soft as she looked.

"What a beautiful day for celebratory ice cream," Zoey said, beaming and breaking Mina's train of thought. The buckles on Zoey's strappy black sandals made little *tink* noises as they walked toward Main Street. If Mina didn't know any better, she'd think Zoey was the one celebrating a new job. "What flavor are you going to get?"

The question took Mina aback, and she had to think for a minute. Christian usually ordered for her when they went to Flora's Dairy Barn together, and he got her cookies and cream every time. She liked cookies and cream, but not *that* much. And this was the first time she'd be visiting the ice cream shop since their breakup.

"I'm not sure. I might get their seasonal special."

"Oh my god! It is *so good*. It's called Harvest Spice, and it's got pieces of apple in it and lots of cinnamon."

"That sounds amazing. Don't you sell a candle that's similar?"

Zoey stopped for a second and looked at Mina with narrowed eyes, but she was smiling. She looked surprised but pleased. "Yeah, I do. It's called The First Bite of Your Grandma's Apple Pie."

Mina felt the need to defend herself—it's not like she had all of Zoey's candle scents memorized. "I almost bought that one at Pumpkin Days last year, but I went for Whiskey on a Cold Night instead."

"Ooh, that's a good one. Thanks for buying a candle, by the way. That's really sweet of you."

"Yeah, of course."

The fact that Zoey called her sweet made the tips of her ears burn.

"Are you selling your candles again at Pumpkin Days this year?" she asked.

"Yep, at the market on the third weekend." For the rest of the walk to Flora's Dairy Barn, Zoey mused about the new fall scents she was experimenting with. They all sounded good to Mina, who loved fall more than any other season. It was one thing she missed about living out east—the trees turned the brightest colors there, painting the landscape in autumn vibes. The Fraser Valley got lots of yellow, but Mina longed for the bright reds and oranges of an Ontario autumn.

They arrived at the ice cream shop an hour before closing time. A waist-high cardboard cow greeted them when they walked in. Zoey got mint chocolate chip and Mina went for the Harvest Spice, both in waffle cones.

"Do you want to sit or walk back while we eat?" Zoey asked.

Mina caught a drip of melted ice cream with her tongue. "We should probably walk back. It'll start cooling off soon."

Zoey hummed in agreement and the two of them headed toward home as they ate their ice cream.

Warmth filled Mina's chest. With the sun setting above them, the warm air cooling around them, the ice cream in her hand, and her footsteps slapping the sidewalk next to Zoey's, she felt at peace in a way she hadn't in a long time. She wished she could bottle the feeling to use in place of her anxiety medication. Her anxiety had certainly quieted in the moment, still there but only if Mina searched for it.

They both finished their ice cream before they reached their townhouses. "That was delicious," Zoey said.

Mina popped the last piece of her waffle cone in her mouth. "Celebratory ice cream was a good idea."

"Thank you." Zoey flipped her ponytail in exaggerated pride.

"Oh, um . . . you have ice cream on your nose."

"I do?"

Zoey stopped and looked comically cross-eyed at her nose, trying to find the offending spot of dairy. Mina laughed and leaned in, swiping a thumb over the tip of Zoey's nose. "Got it."

She didn't realize how close the movement put them until Zoey's breasts brushed her arm, and her heart thumped hard against her ribs.

"Thanks," Zoey said, her voice breathy and her cheeks pink. For the first time, Mina noticed how many freckles she had, as if the sun had brushed her face with the tiny brown dots.

"No worries."

Mina kept walking to resist brushing a finger over Zoey's cheek, and Zoey followed a step behind. Their houses were just down the street, the orange Little Free Library in front of Zoey's house a clear marker of where she lived.

"Well, this is us," Zoey said once they reached it. "I guess I'll see you tomorrow."

"Yeah. Thanks again for the ice cream idea."

They walked up their parallel front walkways, each of them reaching their respective front doors at the same time. Mina put her key in the lock then looked over to see Zoey doing the same. Zoey returned the look, and they both laughed.

Mina couldn't have imagined a better way to celebrate her new job.

To keep herself busy and distracted the next morning, Mina worked on another model for her portfolio. She wanted to have at least two more pieces to show potential employers the breadth of her skill. She wanted to highlight different textures and poses and give them an idea of what types of programs she could work on. She'd heard that quality was better than quantity, but she still felt like what she had wasn't enough.

Her alarm went off to remind her it was time to get ready for her shift at her new workplace. Eleanor had emailed her more information about her job, and there was no uniform at Thistles and Stems. But Mina wanted to make a good impression, so she wore her dark green chinos and a white button-up shirt with little yellow suns dotting it. She saved white shirts for special occasions because of the inevitable sweat stains, and the first day of a new job fit the bill. The outfit felt like her while being professional and bright enough for a flower shop.

Her shift was only four hours today, so she didn't have to pack a lunch or anything. Going to work with so little in her bag felt strange—she hardly ever worked less than six hours at Juniper Foods—but she supposed most of her shifts at the florist's would be shorter.

Clouds filled the sky on her walk to Main Street, and she hoped that wasn't an indication of how her first day would go.

She pushed open the front door of Thistles and Stems, and the earthy smell of freshly churned soil washed over her. Zoey stood at the front counter, her back to the door. Her tight dark blue jeans hugged her ass, and Mina couldn't help glancing at it. Zoey's blouse wasn't much better, the V at the front showcasing her cleavage as she turned around. As soon as she registered who Mina was, her face lit up. "Welcome to your first day! Here, I'll show you the back room."

"Thanks." Mina hoped her blush didn't go beyond her ears. She was here to work, not ogle her unfairly hot neighbor.

Zoey took Mina to the back, where Eleanor was tying together bundles of dried plants. The long sleeves of her blue dress were pushed around her elbows, likely to keep them out of the way as she worked. "There's our new employee. Welcome to the team."

"Thank you. I'm excited to be here." Mina might not have been looking for a job with a florist, but she was genuinely looking forward to working at Thistles and Stems. She knew Eleanor was progressive and quirky, and the stock reflected that. She liked how Eleanor focused on greenery and eccentric plant pots over flowers, and the boho décor felt calming. Plus, she got to work with Zoey.

"Zoey, why don't you give her a tour then get her set up on cash?"

Zoey nodded. "On it."

The shop was small, so there wasn't much to tour: a front

room, a back room, and a small cooler room for the few flowers they had on site. Zoey stood at Mina's elbow as they set her up to use the cash register. Their arms brushed, Mina's entire left side tingling at Zoey's presence. She tried her best to focus on everything Zoey showed her, but she was hyperaware of Zoey's every move and how much space was between them at any given moment.

She was grateful when Zoey gave her a binder full of info about closing and various other store procedures and told her to familiarize herself with it. "You probably won't need to know all of it, but it doesn't hurt, right?"

Mina nodded and took the binder to the back to read through it.

"How's it going?" Eleanor asked. She was arranging the dried plants in a vase now. It looked ready for the pages of a boho magazine, just like the rest of the shop.

"Good, I think. Everything seems pretty standard, except all the plant stuff. That will take time for me to learn."

"Of course. I think you'll pick it up quickly, though. And I can walk you through most of it."

The rest of her shift flew by as Eleanor explained different types of plants to her. She had no idea how she would remember everything—what light each plant preferred, how much water they needed, when to repot everything, which plants were pet-friendly. She made notes in her phone to study later.

She and Zoey got off work at the same time, and Mina's head swirled with everything she'd learned as they grabbed their things from the back room.

"Want to walk home together?" Zoey asked.

Mina suppressed the urge to say *yes, please* and instead said, "Sure."

It seemed like Zoey was becoming a larger part of her life, and she wasn't at all upset about it.

TEN

ZOEY

"So, tell me again why you think I'm a good person to help you with business stuff?" Wren asked, popping a few M&M's in her mouth.

They were sitting on Zoey's couch with her laptop open in front of them. *Border Security: Canada's Front Line* played quietly on the TV. Wren seemed more interested in watching the show than helping Zoey with her business proposal, and Zoey didn't blame her.

Wren had driven from Bellingham to spend her day off with Zoey, and helping Zoey get her shit together was not the most fun activity. Not to mention that Zoey hadn't even been able to get *herself* to work on the damn thing. Just the previous evening, she'd intended to create a template or google things to include in a business proposal, and she'd ended up doing a deep dive on the Hinterkaifeck Murders instead.

"I don't know," Zoey replied. "Because you work full time at a public-facing business, and you support yourself independently without needing your aunt to give you a discount on rent."

Wren shot Zoey an unimpressed look. "Dude, I love you, but you've got to stop that. I work at a business, sure, but I don't *own* a business like you do. It's a totally different ball game. And you know you're happier doing that than you would be working for someone else. Except Eleanor, who you seriously lucked out with."

"Yeah, I know." Zoey sighed and grabbed a handful of M&M's from the bag in Wren's hand. "I'm just being whiny."

When she'd moved to Juniper Creek, she'd hoped her candle business would keep her afloat, but it hadn't been enough. Markets brought in sporadic income boosts, but she needed steady income, which is why she'd started working at Thistles and Stems. And while she loved that job, she still wanted to improve Bell Lights. She wanted that to be her primary source of income, and to do that, she needed to get herself out there more.

"You're allowed to complain," Wren said, crunching the chocolate candies between her teeth. "Having your own business is not easy. But you worked hard to get where you are, and you're doing pretty good. Don't beat yourself up too much."

"I'm trying."

"Have you thought of hiring a business consultant?"

"With what money?"

What she didn't say was that the idea of hiring a consultant made her uncomfortable. She'd spent most of her life figuring out how to make things work on her own, and the thought of someone telling her what to do with her business bothered her. She needed more time.

"Okay, fair point." Wren shrugged. "I don't understand why you won't just ask Eleanor. She'd have no problem selling your candles, I'm sure of it. She's, like, the chillest human."

"This isn't only for Thistles and Stems, though. I need to have something I can show to other shops eventually."

"Right. Hmm." Wren handed Zoey the bag of M&M's. "Take these away from me. I'm gonna be sick if I eat anymore." She laid against a cushion with her hand on her stomach.

Zoey closed her laptop with a sigh and pulled her feet onto the couch. She'd worry about her business later.

"So, what do you want to do for the rest of the day?" she

asked after the current episode of *Border Security* finished. She didn't think Wren had driven two hours up to her house just to lounge around and eat too much chocolate.

Wren stretched and yawned. "Board game?"

"Sure. Which one?"

It was no surprise when Wren said, "Calico."

Wren was weirdly obsessed with cats for someone who was allergic to them, and Calico had an adorable orange cat curled in a ball on the cover of the box.

Zoey went downstairs to grab the game. Since she'd moved in, she'd thrown an orange shag rug on the cement floor in the basement along with a purple bean bag chair, and she'd strung fairy lights along the ceiling. She still only went down there to do laundry, but at least now it felt cozy and not like the lair of a serial killer.

When she returned upstairs, Wren had put the kettle on and was sitting at the table, looking out the kitchen window. Zoey followed her gaze to see Mina grabbing a container from her fridge and shoving it in her backpack. Likely her dinner since she was on the closing shift today at Thistles and Stems.

Zoey willed Mina to look over and wave, but she didn't.

"So, how's that going?" Wren asked, drawing Zoey's attention.

"What?"

"You and Mina. How's it going?"

"We're still neighbors." Zoey knew what Wren meant, but she didn't want to go there. Mina was her neighbor and her coworker. And maybe her friend. But nothing more.

Wren rolled her eyes. "Yeah, okay, I can see that. But how's working with her? Is she good with the plants?"

The plants sounded like an innuendo, and Zoey chose to ignore it.

"Working with her is fun. She learned everything quickly, and now she can do the closing shifts by herself."

"Nice. I'm sure you've gotten to know her better in the past couple weeks then, right?"

"Yes." The word was clipped.

Wren was pushing, but Zoey wouldn't indulge her. Instead, she tossed one of the player boards for the game at Wren, then she dumped out the bags of cat tokens and picked three.

"Why won't you admit that you like her?" Wren said as she placed her score tiles on her board. "Having a crush is not something to be ashamed of."

Zoey paused setting up her board to glare at Wren. "I'm not ashamed of the crush because it doesn't exist, thank you."

Wren snorted. "It doesn't exist, my ass. Every time you get the chance to ogle Mina through the window, you take it. And you find ways to talk about her almost every time we video call. I don't think I've *ever* seen you like this. Why don't you ask her out? You have so many opportunities now. Think of how great it could be to date her while you work together!"

"You know I don't do relationships."

With a sigh, Wren got up to make them tea. "I know. I know that's what you keep saying, anyway. What I don't understand is *why* you don't do relationships, especially when you so clearly like Mina, and she is objectively an attractive human who also seems really nice. You ruled out that you're aromantic or asexual, so what's your hang up? It's not like you even have a terrible dating history like mine."

Annoyance had been crawling up Zoey's spine throughout this conversation, and she finally snapped. "Not everyone has happily married parents like yours, Wren. Some of us didn't get a great example of relationships growing up. Some of us had to take care of their depressed mother and pretty much raise themselves because their father left and ruined their childhood. So sue me if I don't worship romantic relationships like the rest of society." She reached into the purple tile bag and threw down two tiles for herself and two for Wren, then she placed three in the middle.

"Why are you bugging me about this, anyway, when you're also currently refusing to date?"

Wren set a mug of tea on the table in front of Zoey, and her voice softened when she spoke. "I'm not refusing to date, I'm just not actively looking for anyone right now." She paused. "I'm sorry. I verged into your mom's territory there, didn't I?"

"Yeah, you did."

Zoey kept her eyes on the table as Wren walked into the living room and returned. She set the half-eaten bag of M&M's in front of Zoey then sat down. Zoey took a few of the chocolate candies and shoved them in her mouth.

"I hope you get only pink tiles," she said. "And I'm going first."

ELEVEN

MINA

Mina's next day off from both Juniper Foods and Thistles and Stems happened to fall on Saturday, October 11—her thirtieth birthday. Her parents were flying into town that afternoon to celebrate, and she'd filled her fridge and pantry with ingredients for all her favorite Persian foods.

Maybe the familiar food would soften the blow when she'd tell her parents that Christian left. She wasn't sure they'd notice, and she could easily lie and say Christian was out of town again. The house looked more-or-less the same since he'd left, other than some new turquoise-and-yellow geometric throw pillows she'd bought for the living room.

But she needed to tell her parents about the breakup sooner or later, and this was as good an opportunity as any.

Mina made herself turmeric eggs and tea for breakfast. The meal always reminded her of growing up, of the rare days when everyone in her family was home in the morning and Mina would help her father prepare their food. Her entire family bonded over food, and Mina was good at cooking, especially Iranian dishes. It was the one thing she could do that her parents were proud of.

She put on an episode of *Schitt's Creek* to start her day off right. She had just finished eating when her phone chimed with a notification from Discord. Declan had sent her a *Schitt's Creek* "happy birthday" GIF. Mina laughed and sent him a photo of her TV.

DECLAN

Somehow I knew you'd be watching that right now

MINA

Are you psychic?

DECLAN

No, just super smart

If I was psychic, I'd have more money

MINA

I'd hope so

DECLAN

Going to work now, but I hope you have a good birthday

Don't die out there

Mina snorted. Before she put down her phone, she opened her text app to see if she had any other messages. Farrah had wished her a happy birthday first thing that morning, and Yasmin had messaged her shortly after. Nothing from her parents though.

It wasn't necessarily odd since they were flying out to see her in a few hours, but her anxiety flared anyway. She pressed a fist to her sternum to make the feeling go away, and when that didn't work, she went upstairs to shower.

She had just turned the water on when her phone rang. With a sigh, she switched the water off again and wrapped herself in a towel.

A black-and-white selfie of her with her father showed on her screen. She'd taken that photo on his fiftieth birthday when she'd managed to get him alone for a few moments. The two of them had always gotten along better when her mother wasn't around.

"Hi, Baba," Mina answered.

"Tavalodet mobarak, Mina joon!" he replied in a singsong voice. "I hope your day is good so far."

Mina smiled. "It is. Are you on your way to the airport?"

"That's why I'm calling, joon," her father continued, and she didn't like the shift in his tone. "Your mother and I won't be able to make it out to visit you. I'm sorry we're cancelling so last minute, but we only found out this morning."

The smile faded from her face. "Found out what? Is everything okay?"

"Yes, everything is great, actually! Yasmin is receiving an award from the Canadian Neurosurgical Society, and the ceremony is tonight. If we had known earlier, we would have celebrated with you a different day, but Yasmin only just told us. She's been so busy, you know. So much on her mind."

"Right." Mina's heart was in her throat, and she struggled to speak around it. "That's great. Give her a hug from me."

She couldn't begrudge her sister winning an award, but it stung that her parents had cancelled their flight last minute because of it. Not for the first time, their favoritism was showing and Mina was low on their priority list. So low that they didn't even blink at losing hundreds of dollars cancelling their flights so they could celebrate with her sister. And her sister hadn't even told Mina about the award.

"I will. Love you, joon. Hopefully we'll see you at Christmas, right?"

"I hope so, yeah."

Mina still hadn't asked for Christmas off, and she didn't know if she wanted to now that she'd started another job. She would barely be past her three-month probation period by then, and she didn't want to give Eleanor any reason to question her work ethic.

Neither of her parents had even celebrated Christmas growing up, but Mina knew they'd wanted their kids to celebrate the holiday that took over December for most of Canada. When Mina was younger, she'd looked forward to the gifts and the food, but now her parents' version of Christmas was more about solidifying their reputation in the law community than spending time with family.

At least now she didn't have to tell them that she and Christian broke up. She could defer that to a later date, yet again. The silver lining of a writhing dark cloud.

So that was that. Mina had the rest of the day off with an empty house and a bunch of food she would have to eat by herself.

She decided not to shower, and instead slid into a pair of black sweatpants and an artfully ripped gray tank top. She tried to think of something to do that could be fun, something that would make today not as crappy.

Declan would be at work, and she didn't want to play video games on her own. She could work on her current 3D character, but today wasn't supposed to involve work. She was supposed to be *relaxing*.

Tell that to her anxiety.

She flopped onto her couch and stared at the ceiling, and Zelda jumped onto her stomach. "It's just you and me," Mina said, running her hand down Zelda's back.

Zelda purred and settled on Mina's chest. She started making biscuits against Mina's neck, each claw a tiny pinprick of pain that Mina was used to.

"Today is supposed to be amazing," she said. "I just turned thirty, for fuck's sake. Am I going to let my parents ruin that?" Zelda didn't answer, but Mina took her continued purring as a good sign. "You're right. I'm not. I'm going to the store, I'm getting myself a gift, and I'm going to have fun. *We* are going to have fun."

Zelda complained as Mina sat up and planted a kiss on her head. "I'll be back in a bit."

She was going to the liquor store. Today called for tequila.

TWELVE

ZOEY

Eleanor had sent Zoey home at two o'clock since the store was slower than usual—so slow that Zoey had been listening to a podcast all morning. It had been about the sketchy Dyatlov Pass case, which made her extremely wary of cross-country skiing. Now she needed something brighter and less complex to fill her brain. A light romance read to match the warm October weather.

It was unseasonably hot, perfect for an afternoon of reading steamy romance in the sun. So she picked up *The Pairing* by Casey McQuiston, made herself lemonade—the audacity of lemonade in October!—grabbed her sunglasses, and sat on her back porch.

She had gotten cheap patio furniture from Get Your Gear when it was on sale the previous Christmas, and it fulfilled her needs well enough. She set her lemonade on the table and propped her feet on another chair, leaning her book on her jean-clad knees as she read.

It didn't take long for the book to absorb her, and the sounds of rustling leaves in the gentle breeze provided a soothing sound-track. The lemonade she'd made was a touch too sweet, but it was cold and refreshing, and she drank the entire thing within half an hour. When the sun became too much and she needed another drink, she slid her bookmark between the pages and stood to stretch.

Just as she turned to go inside, she heard Mina's back door open, and Mina stepped out. She wore black sweats and a tattered gray tank top that showed off enough skin to make Zoey flush, and she held a red slushy drink that made Zoey's mouth water. It looked way better than her half-assed lemonade.

Mina slumped into one of the two lounge chairs on her back porch, her black sunglasses obscuring her eyes. She huffed a loud breath, and Zoey got the feeling that something wasn't quite right.

"Hey," she called tentatively.

Mina turned to her and lifted her drink in greeting. "Hey." Her voice sounded thick, almost as if she'd been crying. "Nice day, huh?" She sniffed.

"Yeah." Zoey shifted back and forth on the balls of her feet, trying to decide if she should make more lemonade or talk to Mina. Whatever had upset Mina wasn't her business, but what if Mina wanted to talk about it? Zoey should at least give her the choice. "How are you doing?" she asked, cursing herself for how stilted the question sounded.

Mina laughed wryly. "I'm pretty sure this margarita has more tequila in it than sugar. That's how I'm doing." She sipped her drink then made a face. "Yep. That's good stuff."

Instead of asking what was wrong, Zoey waited. She knew from experience with her mom that staying quiet left space for the other person to open up.

Sure enough, after a few seconds Mina said, "Today's my birthday."

"Oh my god, happy birthday!" Although it didn't seem happy, not with how Mina was acting.

"It should be, shouldn't it?" Mina sipped her drink again and grimaced. "It's my thirtieth. It was supposed to be a big thing. I mean, I bought myself a cupcake from the bakery, so it's not like the whole day is a bust. But my parents were going to come to town for the weekend, and I thought maybe we'd go into Vancouver tomorrow after work. They were supposed to arrive this afternoon. I bought all the ingredients to make some of my favorite foods." She scoffed. "Then I get a call from Baba this morning saying that Yasmin won an award for neurosurgery, and she's receiving it tonight, so they're going to support her instead of flying out here. An award! In neurosurgery! My sister is saving lives." Mina waved her margarita around, almost slopping it over the side of the glass. "And I'm just turning thirty."

Zoey had never heard Mina say so many words at one time.

Mina continued, "Maman said they'd pick up a cake. So much for that. And now I have all this food to cook and eat by myself. Because that's exactly how I wanted to spend my thirtieth birthday. Alone." She sipped her margarita again and coughed.

"I'm so sorry," Zoey said, her heart going out to Mina. She couldn't let Mina wallow on her thirtieth birthday, of all days. "I don't usually invite myself to other people's houses, but what if I came over and celebrated with you?"

Mina leaned forward and peered at Zoey over her sunglasses. "Are you serious?"

"Yes, of course! If you want." Zoey's heart thudded against her ribs.

"Do you like Persian food?"

"I don't think I've ever eaten Persian food before. I'd love to try it."

"I mean . . . okay. Yeah. Yes, come on over. Please!" Mina hopped up and stumbled over her feet on her way to the door.

Zoey changed into something nicer that suited the weather and the occasion—a blue linen sundress with a bow at the back. She didn't have cake readily available, but she had just bought herself a giant tub of cookie dough ice cream, so she grabbed that and headed over.

At her knock, Mina swung open the door.

"Happy birthday!" Zoey said, holding out the tub. "I brought you ice cream."

"Oh." Mina had taken off her sunglasses, and she swiped at her eyes. "You're a gem, Zoey Bell." She pulled Zoey into a slightly sweaty hug. "And you look nice." She looked down at her sweats and tank top. "I should probably change."

"No, you look great." *More than* great. Those peeks of Mina's bare skin through the rips in the fabric did something to Zoey's pulse.

Mina made a *pfft* noise and ushered Zoey in, taking the ice cream from her.

Zoey slipped off her shoes and followed Mina into the kitchen. This was her first time in Mina's house, but it felt familiar enough. Especially the kitchen, which Zoey had glimpsed too many times to count.

Mina had clearly been preparing for a big meal. Ingredients sat in haphazard order on the counter: rice, a couple of pomegranates, walnuts, tomatoes, onions, and various herbs and spices.

"Are you sure you want to eat this?" Mina gestured at the food. "We can order pizza or something instead."

Mina sounded sincere, but she had said she bought ingredients for her favorite foods.

"No. If this is what you want, this is what we'll make. I'm not a top chef or anything, but I can cook. Put me to work."

The smile that broke across Mina's face lit the whole room, and affection blossomed in Zoey's chest. Wren was right. Zoey had a crush that was only growing now that she saw Mina on a more regular basis.

"Alright, you can be my sous chef. Do you eat chicken?"

Zoey nodded. "I love chicken."

"Perfect." Mina opened the fridge and took out a pack of raw chicken. "We don't need to make as much since there's only two of us. Let's get the rice going first."

Mina washed the rice and left it to soak, then had Zoey dice an onion while she prepared the chicken.

Zoey's eyes watered as she worked. "Of course, you'd give me the difficult job," she joked.

"I'm sorry!" Mina said, looking pained.

"It's fine." Zoey bumped her lightly with her hip, which made Mina smile again.

They worked well together at Thistles and Stems, and they also worked well together in the kitchen. Zoey wondered if they'd work well together in other ways too.

Once the onion was frying, Mina added turmeric and pepper, the savory smells filling the air and making Zoey's stomach growl. She hadn't realized how hungry she was, and now she couldn't wait to try the food, which Mina had called zereshk polo.

They seasoned the chicken and pre-heated the oven. "I should have left the chicken to marinate overnight, but oh well. We have to wait for a while now, but we can start the barberries," Mina said.

"What's a barberry?"

Mina raised her eyebrows. "You've never had a barberry? They're like cranberries." She scooped a few of the red berries out of a bowl of water where they were soaking and held her palm out to Zoey. "Want to try one?"

"Are they tart like cranberries?"

Mina nodded. "We cook them with sugar before they go in the rice."

"I'll wait then," Zoey said. While Wren loved sour candies and fruits, Zoey was more of a sweet person.

"Suit yourself."

Zoey made herself comfortable at the kitchen table while Mina cooked the berries and set a timer to go off when the rice needed to start cooking.

"Do you want a drink while we wait?" Mina asked. Her margarita from earlier sat on the table, untouched since Zoey had come over. "I can make you a less tequila-y margarita."

"Yes please." Zoey was sweating, even more now that the stove was on, and a cold drink sounded wonderful.

"I think I'll make myself a new one too," Mina said, dumping her half-melted margarita down the sink. "That was a lot of tequila." She laughed and rinsed the blender that had been sitting on the counter.

"So, your family is Persian?" Zoey asked as Mina gathered the ingredients for their margaritas.

"Yeah. My dad moved here with his family when he was a kid, then my mom came over when she was seventeen. They met in Toronto, and they've lived there ever since." Her voice had lost some of the life it'd had when she'd been talking about food. Maybe family wasn't the best choice of conversation topic, but Zoey wanted to know more about Mina.

"And you have a sister?"

Mina nodded but didn't answer as she blended their drinks. "Two sisters, actually," she said, pouring the slushy mixture into two glasses. "You might have heard of one of them. Farrah Hasanza? She used to be a competitive swimmer."

Zoey shrugged apologetically. "I'm not much of a sports person. I think I watched the Olympics on TV once with my mom and my aunt, but that's about it."

"No worries." Mina placed a glass in front of Zoey. "It's actually kind of nice that you don't know who she is. Then you won't compare me to her." She lifted her glass. Zoey clinked hers against it, feeling the weight of Mina's words even though Mina had said them as if they meant nothing. "Cheers."

The margarita was fresh and bright on Zoey's tongue, the strawberry flavor reminding her of sticky summers with Wren when they were kids. She hummed in contentment. "Does Farrah still swim?"

"For fun sometimes, yeah. But now she's a dentist." Mina perched on the chair across from Zoey. "Yasmin—my oldest sister —is a neurosurgeon, and both my parents are lawyers. And then, here I am. Working at a grocery store and a flower shop. And making art."

She said *art* as if it were a derogatory word. As if it meant nothing, and the fact that she was an artist made her worthless.

"What's wrong with working at a grocery store or a flower shop? I worked as a waitress for years before I opened my candle business, and now *I* work at a flower shop."

Mina's eyes widened. "Nothing. God, that's not what I meant. I just mean that my sisters are doing important things they've always wanted to do. Improving people's lives and shit. Making my parents happy."

"I think what you do improves people's lives," Zoey said firmly. "People need groceries. And good customer service is not something to scoff at, especially considering the crap we go through."

"That's true."

"And art? Making art is so important."

"Is it?" Mina's brow furrowed.

"Yes, it totally is. Why do you like making 3D models?"

Mina looked at her, her margarita-stained lips parted slightly, and even more red than her usual lipstick. Zoey had the urge to lean forward and kiss her, to lick the color right from Mina's lips, but she held herself in check.

"I guess . . . I like seeing my ideas brought to life. When I finish a project, I feel like I've accomplished something."

"So, art gives your life meaning, right?"

"I suppose," Mina said softly, looking at her drink through her thick dark eyelashes.

"Then it's important. Art gives people purpose, and it has the potential to bring joy. Just like my candles."

Mina gave a small nod. "Yeah."

"I mean it," Zoey said, feeling an urgent need to get this point across. "Your art will be in a video game one day, and someone will love that game. You're making something that matters."

When Mina looked at her once more, her eyes shone. "Okay. I believe you."

Something hung between them in that moment, and Mina's gaze jumped to Zoey's lips. Zoey's heart raced as she leaned forward . . . and the timer went off on Mina's phone. Zoey startled, almost falling off her chair.

Mina set down her drink. "Time to start the rice!"

THIRTEEN

MINA

Mina couldn't believe how quickly her day had shifted from low to high when Zoey came over.

As they waited for the rice and the chicken to finish cooking, they took their margaritas outside to the lounge chairs.

"I feel like we've only been talking about me," Mina said. "What about you?"

"I mean, it is *your* birthday," Zoey said. "It makes sense to talk about you."

Mina squirmed under the attention. "Since it's my birthday, I get to pick the topic of conversation, and I no longer want to talk about me."

Zoey laughed. "Okay, fine. What do you want to talk about, then?"

"I don't know." She bit her lip and stared at the sky, squinting even with her sunglasses on. There wasn't a cloud in sight, the blue expanse above her so saturated that it almost looked fake. Wasn't October supposed to be gloomy? "How's your candle business going?"

"I've got a booth at the Pumpkin Days market next weekend, but other than that . . . Honestly, it's been slow." Zoey blew out a stream of air, her lips fluttering like a horse's. "I feel like I've made barely any progress."

"Really? Haven't you sold at like . . . every market in the area in the past year?"

"Yeah, but that doesn't make as much money as people think. Especially since I'm a one-woman business. Wren drives up to help when she can, but it's a lot of work. I finally got my online store running last year, which has helped a bit. But I still need to make more money if I want to keep doing this." The frustration in Zoey's sigh was almost tangible. "My aunt owns the house and charges me so little rent, and I'm super grateful, but living in this town is not cheap."

Mina nodded and took a long sip of her margarita. "I feel you."

"I've been thinking of expanding my business, trying to get my candles into other shops," Zoey said, stirring her drink. She pressed her lips together thoughtfully.

"That sounds like a good idea. Do you know where you're going to start?"

"Yeah, actually. I was hoping to start with Thistles and Stems." Zoey turned to her. "Please don't tell Eleanor, though. I want to put together a proper proposal so she knows I'm serious."

"Totally. That makes sense."

Zoey hummed and wiped a bug off her thigh, leaving a streak of water from the condensation on her glass. The droplets glistened on her skin, and Mina couldn't tear her eyes away from the wet streak. If Zoey kept wearing dresses that showed off her thighs like that, Mina would be in trouble.

"I'm honestly at a loss with the proposal, though. I'm a self-made business person, and I have no training whatsoever when it comes to stuff like this."

Mina sat up and swung her legs over the side of her chair so she was facing Zoey. "I can help if you want. I have a bachelor's in business administration, and I had to put together a few business proposals throughout my degree."

Zoey's jaw dropped. "Seriously?"

"Yeah. It wasn't exactly what I wanted to do, but it made my parents happy. Even if I've done pretty much nothing with it." To her parents' chagrin.

"You're telling me I've been struggling with my business, and I've been living next to someone with business management experience for three years now?"

"I guess so, yeah. I think I mentioned it to you at some point."

"Fuck." Zoey facepalmed, which Mina had never seen someone do in real life before. She stifled a laugh.

"My degree was also on my resume," she said.

"You think I read that? I was so sure you'd get the job, I just handed it off to Eleanor." Zoey groaned. "Okay, whatever, past failure to be observant aside . . . You'll help me?"

"Yeah, if you want."

"Mina Hasanza, *you* are the gem in this friendship." The way Zoey looked at her made Mina's ears warm.

The timer went off for the food, startling both her and Zoey. "Shit," Zoey said, looking at the spilled drink on her hand. She licked it off, the action making Mina swallow—hard.

"I'll get paper towel," she said, running inside. Why did Zoey have to be so attractive? The image of Zoey licking her skin stuck in Mina's brain.

Mina practically threw the paper towel at Zoey then returned inside to check the chicken and rice. She poured a bit of saffron water on the rice. Everything was ready, so she busied herself with plating their food.

Zoey entered the kitchen, brushing past Mina to throw out the now-red paper towels. "Can I help?"

Mina kept her eyes on the food. "No, I've got it. You can sit if you want. Do you need another drink?"

"I think I'll just have water, if that's okay."

"Sure. Glasses are in there." Mina gestured with her nose, her hands currently occupied. She arranged the chicken around the rice on each plate, the barberries adding bright splashes of red to the dish. As a finishing touch, she added chopped pistachios. Her favorite.

"This looks delicious," Zoey said as Mina set the two plates on the table. She closed her eyes and inhaled. "And it smells even better."

Mina couldn't help the happiness bubbling through her. "Let's hope it tastes good too."

It did, and Mina's pride in it was boosted by the somewhat obscene moaning noises Zoey made as she ate. "Are you always this enthusiastic about your food?" Mina asked, suppressing a laugh.

"Only when it's this good." Zoey winked at her, and Mina ducked her head as she continued eating.

She'd never been able to share Persian food like this with Christian because he wasn't a fan of all the herbs and spices, and Mina refused to make the food without flavor. It made her happier than she expected to see someone who wasn't in her family enjoying it so much. This was food that Mina and Zoey had made together. Food that reminded Mina of the best parts of her family, of the good memories she had of growing up, which were few and far between.

This meal felt like home, and it was the best gift she could have given herself—and that Zoey could have given her—for her birthday.

"That was so good," Zoey said when their plates were empty. She sat back in her chair, her hand on her stomach. "I don't think I have room for ice cream right now."

Mina shook her head. "Me either."

"Do you want to watch a movie or something until we're ready for dessert?"

That sounded great, if Mina was honest, but Zoey had already spent a couple of hours with her. "Are you sure you want to stay longer? I feel like I've taken up so much of your day."

Zoey shrugged. "I can go if you want, but I have nowhere to

be and nothing urgent to do. Plus, it's not a true birthday celebration without dessert, right? Leaving now would be practically blasphemous."

"I had a cupcake earlier."

"Doesn't count. You have to eat the dessert *after dinner*."

"If you say so." Mina gathered their dishes so she could turn away from Zoey. She didn't want Zoey to see the ridiculous happiness likely shining on her face.

"So what do you want to watch?" Zoey asked. "A movie, a TV show . . . or a video game! I can totally play a video game, as long as it's not too difficult. I haven't played one in years."

Mina bit her lip, trying not to smile too big. "We can watch something, it's fine. Have you seen *Schitt's Creek*?"

Zoey shook her head. "I've heard of it. It's a comedy?"

"Yeah. It's about a rich family that loses all their money and moves to a small town, kind of like Juniper Creek, but not as nice or as touristy. Declan got me into it a while ago. I've seen all the episodes, but it's my favorite show."

"That sounds fun. I'm down."

They started from the beginning, Mina sitting at one end of the couch and Zoey at the other. Zoey cringed and laughed in all the right places, and Mina enjoyed watching her reactions more than she enjoyed rewatching the show. By the third episode, they were ready for ice cream. By the fifth episode, they had made tea.

During episode six, as they watched one of the characters attempt to film an ad for a local wine company, it hit Mina that this was the best birthday she'd had in years. Even with her parents' cancelled plans, she was happy.

She looked at Zoey, who threw her head back in laughter, her smile wide as she enjoyed Mina's favorite show. In that moment, Mina couldn't express how grateful she was for the woman who had moved in next door.

She thought about what Zoey had said earlier.

Mina Hasanza, you are the gem in this friendship.

They had truly become friends. Friends, coworkers, neighbors. And, if Mina let herself think about it, something even more simmered beneath the surface.

FOURTEEN

ZOEY

Zoey had enjoyed celebrating Mina's birthday more than she'd expected. She wanted to eat dinner with Mina again soon, maybe even watch more *Schitt's Creek* with her. And the fact that she wanted that scared her.

As much as it pained her to admit that Wren had been right, she needed to talk to her best friend. As soon as Wren answered the video chat, Zoey went straight into it. "I like Mina, and I don't know what to do about it."

"Ha! I knew it!" Wren said, her expression smug. She was in the midst of doing her makeup, getting ready for her shift at the salon. "I knew you had feelings for her, you fucking liar."

Zoey rolled her eyes. "Yeah, whatever. Crow about it all you want *after* you help me. What do I do?"

"Ask her on a date," Wren replied as if it were obvious.

For anyone else, Zoey supposed it would be obvious. But for her, asking someone out was a huge step from everything she thought she knew about herself. She did not do romance. Hookups, yes. But romance meant a meaningful connection with someone, and it was way too risky. She wouldn't put herself in that position. She wouldn't allow herself to get attached when she knew what would happen when the relationship crumbled.

As if Wren was reading her mind, she said, "It doesn't have to mean anything. You can date casually, no labels. Hang out with her because you like her. No one is saying you have to be or do more than that."

Zoey's nerves calmed at that. One date. One *casual* date. That didn't sound so bad. Now that she thought about it, she could spend more time with Mina without even needing to formally ask her out because Mina had volunteered to help with her business proposal.

It was perfect.

Although Zoey had been reluctant to hire a consultant, working with Mina didn't scare her. She already trusted her, and she highly doubted Mina would try to take the reins on the project. Her business would remain safely in her control.

After she finished her call with Wren, she pulled up Mina's text thread. They'd texted a few times about florist-related stuff, but this was the first non-work-related text, and it felt momentous somehow. Zoey bit her lip.

ZOEY

Hey! Would you be able to come over after work on Saturday to help with my proposal? The market ends at 5, so I can make dinner for around 6:30

Mina's response was almost immediate, sending a thrill of excitement through Zoey.

MINA

Sure! Want me to bring anything?

ZOEY

Dessert? Wine? Whatever suits your fancy

MINA

Wine it is

ZOEY

Great! See you then

They'd see each other before Saturday at the shop, but now they had an official date to work on Zoey's business proposal, and it was definitely leaning toward a *date*-date. Dinner, wine, maybe Zoey would light a candle . . .

No matter what happened, she had to keep it casual. She didn't want to ruin her friendship with Mina, and she wasn't about to launch herself into a deep relationship that could tear her life apart.

With that settled, she pulled out her planner to figure out Saturday's menu. She wanted it to be delicious.

THE WEATHER HAD COOLED BY SATURDAY, AND ZOEY pulled her jean jacket closed over her vintage plaid dress as she sat at her market table. The park was full of vendors and Halloween-themed game stations, the smell of freshly popped popcorn floating on the breeze. Kids ran around in their Halloween costumes, laughing and shrieking, as parents perused the goods available. Zoey smiled at everyone who walked by, trying to entice people to look at her candles. She'd sold a few so far, but not as many as she'd hoped.

A familiar face made her smile turn more genuine. Mina approached her table, waving. She must have been on her break. Black ripped jeans hugged her legs, a pastel color-block button-up shirt tucked smartly into them. A pair of black Chuck Taylors made the entire outfit look effortlessly casual, even with the dash of silver glitter Mina had used at the corners of her eyes.

Zoey hoped she kept that outfit on for their date/meeting/get-together that night.

"How's it going?" Mina asked, sticking her hands in her jean pockets.

"Not too bad. You?"

"Work is slow. I think everyone is over here." Mina picked up one of the candles and took the lid off so she could sniff it. "Is this a new one?"

Zoey nodded. "Pumpkin Spice Latte Dreams. What every basic White girl needs."

With an amused twitch of her eyebrows, Mina said, "I don't fit either of those categories, but I like it."

Zoey laughed. "Good." She shifted in her chair as Mina sniffed another candle. "Looking forward to tonight?"

"Yeah," Mina said, setting the candle down again. "I emailed you a business proposal template this morning, so we can use that to work from. It shouldn't take long."

"Okay. We'll have plenty of time to eat dinner then." And maybe do more than that, if the atmosphere was right.

Ever since Wren suggested that Zoey ask Mina out, she couldn't stop thinking of the possibilities. She'd never let herself consider them before because if she thought about it, there was no going back.

And now it was too late.

Her brain was full of Mina all the time.

She wondered how Mina would react if Zoey kissed her. She wondered how Mina's lips would feel against hers, if her red lipstick would bleed into Zoey's skin, making both of them look scandalously disheveled. She wondered how Mina would taste.

"Yeah." Mina gave her a close-lipped smile, and Zoey reminded herself that Mina knew nothing about her current fantasies.

This wasn't really a date. Not unless Zoey made it one, and she didn't want to come off too strong.

Maybe she'd save the potential *other stuff* for later.

"Anyway, I should probably get back," Mina said, gesturing over her shoulder toward Thistles and Stems. "Eleanor is covering for me, but I know she wants to come say hi too."

"Okay. Well, I'll see you tonight."

With an endearingly awkward thumbs-up, Mina turned on her heel and walked back to the store. Zoey forced her gaze back to the potential customers walking by. She could look at Mina all she wanted later.

ZOEY HAD GRABBED GROCERIES EARLIER THAT WEEK TO make caprese chicken with a balsamic glaze, with roasted vegetables and a salad on the side. The meal was easy enough to make, and Zoey had the table set and the food ready when Mina rang the doorbell around six-thirty.

"Hello!" Zoey singsonged as she opened the door. The market hadn't gone as well as she'd hoped, but cooking while listening to a murder podcast had put her back in a good mood.

"Hey." Mina grinned, her backpack slung over one shoulder and a bottle of wine in hand.

Zoey stepped aside. "Come on in."

Mina slipped off her shoes and leaned her bag against the wall. "It smells amazing in here."

"Thank you. I made caprese chicken. I thought you'd be hungry, so we can eat first then work on my stuff."

"Sounds great."

Mina followed Zoey to the kitchen, and Zoey gestured for her to sit. Mina poured them both wine while Zoey brought the food to the table.

"How did the market go?" Mina asked.

Zoey shrugged. "Not the worst. Not the best. The new scents sold well at least, so that's a plus. Oh, but guess what? Someone proposed in front of the haunted house!"

"Really?" The glitter by Mina's eyes sparkled as she raised her eyebrows. "Please tell me their partner said yes."

"They did." Zoey beamed. Just because she didn't want a relationship for herself didn't mean she begrudged seeing other people happy in love.

"That's cute. Maybe they'll have a Halloween wedding, with black outfits and creepy music and stuff."

Zoey laughed. "That'd be a unique wedding, for sure."

"Have you been to many weddings?" Mina asked.

Zoey was pleased to see Mina had finished almost all her food, which meant she probably liked it. Since Zoey cooked only for herself most of the time, she usually didn't put in much effort. The last time she'd cooked regularly was when she was taking care of her mom. She was sure her cheeks were practically glowing with pride at the sight of Mina licking her fork clean.

She swallowed. "A couple. You?"

"Yeah." Mina's nose wrinkled. "My parents used to stuff me into frilly dresses and parade me around with my sisters. We had to be on our best behavior at all times. I always wanted to run around with the other kids, but if I got caught . . . I'd regret it."

Those words made Zoey's eyes widen.

When Mina saw her expression, she said, "Whoa, not like that. My parents didn't hit us or anything. They just took away our stuff. For me, it was my video games. I rarely got time to play in the first place, so it was like the end of the world."

Zoey relaxed, but she didn't like the thought of anyone hurting Mina in any way.

"What were your favorite games when you were a kid?"

She knew they were supposed to work on her business proposal at some point that evening, but all she wanted to do was drink wine and listen to Mina talk about her childhood.

Especially with the look of fond nostalgia that stole over Mina's face.

"I loved *The Legend of Zelda: Ocarina of Time*, *Donkey Kong 64*, and *Mario Party 2*."

"That's why you have the tattoo!" Zoey gestured behind her ear. She'd caught sight of Mina's tattoo a few times in the past couple of years, but she'd only recently figured out what it was.

"Yeah, Navi. A lot of people hate her and find her super

annoying, but I like how she demands attention. It's a skill I lack." She let out a wry laugh.

Zoey didn't know what to make of that, so she stuck to the video game topic. "I also had an N64. Those were the days."

Mina nodded. "My parents got us a Nintendo 64 and a few games, but we were only allowed to play for an hour every Saturday. That hour was like heaven on earth."

"One hour a week? Damn, I thought my parents had been strict."

Zoey's mother had insisted that she spend an hour a day outside, and her dad—before he left—told her that too much time in front of the TV would burn out her eyeballs. She hadn't fully believed him, but the warning never left her. She sometimes wondered if it was why she preferred podcasts over TV shows or movies these days.

Mina sat back in her chair and swirled her wine in her glass. "Yeah. They got me a Game Boy to keep me out of our nanny's hair at Farrah's swim practices. And they caved and got us a PlayStation when we were older, but that was because my cousins came over and laughed at us for not having one. God forbid we didn't meet the expectations of other children, much less adults."

The more Mina talked about her parents, the less Zoey liked them. She knew what being under pressure felt like, and Mina had clearly been under *a lot* of pressure.

Mina smirked. "I found ways around their time restrictions, though."

"Oh? Do tell." Zoey leaned forward with her elbows on the table, loving that glint in Mina's eye.

"Okay, but you have to promise not to laugh."

Zoey narrowed her eyes. "I promise I'll *try* not to laugh."

Mina studied her, and Zoey felt her cheeks turning pink under Mina's gaze. "Okay." She paused. "I started scrapbooking."

"Scrapbooking?" Zoey almost broke her promise.

"I know, it's usually associated with soccer moms or older White ladies. It's coming back into style, though, I swear."

Zoey had to give her that. Crafting was definitely popular again, especially in the queer community. "How exactly was scrapbooking rebelling against your parents?"

"Since I couldn't play video games as much as I wanted, I kind of tricked my parents into letting me make books about them. I told them I needed supplies for an art project at school, which wasn't technically a lie, but then I used those supplies to make books about my favorite games. I wanted to live in those worlds for longer, you know? Escape reality for a while. And then I kept making the books as I got older."

"I love that." Zoey could picture a younger Mina with her arms full of pencil crayons and construction paper, taking back power in her own way. It made her heart squeeze.

Mina huffed out a laugh. "Thanks. That's all the rebellion I could really get away with."

A thought swirled in Zoey's mind for yet another way she could spend time with Mina. She had turned into a fiend—once she started, she couldn't stop.

"Do you still have your scrapbooking supplies?"

"Yeah. Why?"

"What if we had, like, a scrapbooking day? Wren's thirty-first birthday is coming up, and I'd love to make her a scrapbook of our friendship. I hadn't thought of it before now, but you've inspired me."

Mina rubbed the back of her neck and smiled sheepishly at Zoey. "Yeah? I mean, yeah, that sounds fun. You can use me—m-my stuff, whenever you want."

The flub made Zoey's heart jackrabbit against her ribs, and Mina bolted out of her chair to take the dishes to the sink.

Trying once more not to laugh and resisting the urge to make a joke, Zoey said, "Should we start working on the business proposal?"

Mina's voice was small when she replied in the affirmative, and it took all of Zoey's self-control not to smooth her hands down Mina's shoulders and tell her how amazing she was. How she didn't need to be embarrassed.

While Zoey had never liked the language of people *using* each other, if Mina wanted to, Zoey would let her do anything she wanted to her. In fact, Zoey was starting to hunger for it.

FIFTEEN

MINA

Mina wanted to sink through the floor, into the earth's crust and right through to its core. She couldn't believe she'd slipped like that. Well, she could, because Zoey made her nervous and she was bound to do stupid things when she was nervous.

But that statement . . .

You can use me whenever you want.

What the fuck was that? The two of them spent all of two dinners together, and suddenly Mina wanted Zoey in her pants. She'd always found Zoey attractive, but this was next level. And now she was spewing her horniness by accident at the first opportunity.

Thank god Zoey had suggested they work on the business proposal. Maybe she hadn't even noticed the slip. But of course she had—there was no way she hadn't. At least she didn't say anything about it.

Zoey put the kettle on and grabbed her laptop, putting it on the recently cleared kitchen table.

Mina took a deep breath to pull herself together, focusing on the cold wooden floor under her feet and the hardness of the chair under her butt. She hadn't taken her extra anxiety meds, and now she was regretting it. Once she felt more situated in her body, she said, "So, show me what you've got so far."

Zoey snorted. "Alright." She pulled a blank document up on the screen and gestured to it as if she was showing off. "This took hours and hours of work."

"Impressive."

"Thank you." Zoey sighed dramatically. "There were words on it once upon a time, but alas, they disappeared."

"They do that sometimes, I've heard."

"Yeah, I think they hate me. I can't make them stay."

"They just haven't gotten to know you yet." Mina winced. She didn't know what had come over her, but the sentence had come out of her mouth before she could stop it.

Zoey's lips parted, as if whatever witty remark she'd prepared had fled her mind. Her eyes locked on Mina's, her blue-green gaze soft, and heat shot through Mina's lower belly.

They needed to get back to business.

"Did you get the email I sent?" Mina asked.

Zoey rocked back as if jolted. "Yeah, I did." She opened the email.

"Awesome. We can work off this to get going. I put in everything I think you'll need as a freelance candle business, so all you have to do is replace the template text with your specific information."

"You make it sound so easy."

Mina shrugged, and her shoulder brushed against Zoey's, sending sparks down her arm. "It should be, as long as we aren't missing any info."

"Okay." Zoey straightened and rolled back her shoulders. "Let's do this."

They managed to stay on task for the next two hours. Mina pulled out her laptop, and they decided to compose the proposal on it instead of Zoey's. That way, Zoey could use hers to find the relevant info in her files more easily. Mina felt like she was learning

Zoey's trade secrets, but Zoey didn't seem bothered to show Mina her sales information.

"Okay, now we get to the juicy stuff," Mina said, stretching her arms and trying to avoid hitting Zoey's ponytail.

"Analyzing the market wasn't juicy? I was practically drooling at all that research." Sarcasm dripped from Zoey's words.

Mina rolled her eyes. "That was the groundwork. Now we need to devise strategies for marketing and distribution to show the stores you know what you're doing. And we need to draw up final projections."

"God, you really did take business classes, didn't you? Listen to all that—*devise strategies*, *draw up final projections*. Why aren't you a business consultant or something?"

That hit a nerve, and Mina tried not to let it show. "It's not exactly fun, as I'm sure you've noticed."

Zoey nodded. "Oh, I have. I'm sure it gets some people going, but I am not one of them."

"Me either." Mina yawned, covering her mouth.

"Don't do that . . ." Zoey yawned too and ended it with a groan. "Okay, I think we're done with this for the night. This is way more than I had before."

"Even before the words fled the document?"

"Yep. Do you mind coming back again to help me finish it? Or I can go to your place, if you want."

"I'm not sure there's much difference," Mina said, looking out Zoey's kitchen window at her own dark kitchen. "But yeah, I don't mind."

In fact, she looked forward to it. Even doing something boring with Zoey meant spending time with her, which was one of Mina's favorite new activities.

Zoey put their empty mugs in the sink while Mina packed up her laptop, then they had an awkward goodbye before Mina left. A few seconds later, she was in her own kitchen, trying to avoid staring longingly out her window. It was convenient to spend time with someone who lived so close.

Mina found herself humming tunelessly as she prepared Zelda's dinner. She'd just put Zelda's bowl on the floor when she remembered Zoey's scrapbooking request. She grabbed her phone.

MINA

When is Wren's birthday?

When Zoey didn't answer right away, Mina pocketed her phone and went to make herself a cup of tea. She was tired, but she wanted to squeeze in game time with Declan if she could. He'd probably be awake.

She plugged in the samovar and turned to see Zoey with her hands in the sink, bubbles climbing her wrists. Mina let out a huff of amusement through her nose, and Zoey looked over as if she heard. A grin grew across her face, and she waved with one soapy hand.

Mina waved back and pulled out her phone, pointing to it.

Zoey raised a brow then made an *aha!* face and dried off her hands. She disappeared from the window frame and returned a second later. Mina's phone pinged.

ZOEY

Next weekend. Why?

MINA

You want to make her a scrapbook, right?
Gotta do it before then

ZOEY

Oh yeah! When works?

MINA

Tomorrow evening?

It was entertaining to text someone while looking at them through a window. Zoey gave Mina a thumbs-up.

MINA

I'll make dinner this time

ZOEY

Can I bring anything?

MINA

Drinks?

Another thumbs-up. Mina idly wondered if this would be their new primary form of communication—half text, half charades.

Instead of texting goodnight, Mina waved. Zoey mimed sleeping with her hands together as the pillow, making Mina laugh.

While she did manage to fit in a game with Declan before she got too tired, her mind was otherwise occupied. She couldn't stop thinking about Zoey.

MINA'S STEPS FELT ODDLY LIGHT AT JUNIPER FOODS the next day. She seemed to float around the store, humming as she took inventory and cleaned up a jug of spilled milk. She'd been hired only for cashier duties. But Vera had soon realized that Mina would do whatever was needed, and she'd quickly promoted Mina to supervisor.

"What's got you in such a good mood?" Vera asked, her arms crossed as she looked at Mina with narrowed eyes. A smile hovered around her lips.

"I'm just having a good day," Mina replied, shrugging. A good day that would get even better when Zoey came over later that evening.

"And what makes today so good? I can't remember the last time I saw you like this—tapping your toes and practically dancing around. And are you singing under your breath? I don't think I've *ever* seen you like this, come to think of it."

Mina bit the inside of her lip, trying to decide if she should tell Vera about Zoey. Not only about Zoey being in her life more, but about how she was developing feelings she could no longer easily ignore.

Not after yesterday.

Not after how she'd wanted to kiss Zoey multiple times in one evening.

"Oh, you know. This and that."

She couldn't own up to it out loud yet. It scared her that she was catching feelings for someone else only a couple months after Christian had left. It seemed like she should need more time after a nine-year relationship. But then again, she hadn't exactly loved Christian in the same way for the past couple of years. Something had soured between them long before he left, and she'd felt it even if she hadn't done anything about it.

That was what scared her about what was happening now with Zoey.

Zoey wasn't the same as Christian. Not even close. But Mina and Christian's relationship had started out with stomach butterflies, longing glances, and the desire to spend all their time together too.

Sunshine and rainbows could quickly turn dark and stormy.

Vera's eyes sparkled just like Eleanor's did. "Does *this and that* have a name?"

"Maybe."

Of course, Vera saw right through her.

"Alright, well, I hope it goes well. I'm patient. I can wait until you're ready to tell me about them."

Mina tried unsuccessfully to suppress her grin, and Vera squeezed her shoulder. "It's good to see you smiling again," she said.

It felt good to be smiling again, and Mina could only hope it would last.

AFTER WORK, MINA PREPARED SOME SALMON, RICE, AND vegetable sabzi to feed herself and Zoey. Once the fish was in the oven, she pulled out her giant bin of scrapbooking supplies. Zoey would be there in half an hour or so.

Mina was jealous that Zoey had enough photos of her and Wren to make an entire scrapbook about their friendship. She didn't have any friends like that—people close enough to have years' worth of photos with. She had a few acquaintances in town and friends from university who were now scattered around North America, but she wasn't close with any of them. She'd known Declan the longest, but their relationship was mostly online through video games. They didn't have many photos with each other from after high school.

The closest she got would've been Christian, and she *had* made a scrapbook of their relationship for their last Christmas together. He'd barely even looked at it, and he'd called it *neat*. That should have been a sign that things between them were going south, but he'd become so dismissive and busy with work that Mina had brushed off his reaction even though it had hurt. Now that scrapbook was in the trash with the rest of her Christian-related artifacts.

Luckily for Zoey, Mina had an empty coil scrapbook ready to be filled that she could use for Wren's gift.

Mina washed the dirty dishes in the sink and wiped the counter, then checked the rice. She'd used her Persian rice cooker tonight so she could easily get perfectly golden tahdig. Everything looked good and the smell of baked salmon, honey, and spices filled the air.

She started laying out the scrapbook materials on the table: a stack of different colored and patterned paper, tape and sticky tabs, glue sticks, stickers for all occasions, a variety of crafting scissors, boxes of pencil crayons and markers, and rolls of washi tape.

Zelda hopped on the table, sniffing at the glue sticks. "This isn't for you," Mina said, shooing her off. With her nose in the air, Zelda sauntered away as if she couldn't care less about the craft supplies.

Mina rolled her eyes. A knock on the front door startled her, and she dashed to answer it.

"Hey," she said, opening the door to reveal Zoey with a grocery bag full of drinks over her arm and a laptop bag over her shoulder. It was white and patterned with bright orange foxes. "Come on in."

Mina took the drinks from her so she could take off her shoes and coat, then Zoey followed her through the living room to the kitchen. Mina set the drinks on the table, and Zoey let her bag slide onto a chair.

"Eesh, you really do have a lot of scrapbooking stuff," Zoey said.

"I don't use it as much as I used to, but I collected it for years. How was work?"

"Good. Nothing special to report." She pulled out her laptop then set out the drinks. "I brought a variety of options for us this evening," she said in a posh-sounding voice. Mina assumed she was trying to mimic a fancy British waiter, and the lack of accuracy was amusing. "We've got a smattering of choices for Bubly, pop, and beer."

"Wow, you really committed."

Zoey dropped the accent. "I was out of drinks at home, so I stocked up on the way here. I'll be taking whatever's left with me, don't worry." She winked at Mina. "So where's your secret shelf of scrapbooks?"

Mina snorted. "It's not a secret. They're on a shelf in the office." The office she'd taken over once Christian had left. With him gone, she no longer had to work in a corner in the living room. She could put her artwork on the walls and her scrapbooks on the shelf where his figurines had been. It was nice to have a real workspace for once.

"Can I see them?"

She wasn't sure why Zoey wanted to see them, but it wouldn't do any harm. "Sure, I guess." While she was in her office, she also grabbed her small photo printer and a stack of photo paper.

"Here," she said, handing one of her newer scrapbooks to Zoey. "I started this one right before my 3D modelling classes." As Zoey flipped it open, Mina set up the printer so Zoey wouldn't feel like she was hovering.

"This is so cool." Zoey turned the book around to show Mina a page filled with pictures of fantasy elves with delicate ears. "Is this your favorite artist?"

"One of them, yeah. We had to pick an artist as inspiration in our first class."

Mina grabbed a lime Bubly and moved the drinks to the counter while Zoey kept flipping pages. When Mina glanced over at her, she was smiling fondly, and Mina's heart fluttered.

"I'll be honest. I didn't know what to expect when you said you enjoyed scrapbooking, but I get the appeal now. This is a nice keepsake. I feel like we've moved to online albums these days, which don't have the same weight, you know?"

"Yeah, exactly. It's more fun when you can look at something you made with your own hands."

Even Declan had seen the appeal. One year in high school, they'd made each other lore books for Christmas. Hers was about *The Elder Scrolls* and his was about *Dark Souls*. The book he'd made her still had pride of place on her scrapbook shelf, its cover facing out instead of only the spine showing like the rest of them. Memories like that made her miss Declan fiercely, even though she'd played *Elden Ring* with him the night before.

"I love that," Zoey said.

"So, should we eat then work?"

"Sounds good. What will you work on while I make Wren's gift?"

"I have stuff to do on my computer, if that's okay."

"Totally. Whatever you need to do. I'm just here for the food and to mooch off your art supplies."

Mina loved that they were close enough now for Zoey to mooch off her. "Mooch away."

SIXTEEN

ZOEY

Zoey devoured the salmon, rice, and sabzi Mina had made. She didn't love seafood, but whatever Mina had spiced the salmon with made it so good that Zoey took seconds. And the crispy rice! Zoey couldn't believe she'd been missing out on that her whole life.

"My god," she said after dinner, leaning back in her chair and patting her stomach, "you'll have to roll me home later. I don't know if I can even lean forward to work on the scrapbook."

"I'm glad you liked it."

Zoey saw the delighted expression on Mina's face before she carried their dishes to the sink, and warmth flowed through her. She loved how she could make Mina smile like that so easily.

"What music do you like?" Mina asked, wiping her hands on a towel.

"Umm." Zoey hadn't been thinking about music at all, and every band she'd ever heard of fled her brain. "Doesn't matter. Nothing screamy."

Mina nodded, and a few seconds later, an indie rock band Zoey hadn't heard before started playing from a speaker on Mina's counter.

"I don't listen to music much these days," Zoey said. "But I've got a never-ending queue of podcasts."

Mina glanced at her while she pulled a few glass containers out of a drawer. "What kind of podcasts?"

"True crime." Zoey took a container from Mina to pack up the leftover rice.

"Seriously? Doesn't that stuff make you paranoid?"

"Not really? I mean, it can sometimes. But mostly it makes me feel secure. Like if I know what could potentially go wrong, I can prepare for it. If that makes sense."

"It does, sort of. Still weird."

Zoey stuck her tongue out at Mina, who returned the gesture.

The two of them finished cleaning the kitchen together, and the whole scenario felt so pleasantly domestic that Zoey thought of Mom. When Mom's depression hadn't kept her in bed, the two of them would cook together almost every night.

"Alright, time for the fun stuff," Mina said, grabbing a beer from the pack Zoey had placed in the fridge.

"Hand me one, please."

Their fingers brushed as Mina gave Zoey the can, and Zoey swore tiny fireworks went off where their skin touched. Eventually, she'd need to do something about that.

"So, what photos do you want to use?" Mina asked, sitting at the table.

"Right." Zoey sat too and turned to her computer, feeling the absence of Mina's touch keenly. "I've got a heck ton of photos. Maybe I should pick, like, one from each year or something?"

"Sure."

"Want to help me choose?"

"If you want me to."

The thought of Mina seeing pieces of her past was oddly exciting, and Zoey didn't want to analyze that feeling too much. She scooched over so she was closer to Mina, turning her computer so Mina could see the hundreds of photos of Zoey and Wren.

"Oh my god, how old are you here?" Mina asked, pointing at

a photo of a young Zoey with a missing front tooth. She and Wren smiled at the camera, holding ice cream cones.

"Seven or eight, maybe?" Zoey laughed. "Wren and I had a competition to see who could lose all their baby teeth first, and I was definitely falling behind. Losing that front tooth was a serious accomplishment."

"Did you use the slam-the-door trick?"

Zoey shuddered. "I did, and I never want to think about it again."

"Ice cream is clearly a thing for you two," Mina said, pointing to another photo of Wren with melted ice cream dripping down her hand.

"Yeah, it is. We used to go to Birch Bay every summer with Wren's parents, and there was an ice cream store by the beach that had the best raspberry swirl ice cream. It was our favorite."

"Was?"

Zoey nodded, her smile faltering. "We haven't been there in ages. I don't even know if that shop exists anymore." She hummed thoughtfully then continued scrolling through the photos, through the snapshots of her life. All the photos had happy subjects, none of them betraying how stressed Zoey had been and how bad her mother's depression had gotten.

None of them featured her dad.

She started selecting photos, aiming to get one for each year. She'd organized them chronologically, which helped.

"I think I've got all the pictures," Zoey said, sipping her beer. She'd bought craft beer that was sweeter than she was used to, but she didn't mind.

"Okay, let's get them printed."

It took another few minutes to size them all, then Mina printed them out. "I can cut them out, if you want to start picking papers," Mina offered.

"Don't you have your own stuff to work on?"

Mina shrugged. "It's not urgent." She picked up one of the

photo pages. "You two are so cute. How did you become friends?"

Zoey paused her paper browsing, a smile bursting across her face. "It was our first day of kindergarten. My mom didn't work at the school then like she does now, and I didn't want her to leave when she dropped me off. I remember clinging to her skirt, determined not to let go no matter what. Then this other girl comes over—she was wearing a pink sparkly jacket, and it was the coolest thing I had ever seen—and says something like, 'It's okay. Your mom will be back. Do you want to build a tower with me?' And that was it."

She blinked back to Mina's kitchen to see Mina smirking at her. "What?"

"You're won over pretty easily, aren't you?" Mina said, a mischievous glint in her eyes.

Zoey scoffed. "I can just tell when someone has a good vibe."

"Yeah? What's my vibe? What was my vibe when you first met me?"

There was no way Zoey could make any progress on this scrapbook with Mina asking her questions like that. And yet, she wanted to answer. She wanted Mina to keep asking questions, to keep talking to her.

"Honestly?" Zoey pulled out a piece of yellow paper with abstract white lines on it. It felt happy, perfect as the backdrop for the first photo of her and Wren. She set it aside and kept her eyes on the other papers as she flipped through them, not thinking too much, just going for the ones that gave her a good feeling.

"No, I want you to lie to me." Mina looked even more mischievous when Zoey frowned at her, and she couldn't help but think that roguishness suited Mina. Her neighbor wasn't usually this sassy. "Of course, honestly." Her face transformed as she laughed, becoming somehow more striking than usual.

Zoey's heart fluttered. She didn't know if she was ready to tell Mina the whole truth about her feelings, but she could tell her part of it.

"When you came over with cinnamon buns, I knew you were a good person," Zoey said, grabbing a pair of scissors to cut squiggly edges for her first photo frame.

Mina snorted.

"No, seriously. Anyone who can bake like that has good vibes. Also"—she looked at Mina, her mouth suddenly dry—"I liked you. You made me feel comfortable, like I'd picked a good place to live."

Mina huffed a laugh through her nose. "Really?"

"Really." Maybe that had been too much. "What did you think of me?"

Mina handed her a stack of the first few photos she'd cut out, and their fingers brushed again. The tiny fireworks returned.

If Mina noticed, she didn't say anything about it.

When she spoke next, her voice was softer than Zoey had expected. "You made me comfortable too. I don't know why, but whenever I saw you through your window back then, I felt safe. Like I knew you'd be there if I needed someone. Which sounds stupid because we didn't even know each other."

Zoey's lips parted as she let out a quiet, surprised breath. "That's really sweet."

Mina looked at her, her gaze so earnest that Zoey's chest ached. "I still feel that way, really. Maybe even more now that Christian doesn't live here. And now that I know you better." Her words still had that soft quality, as if she was scared to share this but wanted to all the same.

Zoey couldn't help herself. She reached out to grab Mina's hand, to feel Mina's smooth skin against her own.

The air between them was like a live wire, as if the tiny fireworks had grown. Zoey leaned forward, just a few inches, but Mina's phone went off and they both snapped back to their own chairs.

As Mina looked at her phone, she frowned.

"Everything okay?" Zoey asked.

"It's my mom. She keeps nagging me to visit them for Christmas, and she said she'll pay for the flights. But if I go, I'll have to tell her that Christian and I broke up."

Zoey had admittedly forgotten about Christian. He'd been out of the picture for a while now, and she'd never liked him anyway. "You haven't told them yet?"

Mina shook her head and bit her lip. "They aren't going to react well. They really liked him."

"Seriously? I didn't really know the guy, but he seemed like an asshole."

Mina looked incredulously at Zoey then burst out laughing.

"Oh my god." Zoey covered her mouth. "Sorry, that was totally uncalled for."

Swiping her fingers beneath her eyes, Mina said, "No, I agree. He was. I didn't really see it until he left, but he was definitely an asshole. Did I ever tell you how he broke up with me?"

"No. You just said he left."

"That's true, technically speaking. He literally packed most of his shit and left while I was at work one day. I came home to a letter on the table and instructions about paying the bills."

Mina said it so casually, as if it didn't matter to her anymore, but Zoey's jaw dropped.

"He did *what*?"

"I know, right? He was a charmer, that one."

"That's awful, Mina! I am so sorry."

Mina waved her off. "I'm not. I mean, yeah, it hurt in the moment. But it didn't take long for me to realize we'd both been unhappy for a long time. We lived in the same house and barely saw each other. When he was home, he stayed in his office and pretty much only came out for meals. We never did anything together anymore. And when he was home . . . I felt like I was walking on eggshells. Like everything had to be exactly how he wanted it, or he'd get upset."

Zoey's throat thickened as she listened, hating what Mina had gone through.

"I don't know when it happened, but he'd gotten really

controlling. I think he might have always been like that, actually, and I just didn't notice somehow. I was too caught up in the things I did like about him to see the things I didn't. And then we were kind of stuck together."

Zoey wondered if that's what had happened to her parents. The way Christian had left Mina sounded similar to how her father had left. Her mother hadn't seen it coming at all, and Zoey had been heartbroken. They'd both trusted and relied on him.

When Zoey was sure Mina had finished speaking, she said, "So why the hell did your parents like him?"

Mina blinked at the ceiling. "Because he had money. He was responsible and had a well-paying job. Now that I think about it, they might have seen him as someone who could keep me in line."

"Excuse me?"

"I've never fit neatly into the boxes my parents want me to fit in. I've never wanted to be a doctor, or a lawyer, or a dentist. I never got into sports. I hate wearing dresses. I cut my hair like this." She pointed to her ruffled hair, which Zoey always wanted to run her hands through. "I came out as pansexual in high school, and I've got bad anxiety. My sisters followed the path my parents laid out for them, but I veered right off it. There's a reason I cover my tattoos when I visit home."

Zoey was absorbing a lot of information in that moment, and for some reason she blurted, "Tattoos? As in, you have more than one?"

One corner of Mina's mouth ticked up. "Yeah, I do."

"Where?" Zoey ran her eyes down Mina's body as if she could find it.

"Maybe one day you'll be lucky enough to find out."

Challenge accepted. "Maybe I will be."

SEVENTEEN

MINA

The more time Mina spent around Zoey, the bolder she seemed to get. Mina from a couple months ago wouldn't have taunted Zoey with the bait of seeing her tattoos in a million years. She would have thrown up before the sentence even left her mouth.

Now, a frisson of delight shot over her skin at Zoey's response, at the thought of what they would be doing to give Zoey a glimpse of the tattoo on Mina's thigh. She hadn't had sex since long before Christian left, and she was feeling it.

It didn't help that she spent so much time around Zoey these days.

Zoey, with her short dresses that would be so easy to get underneath. With her witty comebacks that kept Mina on her toes.

Mina's ears were hot, and she was sure the kitchen had become a few degrees warmer.

"I'm out of beer," she said a few minutes later, chugging whatever was left in her can. "Want tea?"

"Sure. Thanks."

She could practically hear the smirk in Zoey's voice.

Mina plugged in the samovar and prepared the tea, and when

she returned to the table, Zoey was working on the scrapbook again. She paused and looked up at Mina, a gentleness in her eyes that hadn't been there before. "If you want me to be there when you tell your parents about Christian, I can do that," she said.

Every word out of Zoey's mouth lately made Mina want to kiss her.

Instead, she said, "Thank you."

The two of them settled into a rhythm of cutting and pasting while the music played in the background. Their conversation revolved around what they were making, which was safe territory. No feelings involved. Once Mina had finished cutting out the photos, she swapped jobs with Zoey, adding the frames Zoey chose to each picture while Zoey pasted photos in the book.

"Is this your mom?" Mina asked, holding up a photo of a smiling woman who looked a lot like Zoey.

"Yeah." Zoey's smile was full of affection. "She spent a lot of time with me and Wren in junior high and high school."

"She was the *cool* mom then," Mina said.

Zoey winced so slightly that Mina almost didn't catch it. "I wouldn't say that, exactly. More like she was the depressed mom. It was easier for me to make sure she was doing okay if we invited her along with us."

"Oh." Mina winced now too. "Sorry."

"It's okay. You didn't know. My dad left when I was thirteen, and she sort of . . . collapsed. It wasn't great, and it honestly ruined the idea of romance for me. Like, why put the effort into loving someone when they can leave you so easily and bring everything crashing down? But things are better now. My aunt lives with her, we have weekly video calls, and we see each other in person at least once a month."

"That's good. I'm glad she's doing better."

Zoey nodded. "You're sure you don't mind me using this stuff?" she asked as she pasted another photo in, clearly changing the subject. "I can pay you for all of it."

Mina shook her head, a few strands of her dark hair falling

into her eyes. "Don't worry about it. Most of it has been sitting in the bin for ages, so it's nice to see it put to use."

After a few minutes, Mina realized she'd been sitting there doing nothing but watching Zoey work. Zoey pressed each photo down lightly, gently, so she didn't bend or wrinkle anything. After that, she picked an assortment of colored pens to write notes and draw doodles between the photos. Her handwriting was messy but in an endearing way, all loops and flourishes that put Mina in mind of fairy tales.

Zoey took her time to make each page pretty, choosing stickers to fit the colors and themes. Her care for Wren showed on every page.

Forcing herself to stop being creepy, Mina looked out the window. Straight into Zoey's kitchen. She smiled wryly to herself. Even when she tried not to look at Zoey, she couldn't avoid her altogether.

"What are you smiling at?" Zoey asked before turning her gaze back to a sticker sheet.

"Nothing."

Zoey narrowed her eyes at Mina but let it go. "If you say so."

Mina thought back to the scrapbook she'd made for Christian. She'd spent hours making it, going through the photos, picking out things to write. She'd given herself a paper cut and had to run to the store when she ran out of washi tape.

He'd flipped through it in less than ten minutes then set it aside.

She hoped with all her heart that Wren would cherish this scrapbook and look at it often, thinking fondly of her relationship with Zoey and maybe even calling her to laugh over old stories when they missed each other.

Zoey deserved that kind of love.

A meow drew their attention away from the table. Zelda sat by her food dish, staring forlornly at Mina.

"I guess it's dinner time," she said, looking at her phone. It was nine-thirty already.

"I should get out of your hair, anyway. I think the scrapbook is finished," Zoey said, gesturing at the book on the table in front of her. "Want to see?"

"Sure." Mina's hands trembled as she picked up the scrapbook. She already knew it would be beautiful, and it was. Every single page highlighted Zoey and Wren's friendship, and it made Mina smile. "There's no way Wren won't like this."

"Yeah? It's not too messy?"

"It's just messy enough." Mina returned the book to her.

Zoey grinned. "Thank you. I had a lot of fun with this." She gestured at the supplies scattered on the tabletop. "I'll help clean before I go."

Mina fed Zelda then helped Zoey tidy the table. It didn't take long, and they were standing by the front door only a few minutes later.

After all that had happened that evening, Mina thought maybe Zoey would kiss her. She didn't have the courage to kiss Zoey, even though she wanted to. She ached for Zoey's touch, and it was maddening.

And while Zoey did hug her, giving Mina the opportunity to breathe in her sweet vanilla and coconut scent, nothing more happened.

Zoey left, and Mina let out her breath in a *whoosh* as she sagged against the front door.

She had it bad.

EIGHTEEN

ZOEY

Zoey drove to Wren's for her birthday the following weekend. They went out for dinner with a few of Wren's friends from the salon, then they went to a club. Zoey hadn't gone out dancing in ages and felt out of place, but once she had a drink running through her system, she found herself on the dance floor with Wren.

The two of them twirled around each other, the music so loud that Zoey could feel the bass in her bones. The floor was sticky, the smell of sweat and alcohol and cologne almost over-whelming. Wren laughed, throwing her head back and her hands up, and Zoey grinned. She was having more fun than she'd expected.

A woman with a blond pixie cut and a tight red crop top caught her eye, smirking in a way that made Zoey catch her breath. Wren clearly saw the interaction and nudged Zoey toward the woman, but Zoey hesitated.

Normally, she'd throw herself at a woman like this without a second thought. But something held her back. Some*one*.

The woman quirked an eyebrow and sauntered closer, moving to the beat. She leaned toward Zoey's ear. "Wanna dance?" She had to yell so Zoey could hear her over the music.

Zoey was sweaty and tipsy and high on the atmosphere, so she licked her lips and nodded. The woman linked her arms around Zoey's neck and pressed her body close, and Zoey's heart raced.

She tried to relax into the movement, into the feeling of the woman's body against hers. Their hips moved together, pressed close, the woman's waist hot under Zoey's palms.

A few months ago, Zoey knew exactly how this would have gone. She and this woman would dance together for a while then one of them would offer to get drinks. They'd sit and chat, and Zoey would suggest they get out of there. They'd giggle and paw at each other, barely keeping their clothes on in the Uber to wherever they were going. And Zoey would sink into pleasure for a few hours, losing herself between the woman's thighs. Then she'd clean herself up and leave before the sun rose.

This wasn't a few months ago, though. And while the thought of rolling into bed with this woman was appealing, she didn't really want to. The only person she wanted to kiss, to touch, to taste, was back in Juniper Creek.

When the song ended, Zoey kissed the woman on the cheek and yelled, "Thanks!" Then she ran to the table Wren's other friends sat around. Wren was still on the dance floor, clearly having a blast.

Zoey listened to Wren's other friends chatting, staring at her empty glass. Wren bopped up to them, stealing the empty chair beside Zoey. "What was that about, Zoey?" she asked, out of breath. "That chick was totally into you."

Zoey sighed. "I know. I'm just . . . not into her, I guess."

Wren gave her a look. "Okay."

They called it a night shortly after that, none of them feeling young or spry enough anymore to dance the entire night away. When they returned to Wren's apartment, Zoey was so tired she barely managed to brush her teeth. She fell into Wren's bed and slept like a rock.

The next morning, she and Wren made gluten-free French toast together.

After they were done eating, Wren leaned her elbows on the kitchen table with a steaming cup of coffee in her hands. "Can I have my gift now?" she asked. "I waited all weekend. You have to give it to me before you leave."

"Well, obviously." Zoey grabbed a bag from a nearby chair and pulled out the scrapbook, which she'd wrapped with brown paper and tied with twine. "I hope you think it's worth the wait. Happy birthday!"

Wren wiggled in her seat and took the book from Zoey. She undid the twine and unwrapped the paper carefully, and her face lit up at the sight of the scrapbook cover. "Did you make this?"

"Yeah, Mina helped me. It was her idea, really."

"Oh my god. Okay, we have to look at this together." She scooched her chair so she was sitting right beside Zoey. "Zoey! The ice cream!" She laughed at the photo of the two them standing together with ice cream cones, Zoey with a missing tooth. "God, I miss those summers."

"Me too." Zoey leaned her head on Wren's shoulder as they continued through the book.

When they came to the last page, Wren turned to her. "Zoey, this is seriously the best gift ever. Thank you." She pulled Zoey in for a hug. "I love you so fucking much."

Tears sprang to Zoey's eyes, and she mentally scolded herself for being so sentimental. "I love you too."

Before she drove home, Zoey opened her text thread with Mina.

ZOEY

Wren loved the scrapbook! Thank you sooo so much for helping me with it

MINA

Awesome! I'm glad. You can use my supplies again whenever

ZOEY

You're the best

MINA

Her text exchange with Mina replayed in her mind for the entire drive back to Juniper Creek. That winking emoji could mean so many things, but she didn't want to read too much into it. Then again, maybe she did.

When it came to Mina, she didn't know exactly what she wanted.

THREE DAYS LATER, ZOEY WAS AT WORK, WISHING SHE was having dinner with Mina that night instead of her mother. Except she also looked forward to seeing Mom. And she hated having mixed feelings.

She had thought moving to Juniper Creek would help her worry less about her mom being depressed, but it had done the opposite. Having the house to herself was lovely, and not having to monitor Mom every day was a gift, but the flip side was not knowing how Mom was doing.

Had she gotten up on time? Eaten breakfast? Remembered to pack herself lunch? Was she watching TV after work? Or sleeping more than usual? Zoey knew what to look for with her mother's moods. She knew when to be worried and when to brush it off as a bad day.

Aunt Shannon had probably figured out the same things, and Zoey told her to reach out whenever she needed, but still.

So when Mom had suggested they start weekly video calls, she'd agreed. And then Mom had suggested at least one in-person event every three months, and Zoey had agreed to that too. Sure, Mom had friends nearby and now Zoey's aunt was living with her, but Zoey still felt responsible for her.

She knew what her mother had gone through. She understood her the best.

That's where her mind was when Mina came in early for her five o'clock shift.

"Vera's training a new person, so she told me to leave a few minutes early," Mina said as she hung up her jacket. "There wasn't really a point in walking home."

"Makes sense. Hey, I know you're not clocked in yet, but do you mind grabbing a case of ribbons for me?"

Mina was an inch or two taller than Zoey, and Eleanor kept the ribbons on a high shelf.

"Yeah, I got it." Mina pulled over the stepladder, and Zoey went back to the front to ring through a customer.

Just as she was handing the customer their receipt, a yelp and a crash sounded from the back room. Zoey and the customer froze, looking at each other with wide eyes.

Dropping the receipt, Zoey ran to the back to find Mina sprawled on the floor, holding her ankle. The case of florist ribbons lay wide open beside her, rolls of colorful satin scattered across the room.

"Oh my god, are you okay?" Zoey rushed over to her, kneeling, her hands fluttering uselessly.

"I twisted my ankle," Mina said, wincing. "I must have stepped off the ladder weird or something."

Zoey hadn't even noticed the ladder at first. It was haphazardly on its side next to Mina.

"Ahh, fuck, okay. Let me call Eleanor. And maybe 911? Do you need an ambulance?"

Mina pushed herself up on her hands. "No, it's not that bad." She slid so she was leaning against the wall. "Just give me a minute. I'm fine."

She didn't look fine. She let her head fall back, her eyes closed.

"I'm calling Eleanor anyway," Zoey said. "Don't move."

Mina cracked an eye at her. "I think I can manage that."

Eleanor and Minnie lived close to Main Street, so Eleanor was there within ten minutes. Zoey stayed in the back with Mina, glad there were no customers in the shop.

"I brought an ice pack," Eleanor said, hurrying through the door. She handed it to Mina, who placed it on her now-swelling ankle. She'd taken off her shoe. "We need to get you to a doctor."

Mina groaned. "I'm sure it's fine, really."

"It's turning purple," Zoey said. "I don't think it's fine."

Eleanor huffed. "Zoey, would you be able to take her? I'll handle the store. And I'll work on getting you workers' comp as soon as I can." She clearly worked well in a crisis.

"Eleanor, honestly, you don't need to do that," Mina said. She went to say something else, but Eleanor's glare cut her off.

"Zoey?" Eleanor said.

"Right, yeah, I'll take her to the community hospital."

Zoey felt like her brain had glitched, and she couldn't remember how to do anything. But she had to pull herself together for Mina. She took a deep breath, then grabbed her coat and purse.

"Do you think you can put weight on it?" she asked.

"We'll find out," Mina said.

Zoey slung Mina's arm over her shoulders, aware even in this moment of how Mina smelled faintly like honey, and hoisted her up.

Mina tried to put weight on her ankle and hissed. "Um, that's a no for walking on it."

"Okay. We just need to get you to the car." She groaned. "Shit. I walked to work."

"Take my car," Eleanor said without hesitation. She came around Mina's other side, and they managed to get Mina into the passenger seat of Eleanor's Ford Focus. "Keep me updated, alright? And you keep breathing, dearie," she said to Mina, squeezing her arm.

Zoey glanced over at Mina every few seconds as she drove to the community hospital at the edge of town. Houses decorated for Halloween flashed past the windows, the townsfolk having leaned into the holiday spirit. Mina seemed to be in less pain now, at least when she wasn't moving, but her eyebrows were drawn tightly together.

"Are you okay?" Zoey asked, worry heavy in her chest.

"I feel really stupid," Mina said. "I fell off a *stepladder*. Who does that?"

"It happens. It's not your fault."

"It kind of is. And now Eleanor has to work by herself tonight."

"Hey." Zoey grabbed Mina's hand, keeping her eyes on the road. "It's not your fault."

Mina's voice was small when she replied, "Okay."

Luckily, the community hospital wasn't busy that evening. A nurse helped Zoey bring Mina inside, and Mina saw a doctor within the hour. It was a huge difference from Zoey's experience with Vancouver hospitals, where she'd once waited for seven hours in the ER to get stitches.

While she waited for Mina, Zoey checked her phone. Mom had phoned six times. "Shit," Zoey said, then called her back.

"Zoey? Where are you? Are you okay?" Her mother's voice was breathless, as if she'd been panicking.

"I'm okay. Mina twisted her ankle, and I brought her to the community hospital. I'm sorry, I didn't even think to text."

A huge sigh came from the other end of the line. "I'm just glad you're okay, sweetie. I let myself in, and there's pizza on the counter. Do you want me to bring you some?"

"No, it's okay." With everything going on, food was the last thing on Zoey's mind.

"Okay. Well, let me know what's happening, and I'll come help if you need me to."

"Thanks, Mom. I love you."

"I love you too, honey."

Half an hour later, another nurse brought Mina out to the waiting room in a wheelchair. Mina's foot was now wrapped in a tensor bandage.

Zoey shot up from her chair. "How did it go? How's your foot?"

"Sprained," Mina said. "Not broken, thank god. They told me to ice it and keep it elevated. And I'm not supposed to walk on it for a few days." The way she said that last sentence told Zoey she was not happy about it.

Zoey had the urge to fling her arms around Mina's neck, glad it was nothing worse than a sprain. She restrained herself, settling for a smile instead. "Good thing you have such a nice neighbor, then. I can help you until you're back on your feet—literally. If you want."

Mina's expression softened. "I'd like that."

"Let's get you home."

As Zoey pulled up to their townhomes in Eleanor's car, Mom came rushing outside. The two of them helped Mina into her house, getting her settled on the couch.

"I'm Mandy," Mom said. "It's nice to finally meet you, although I'm sorry about your ankle. I've heard lots about you."

"You have?" Mina raised her eyebrows at Zoey.

Zoey blushed and hoped it wasn't too visible in the dim light of Mina's living room. "All good things," she said before Mom could add something embarrassing.

Mom nodded. "I'll go get the pizza. And I picked up some of those breadsticks with it."

When her mother returned with the food, the smell of greasy cheese and pepperoni hit Zoey, and her stomach growled audibly. Mina's did too, and they both laughed.

Zoey pulled out plates and drinks from Mina's kitchen, and she and Mina ate on the couch in the living room while Mom pulled over a chair. Mina's ankle was propped on a pillow on the coffee table.

"I'm sorry I ruined your mother-daughter evening," Mina said between bites of pizza.

Mom waved a hand. "Not at all. I'm glad I was here to help."

Now that everything had calmed, Zoey had a chance to really

look at her mom. She looked good, her eyes bright with no bags under them. Her brown hair had more gray in it than Zoey remembered, but that wasn't odd for someone her mother's age.

"How are you doing, Mom?" Zoey asked after they'd gotten through the small talk. Her mother could gossip endlessly about school-related incidents if Zoey let her, and she wouldn't talk about herself unless prodded.

"I'm doing well," Mom said. "Shannon got me to start going to this yoga class twice a week with her. I am not as flexible as I used to be, let me tell you, but it's nice."

Yoga seemed like a good thing. It could help Mom stay grounded. "You enjoy it?"

"I do." They munched their pizza in silence for a bit. "I know you're checking on me," she said, giving Zoey an exasperated but fond look. She turned to Mina. "Zoey's a worrywart."

Zoey grabbed another piece of pizza. "I just want to know you're happy."

Her mother smiled. "I am happy, honey. You don't need to worry about me."

Zoey looked at Mom again, more closely this time. Her dangling blue gemstone earrings brought out the blue in her eyes, and her mascara was a bit clumpy. Her cheeks were a healthy pink, and her clothes weren't hanging off her like they had in the past. She had been doing well for years now, and Zoey knew that.

It didn't keep her from staying wary, though.

"So, Mina, tell me all about this 3D modelling you do," Mom said. "I know nothing about it, but Zoey tells me you're a talented artist."

Mina shot Zoey a confused look, but her eyes lit up. "I don't know how accurate that is, but thank you. What do you want to know?"

"What's the process like? It's called *sculpting*, right?"

"Part of it, yeah."

As Mina explained about 3D modelling, the world seemed to narrow to her and her passion for the subject. She became more animated, leaning forward as she spoke, seeming to forget about her ankle altogether. Her love for her art kept Zoey captivated even though she didn't fully understand everything Mina was saying.

Her heart expanded as she listened to Mina talk.

"That's fascinating," Mom said, popping the Mina bubble in Zoey's brain. She'd almost forgotten her mother was in the room. "Can I see some of your work?"

"Sure." Mina looked at Zoey, and she was practically glowing. Although Zoey wasn't happy that Mina had hurt herself, the evening was turning out much better than she'd expected.

NINETEEN

MINA

Mina really liked Zoey's mother. Mandy seemed kind and caring, just like Zoey. And she showed a genuine interest in Mina's work, asking her for details that most people wouldn't bother with.

But watching Zoey interact with her mom was almost overwhelming. The two of them clearly cared about each other. Zoey made sure her mom was comfortable, and Mandy gazed at her daughter with fondness.

Mina's relationship with her mother looked nothing like that. Sure, she respected her mom and everything her mom had done for her—making her meals and ensuring she had a good education —but they weren't friends. They didn't enjoy spending time together, not like Zoey and Mandy.

And while Mina loved seeing Zoey in her element with her family, it also hurt. She had something Mina had always wished for and would never get.

Mandy even helped Mina upstairs to her room, making her tea and bringing her ibuprofen while Zoey washed their dishes.

"I think I'm going to tuck in for the night," Mandy said, sitting on the edge of Mina's bed and helping her elevate her ankle on a pillow. "But it was good to meet you. I'm glad my daughter has such a lovely woman living next door. And I know she'll take good care of you. Are you a hugger?"

Mina accepted the hug, feeling bewildered. To have someone else's parent care for her like Mandy had this evening . . . She didn't know what to do with it.

She heard Zoey coming up the stairs as Mandy left, and the two of them murmured to each other in the hallway. Then Zoey came into view, leaning against the doorframe.

"How're you doing?" she asked, her voice soft yet filled with concern.

"Fine. Good, really. My ankle doesn't hurt unless I try to move it."

"That's good." Zoey sat on Mina's bed where her mother had been sitting a few minutes earlier. The bed dipped under her weight. "I talked to Eleanor already about your shifts for the next few days. Between the two of us, we can cover them."

A twinge of guilt shot through Mina. "I'm sorry. You shouldn't have to do that."

Zoey grabbed her hand for the second time that evening, and Mina's skin reacted immediately, tingling in a pleasant way. The touch sent a thrill up her arm, making her heart flutter.

"It's fine, seriously," Zoey said. "And I can come over tomorrow morning and check in, see if you need anything."

"You're good at taking care of people, aren't you?" Mina swiped her thumb over Zoey's knuckles, her pulse pounding. It had nothing to do with the throbbing of her ankle.

"I have lots of experience," Zoey replied. Mina was sure she was thinking of her mother.

"I appreciate it. It's nice to have someone take care of me. Christian never did."

"Even when you were sick?"

"When I was sick, he wouldn't even come in the same room in case I was contagious. He worked so much that he couldn't afford to get sick."

Zoey straightened and lifted her chin, her gaze fierce. "Well, lucky for you, I am a much better human than Christian."

Mina laughed. "You really are."

Zoey's hair glowed golden in the soft light of the bedside lamp. She was a bit disheveled from the day's events, but she'd never looked more beautiful. "Can I get you anything else before I go? Your game console thing, maybe?"

"No, I think I'm okay."

"You don't want a distraction?"

Mina shrugged. "I'll probably just go to sleep."

"Hmm." Zoey shifted, the side of her leg brushing against Mina's through the comforter. "You don't need something to keep your mind off the pain?"

Mina's lips parted. She had a feeling Zoey wasn't talking about video games anymore.

The two of them locked eyes, and every inch between them hummed with electricity.

Instead of answering, Mina tightened her hold on Zoey's hand and pulled, just a bit. Zoey took the hint, moving closer. Mina's heart beat faster, a restlessness coming over her. An overwhelming yearning filled her, and she leaned forward just as Zoey did, their faces a mere inch away from each other.

They were so close, she could feel the warmth of Zoey's breath, and all she could hear was the sound of their breathing, both of their chests rising and falling in tandem. Everything around them faded away.

Zoey lifted a hand to Mina's face, running her fingers gently from Mina's temple to her jaw. Mina shivered. Zoey leaned forward so their foreheads touched, and Mina's heart just about burst.

Without thinking, Mina closed her eyes. She tilted her head and touched her lips to Zoey's.

Zoey let out a sigh. The kiss was no more than a brush of their lips, but it filled Mina to the brim with happiness.

When Mina opened her eyes, Zoey was looking at her with

molten intensity, her pupils blown wide with desire. She put a hand on Mina's waist and hitched herself even closer. Mina's entire body seemed to melt into Zoey's embrace.

Mina made a low, pleasantly startled noise in the back of her throat. Agonizingly slowly, Zoey moved in to kiss her again. "Is this okay?" she whispered against Mina's mouth.

"Yes," Mina whispered back, gripping Zoey's shirt right above her hip.

Zoey dove back in to kiss Mina, and Mina opened her mouth, allowing Zoey to taste her. Their tongues tangled, and Mina wanted more, wanted everything Zoey would give her.

"Girls?" Mandy's voice echoed up the stairs, and Zoey sprang away from Mina as if they'd been electrocuted. "I forgot my phone! Zoey, I'm going to lock the door when I head back. Do you have your key?"

Zoey blinked, looking dazed. "I guess that's my cue," she said, her voice breathy. "One sec, Mom!" she called. Then she turned back to Mina. "I don't have my key, so I should go. But if you need me . . . you know where to find me."

She brushed aside a lock of Mina's hair before she left, her fingers lingering over the shell of Mina's ear. The feeling of Zoey's fingers ghosting over her skin stayed with Mina until she fell asleep.

MINA COULDN'T STOP THINKING ABOUT KISSING ZOEY. Her lips had been so soft, and she'd tasted faintly like pizza.

Zoey stopped by the next morning to bring Mina breakfast, but neither of them said a word about the kiss. They didn't kiss again either, although Mina desperately wanted to. Especially when Zoey helped her down the stairs. Their faces were so close together, it would have been easy for Mina to turn her head, to pull Zoey's lips to hers.

But she wanted to know what the kiss meant before she made another move.

She knew Zoey didn't like the idea of romance because her father had left her and her mother. There was a possibility that Zoey had changed her mind, though. Or maybe she wanted something casual, like a friends-with-benefits arrangement. Or maybe she wanted nothing at all and had kissed Mina for some unknown reason. Maybe they were just friends. Friends could kiss their friends, right?

Even as she thought it, Mina snorted. What she and Zoey had done the night before had not been a platonic kiss between buddies. She sounded like every heteronormative person that saw two people who appeared to be the same gender heavily making out and put up a *no homo* wall so thick, you couldn't knock it over with dynamite.

So Zoey must have kissed her for a reason.

Mina hoped it meant Zoey returned the feelings that had been swirling inside her for months. Since she'd decided to get a new job and embrace the freedom she'd gained after Christian left. Since she'd started seeing Zoey almost daily either at work or because they were spending more time together. And they were spending more time together because they were helping and supporting each other.

That had to mean something, right?

Mina was so deep in her head that she jumped when her front door opened. "Sorry," Vera said when she saw Mina with her hand pressed to her chest. "I should have knocked. How's your ankle?"

She came inside, setting down a bag of groceries before sitting on the couch.

"It's okay. Still swollen, but it doesn't hurt as much. I'm sorry I couldn't make my shift."

Vera waved her off. "Don't worry about it. I've covered you for the next week. And I brought you a few ready-made meals, so you don't have to be on your feet much."

Tears sprang to Mina's eyes. All the kindness people had shown her in the past couple of days was getting to her. "Thank you."

"Of course. How're you doing other than the ankle?"

Mina thought about Zoey. About that kiss. "My head is in the clouds today, honestly."

Vera leaned back onto the couch and pulled one of Mina's new colorful cushions onto her lap, making herself comfortable. "What do you mean?"

Mina bit her lip. She hadn't told anyone about her growing feelings for Zoey. She knew Declan would be excited for her but would probably push her to ask Zoey out, which Mina wasn't ready for. But Vera had asked about Zoey before. Not specifically, but she knew Mina had feelings for *someone*. It couldn't hurt to get advice.

"Do you remember when you asked me what was making me smile so much a few weeks ago?" She kept her eyes on the ice pack on her foot, not wanting to see Vera's likely smug expression.

"Yes, I do."

"Well . . . you were right that there is someone in my life who . . . I maybe like."

"Go on."

"And we may have kissed last night."

"Mina!" The surprise and excitement in Vera's voice made Mina duck her head. She wasn't used to people being excited for her. About anything. "Sorry, keep going."

Mina straightened to see Vera pressing her lips together, her eyes shining, clearly struggling to let Mina tell the story at her own pace instead of bombarding her with questions. Mina appreciated her restraint.

"I just don't really know what the kiss meant. I want to talk to her about it, but . . . Is that weird?"

"Not at all. I think it's good to clarify what it meant for you both, especially since you like her. Being clear about your expectations will ensure neither of you gets hurt."

Mina nodded. She knew that already, but it was validating to hear it from someone else. Especially from someone older who had more life experience.

"Yeah. How do I approach the subject, though?"

Vera pressed her lips together, thinking. "It will probably feel weird, but I think you need to just come out and ask it. There's no point mincing words in a conversation like that. When my ex-husband and I got divorced, we both knew neither of us was really *in* the relationship anymore. It was still tough to separate, but we had to sit down and talk about it to make anything happen. It wasn't a comfortable conversation, but dancing around the topic wouldn't have helped. That goes for any type of misunderstanding or tension in a relationship. If you don't talk about it, it gets worse. It gets more confusing or it gets buried under other things, and by that point it's even harder to talk about. So your instincts are right to talk to her now, before things have a chance to get messier."

Mina nodded and surprised herself by holding her arms open for a hug. Vera obliged, smiling, and patted her back.

"Thanks," Mina said. "You know, if everyone in romance stories had someone like you to talk to, I don't think there would be all those messy fights and needless third-act breakups."

She could have probably avoided a few unhappy years with Christian if they had hashed things out sooner.

Vera laughed. "Thank you. That's a high compliment."

After she put away the food she'd brought, Vera headed back to work. Mina broke out her Steam Deck so she could easily play video games on the couch while she waited for Zoey to stop by after work. Zelda curled up on her lap, seeming happy with the arrangement.

While she lounged, Mina thought through what she wanted to say and exactly how she wanted to say it. She imagined how Zoey would reply, trying to work out appropriate responses to each scenario so she would be prepared for anything.

Vera's speech had given her a boost of confidence.

Zoey finally came over around six. "Hey," she said when she opened the door. "How are you feeling?"

"Pretty good," Mina replied, her heart pounding. "How was work?"

Zoey shrugged. "Uneventful." She plopped onto the couch beside Mina. "Can I get you anything? I can make dinner."

"It's okay. Vera brought me ready-made meals earlier, so all I have to do is microwave them."

"Oh, great." Zoey seemed disappointed. "That was nice of her."

"Yeah." Mina bit her lip. "I actually wanted to talk to you. If that's okay."

Zoey shifted to face her. Something in her expression told Mina she already knew what Mina was going to say. "Okay. Shoot."

Mina had no idea how this conversation would go. She took a deep breath. "Yesterday evening."

"Yeah?"

"We kissed."

Zoey's gaze shot to Mina's mouth and back to her eyes. "We did."

Mina hoped Zoey would add something to that, maybe answering Mina's question before she had to ask it, but Zoey didn't say anything else. Vera's advice ran through Mina's head again. *Don't mince words, just ask.*

"I was wondering . . . what it meant, exactly. If it meant anything."

Zoey's lips parted, and Mina remembered how those lips felt against her own. She was tempted to lean in and see if they could repeat the experience, but that's not what they needed right now.

"I . . ." Zoey licked her lips, not helping Mina any. "I think it was just the heat of the moment. Not that I didn't like it, but . . . I'm not really looking for anything right now, you know?"

Mina deflated. She thought she had prepared herself for the

full spectrum of answers, but hearing Zoey say their kiss essentially meant nothing was not great.

"Right, yeah. That's totally fine."

"It is?" Zoey's forehead wrinkled.

"Yeah, yeah, I get it. I don't really know if I'm ready for anything either. After Christian. I'm embracing my singleness and enjoying the freedom of it." It wasn't a lie, but it also wasn't the full truth.

"That's great. I'm happy for you." Zoey smiled, and Mina ignored the way her heart fluttered.

"Yeah. Awesome. Okay, so . . . I'm probably going to make myself dinner soon."

"Okay. I guess I'll go then." Zoey went to the door and slipped her shoes on.

"I'll see you around?" Mina asked, hugging a pillow to her chest.

"Definitely. Let me know if you need anything. You know where to find me."

As Mina limped to the kitchen, she tried to tell herself she wasn't upset. Zoey liked her as a friend, and that was good, wasn't it?

If only Mina hadn't been hoping for more.

TWENTY

ZOEY

Zoey had loved kissing Mina. Ever since that night, she'd cursed the fact that her mom had butted in, preventing them from kissing longer, from potentially going further. She wanted to taste Mina again, to slide her hands into Mina's hair. She wanted to do more than kiss her.

And that scared her.

She'd never felt this way about anyone.

They'd only kissed once, and yet thoughts of Mina consumed her. Not just in a horny way, either.

Mina was smart and funny. Although she was usually quiet, she had a lot to say if you gave her the space. She was passionate about her art, and Zoey could listen to her talk about it all day. She was an amazing cook, and she had fantastic taste in TV shows.

And yet Zoey couldn't admit their kiss meant something to her.

She wanted to tell Mina that it meant *everything*. It made Zoey feel alive in a way she couldn't remember ever feeling. It made her want to give romance a chance, the risk be damned, but she couldn't take that leap.

She wasn't ready.

So, as much as she wanted to kiss Mina again, she'd told her the kiss meant nothing. *The heat of the moment,* while a fantastic Asia song, was a terrible excuse.

And she regretted saying that every day when she saw Mina through their kitchen windows or at work after Mina had recovered. They remained friendly with each other, but their conversations became stilted.

Zoey didn't ask Mina to help with her proposal again, even though it wasn't finished, and she didn't tell Mina she had marathoned all of *Schitt's Creek* and adored it. The last episode of the final season made her sob, and she started the series over from the start.

So she didn't expect it when Mina showed up at her front door again three weeks before Christmas. Yet there she stood, bundled in a black winter coat that had floral stripes on the sides. The tip of her nose was pink, and Zoey had the urge to boop it.

"Hey," she said. She didn't know why Mina was there, but she couldn't leave her standing out in the cold. Not to mention she was letting the freezing air in, and Zoey was not prepared for that in her thin yoga pants. "Do you want to come in?"

"Sure. I'll only be a minute." Mina stomped the snow off her boots on the front mat then stepped inside. "How are you?"

Zoey shrugged, hugging her elbows at the chill that had washed over her from the open front door. "Good. I've been working on a few new candles for spring."

"Oh, nice. First Rain of the Season?"

"That wasn't one of them, but now it might be. If you don't mind." Zoey made a mental note to add that scent to her list.

Mina gave her a thumbs-up. "Go for it."

"How about you? How are you doing?"

Mina pulled a hand from her pocket to swipe aside a loose strand of hair. "Also good. I came over to ask you for a favor, actually. About the holidays. Are you going anywhere for them?"

The word *favor* had Zoey intrigued. It implied that Mina still trusted her on some level, even though they'd grown distant in the past month. "No, I'm staying in town. My mom and my aunt are coming here to celebrate."

"Cool. I feel bad leaving work before the holidays, but I'm honestly more scared of my mother if I don't visit my family for Christmas." Mina rolled her eyes. "I'm not bringing Zelda, so I was hoping you'd be able to watch her for me. You can stay at the house if you want, or even pop over there every couple of days. She's pretty independent, so you can leave her on her own for a while if you need to."

"I would love to watch Zelda! It would actually work really well for me to stay at yours. Then I don't have to sleep on the couch while I have company."

"Perfect."

"So . . . did you tell your family that you and Christian broke up, then?"

Mina winced. "Yeah."

"It didn't go well?"

"I don't really know yet. I think I'm going to get an earful when I get there. My dad was the one who called, and he showed the requisite sympathy, but I've heard nothing from my mom. And I'm sure he told her, because my sisters know. They both texted me to say they're sorry, there are other fish in the sea, blah blah blah. I didn't give any details."

"Ah. I hope it goes better than you expect."

"Thanks. Me too, but I'm not getting my hopes up." She sighed. "Anyway. Do you want to come over in the next couple weeks, and I can show you everything you need to know?"

"Sure."

Mina nodded and reached for the doorknob. "Thanks again. You're the best neighbor."

The word *neighbor* echoed in Zoey's ears. She kind of hated it. Maybe watching Zelda and Mina's house while she was away would help repair the cracks in their friendship.

In what Zoey achingly wished was more than friendship.

A week before Mina left, Zoey went to her place so Mina could show her everything. There was something exciting about seeing more of Mina's house than just the public spaces, and Zoey tried not to act weird about it as Mina gave her a tour.

Seeing Mina's room again—when Mina wasn't stuck in bed with a sprained ankle—made Zoey especially giddy. It was Mina's private space, and she was granting Zoey access to it. She'd added a few plants since Zoey had been in there last, and they brought more life to the small area.

Zoey's housesitting duties seemed standard enough: feed the cat, water the plants, get the mail, clean the litterbox, take out the garbage, and make sure nothing was amiss.

"I'll change the sheets for you so you can stay in my room, and you can help yourself to whatever food I have," Mina said. "Feel free to play any of my video games, too."

"I doubt I'll do that, but thanks for the offer," Zoey replied. She wasn't about to tell Mina that she'd started watching playthrough videos of some of the games Mina had mentioned just so she'd understand more of what Mina liked about them. She didn't want to seem creepy.

They stood in the entryway after touring the house. "So"—Mina absently rubbed the back of her neck—"do you have any questions?"

"No, I think I've got it all."

"And you have my number if you need me. I'll leave a list too, and I'll put the vet's number on it."

"Sounds good."

Zoey put her boots and coat on, then fumbled for a second, trying to decide if she should hug Mina goodbye. She wanted to, but she didn't know how it would go over.

She needn't have worried. Mina reached out first, giving her a squeeze. Zoey tried not to hang on too tightly, but she didn't want to let go.

"I really appreciate this," Mina said into her hair, her mouth so close to Zoey's ear that her breath tickled Zoey's skin. Goosebumps ran down her arms.

"It's my pleasure, really."

Later that evening as Zoey made herself dinner, she looked out the kitchen window to see Mina also making dinner. They caught each other's eye more than once as they worked, to the point that Zoey's cheeks were red and the two of them were laughing. Eventually, Zoey went into the living room to eat. She didn't want Mina out of her sight, but it felt weird to share this sort of voiceless comradery.

Not for the first time, Zoey thought that everything would be nicer—easier—if she told Mina the truth. If she admitted that she liked Mina as more than a friend. But every time she considered doing that, she clammed up. What they had as friends was good, and she couldn't risk ruining it.

TWENTY-ONE

MINA

A sense of freedom washed over Mina as she boarded the plane to Toronto by herself. That same feeling had enveloped her multiple times since Christian had left. Part of her was upset that she'd taken so long to realize she was unhappy, but another part of her was relieved they'd broken up before things had gone any further. She could have lived with Christian, mired in an unfulfilling life, for years. She'd *already* been unhappy for years but hadn't been able to see it clearly until she hadn't had to think about what Christian wanted.

With him gone, she'd been able to focus on her own goals. She'd finally finished a couple more 3D character models for her portfolio, and she planned to put her resume together and start applying at game developers after the holidays.

Now she just had to explain that to her family.

At least she didn't have to worry about anything in Juniper Creek. She'd left Zelda and her house in good hands. In Zoey's hands. Those hands that had touched her face so tenderly not so long ago, even though it had only been "the heat of the moment" for Zoey.

Mina turned her thoughts away from Zoey as the plane landed.

Farrah and her husband, Cyrus, picked Mina up from the airport. "There she is!" Farrah held her arms out, enveloping Mina in a jasmine-scented hug then air kissing her once on each cheek. It had been so long since someone had greeted Mina that way, tears sprang unbidden to her eyes. Cyrus hugged her as well, a hint of sandalwood tickling her nose as he patted her on the back.

"Can I take your bag?" he asked.

She let him take the handle. "Sure, thanks."

"How was the flight?" Farrah asked, and Mina suffered the small talk as they headed toward the car and drove to her parents' house. The house she had grown up in.

She knew exactly what it looked like, but when they pulled up out front, it loomed over her. Even though it had been built in the eighties, it still screamed *luxury* with its high ceilings, white walls, large lawn, and tall windows. It wasn't the biggest or most expensive house Mina had ever seen, but she knew it was on the list.

Cyrus carried her bag for her again, and she pushed away all the memories weighing her down as she walked through the front door.

The smell of her childhood hit her immediately: a fragrant mix of spices, cooking meat, basmati rice, and rosewater, all with an undercurrent of orange-scented cleaner. It made Mina feel like a teenager again, as if Farrah had picked her up from school and they would study for an hour before dinner.

No one was waiting to greet her, but she could hear her parents speaking Farsi in the kitchen. Mina couldn't speak the language fluently, but she and her sisters had picked up quite a few words and phrases from overhearing their parents' conversations. She definitely understood more Farsi than she could speak.

"Maman! Baba!" Farrah called as they slipped off their shoes. "Mina's here!"

Something clattered in the kitchen, and Mina headed that direction to meet her parents. Even though she'd largely been dreading this trip, she wanted to see them. She wanted to prepare food with them again, to watch her mother make tea and her father make perfectly shaped zoolbia.

She saw her father first, a wide smile spreading on his face as he came toward her. He looked older than he had when she'd seen him last, the wrinkles around his eyes deeper, his hair thinner. "Mina joon!" He grabbed her firmly by the shoulders then kissed her cheeks and her forehead, and she leaned into it with her eyes closed.

Once her father let her go, her mother said a quiet "salam" and hugged her. "How was the flight?"

Mina waited for her mother to say something about Christian's absence, but so far, she was in the clear.

"Good. How are you? It smells delicious in here." Her stomach grumbled as if to agree.

Her father tugged on her arm, pulling her toward the kitchen. "Come help me with the ash reshteh."

Her mouth watered at the name of the dish, and she grinned. "I'd love to." This visit was off to a better start than she'd expected. She hoped it was a sign of how the rest of the trip would go.

Dinner that night was everything Mina could have asked for: delicious food and light conversation. She, her mother, and Farrah cleaned up afterward, then they sat in the living room with tea while Farrah regaled Mina with stories from her past few months of dentistry. Mina did not envy her sister's job at all. She had no desire to stick her fingers in peoples' mouths or deal with the horror stories Farrah recounted, even though Farrah seemed to find them amusing. Mina worried she'd dream of her teeth falling out that night.

Her mother still didn't say anything about Christian, which both pleased Mina and worried her. The topic hung over her head like the blade of a guillotine, and she had no idea when that blade would fall. If she was lucky, it wouldn't fall at all.

She texted Zoey before she went to bed.

MINA

Just checking in. How are things?

ZOEY

Great! I think Zelda likes me.

Zoey sent a photo of Zelda curled up on Mina's bed at Zoey's feet. The sight sent a pang of longing through Mina's chest. That scene looked perfect, and Mina ached to be part of it.

MINA

I'm glad you're getting along!

ZOEY

How are things there?

MINA

Good so far. Better than I thought they'd be.

ZOEY

Good

Mina waited for more, hoping Zoey would give her something else to comment on. She drifted to sleep with her phone still in her hand, Zoey on her mind.

TWENTY-TWO

ZOEY

The first night Zoey stayed in Mina's house, she tried her best to snuff her curiosity. She wasn't there to snoop; she was there to take care of Zelda. The cat had made herself scarce to start with. All Zoey had seen of her for the first few hours was a flash of her black tail going down the stairs.

But not snooping proved difficult when she was literally sleeping in Mina's room, surrounded by Mina's things. What someone owned and how they decorated could say a lot about them, and Zoey had had an insatiable urge to learn more about Mina since she'd moved in. Since Mina had first shown up on her doorstep with those delicious cinnamon buns.

She decided it wouldn't hurt to look at what Mina had on display.

Mina's room had changed slightly since she'd seen it last, in addition to the new plants. She'd replaced her gray-and-white plaid comforter with a dark green floral one that suited her much better. Two wooden night tables sat on either side of the queen bed, one of them holding an alarm clock and a photo of Mina with a bearded White guy who must have been Declan. Sketches of video game characters Zoey didn't recognize were tacked on the walls, and she was pretty sure Mina had drawn them all. Above the bed hung a large canvas showing a foggy forest-scape that gave the room a moody atmosphere.

Downstairs on the living room shelves, Zoey found more video game memorabilia. She had seen the figurines and framed art before when she came over for Mina's birthday and for scrap-booking, but now she could look at everything without feeling creepy. She didn't recognize some of it, but the *Legend of Zelda* art and the Pokémon figurines were familiar.

A few more plants lived in the room now. Mina seemed to have embraced her employment at Thistles and Stems by buying much of its stock.

There was also a photo of Mina with her sisters, the three of them pressing their faces together as they smiled at the camera. At least, Zoey assumed those were her sisters. They had the same nose shape and the same dark hair and eyebrows. A few poetry books filled the shelf beside the photo, most of them names Zoey didn't recognize: Hafez, Khayyam, Farrokhzad. Rumi was famil-iar, though.

Zelda finally made her presence known as Zoey poked around in the kitchen cupboards for dinner. Mina had gone overboard and left her chicken enchiladas and rice in the fridge, so Zoey didn't have to do much.

"There you are," she said, putting her plate in the microwave. Zelda trilled softly and Zoey made a point of ignoring her as she approached. Zelda brushed against her leg and trilled again. "Are we going to be friends?" Zoey asked, slowly bending down. She held out her hand for Zelda to sniff, and the cat rubbed against her, purring. "I'll take that as a yes."

Zelda sat near her feet as she ate. It was weird to look into her own kitchen while sitting in a house that mirrored hers so closely. Her kitchen lights were off right now since no one was home. Her mom and her aunt would be coming over the next day to cele-brate the holidays, even though Zoey still worked until Christmas Eve.

She was finishing the dishes when her phone rang with Wren's photo appearing on the screen. "Hey," she answered.

"Hellooooo," Wren sang. "So, how's Mina's place?"

Zoey rolled her eyes. "Fine. I've been here before, you know."

"Yeah, but you've never stayed there. Have you explored yet? Found any juicy secrets?"

"No, Wren, I have not. I mean, I've explored a bit, but I'm not about to go poking through her things."

"You're no fun. You'll never know what she's hiding if you don't look," Wren said, her tone taunting.

"You're ridiculous," Zoey replied as she went upstairs to Mina's room. "She's not hiding anything."

"I mean, she probably isn't. But still. Maybe you could find something that would make a good conversation starter so you could finally tell her how you feel. Then I wouldn't have to hear about it *all the time*."

Zoey flopped onto Mina's bed. "I do not talk about her that often! Do I?"

"Okay, no, but when you do, I can tell you're pining. And as your best friend, I just want you to be happy."

The smell of laundry soap surrounded Zoey as she flipped onto her side, leaning on her elbow. "You sound like my mother."

"I am not that pushy. Plus, I *know* you have a thing for this girl." Wren's tone left no room for argument, and she was right.

Their conversation shifted to the latest gossip at the salon and their plans for the holidays. They could have talked longer, but Zoey couldn't stop yawning and needed to be awake early the next day for work.

Except when she finally got into bed, she got a text from Mina. A wide smile spread across her face, and she scoffed at herself. One text from Mina made her light up like a Christmas tree.

She sent Mina a photo of Zelda, but once Mina assured her that she was doing fine, she put her phone down. It wasn't fair to either of them for Zoey to flip-flop about what she wanted. By the time Mina got home, Zoey needed to have her mind made up.

She needed to decide if she wanted to stay friends with Mina or if she wanted something more.

But it might not even matter. Mina had said she was embracing her newfound freedom as a single person. Zoey got the impression that Mina was more open to a relationship than she let on, but she couldn't be sure. She had no idea what Mina would have said if Zoey had answered differently. If Zoey had been honest.

Maybe Mina truly did want to stay single for a while.

To clear her mind for sleep, Zoey opened her meditation app and put on sleep music. A few minutes later, she drifted off to the sound of rain and a gentle piano melody.

SHE COULD TELL SHE WAS DREAMING, BUT THAT DIDN'T dampen the feeling of excitement that shot through her at the sight of Mina beside her in bed. Her body was a warm, comforting presence against Zoey's own.

Mina rolled over and yawned. Her eyeliner wings were perfect, her hair cutely mussed. She lay on her side and smiled at Zoey, her eyes sleepy but inviting. "Hey," she said.

"Hey," Zoey replied, smiling back, her heart pounding.

"Thank you for watching Zelda for me." Mina shifted closer and lifted a hand, pushing aside a lock of Zoey's hair. A pleasant shiver washed over Zoey's body.

"Of course," Zoey said. "I like being able to help you."

"Yeah?" Mina moved even closer, her legs now entwined with Zoey's.

Zoey's next word was barely a whisper. "Yeah."

"Well, I'd like to thank you anyway." Mina brought her lips to Zoey's, and heat shot through Zoey's body. The kiss was soft at first, then Mina deepened it, her tongue swiping over Zoey's.

Zoey moaned low in her throat, and Mina grinned then rolled so she was on top of Zoey, her weight on her elbows.

"Is this okay?" Mina asked softly.

"Yes," Zoey said, desperately wanting more. She wanted to feel every inch of Mina.

"How about this?" Mina asked, slowly sliding Zoey's shirt up her torso. Zoey nodded and lifted her body so Mina could pull her shirt off. She gasped as Mina kissed her collarbone, leaving a trail of fire on her skin.

Zoey writhed with pleasure under Mina's kisses, her underwear soaking as Mina slid down her body.

The dream started to fade as Zoey woke up, but Zoey's pleasure didn't.

Half asleep, she slid a hand down her stomach, even that light sensation on her skin feeling amazing. She found her clit and pressed on it just enough, pulling a soft whine from her throat. She tried to hang on to the dream of Mina as she touched herself, moving her fingers slowly and torturously gently until she came with a soft cry, her muscles twitching.

It wasn't until she woke the next morning that she realized she'd had a sex dream about Mina, and then thought about Mina while she orgasmed. In Mina's bed.

TWENTY-THREE

MINA

The pleasant feelings from the first night of Mina's visit with her family couldn't last forever.

The next morning, Mina's mother woke her early. "We need to go get things for the party," she said. "Up, up, no time for sleeping."

Mina groaned. Since she'd been a teenager, her parents had thrown a Christmas Eve party every year for pretty much everyone they knew, including their colleagues and now Farrah's and Yasmin's too. Mina supposed her colleagues would also be invited —if she had any her parents deemed worth inviting. Yet another way for them to show their peers that they were truly Canadian, that they'd found success. Mina couldn't exactly blame them for it, but that didn't mean she found the party any less stuffy and boring.

"Is that all you brought?" her mother asked, nudging her open suitcase with a toe. "This tiny bag? What are you wearing to the party tomorrow?"

Mina pushed herself up in bed, blinking sleep out of her eyes. "I brought dress clothes," she said through a yawn.

Her mother looked at her with hands on her hips. "Show me."

Rolling her eyes, Mina got out of bed and went to her suitcase. She'd rolled everything to make it fit properly, and she hoped her dress clothes hadn't gained any wrinkles. She pulled out black dress pants and a floral button-up shirt.

"Hmm." Her mother's lips pressed in a tight line, which wasn't a good sign. "That won't do. We'll buy something else for you today."

Mina bit her lip, on the verge of spitting out that she didn't want to wear something else. She'd bring it up later once they were out. If she was lucky, her mother would forget about her outfit altogether in the chaos of getting everything else ready.

But her mother didn't forget, which prompted a hushed argument in an expensive department store, frustration saturating Mina's veins. The only thing preventing the argument from escalating was Farrah, who managed to convince their mother to let Mina get a dark gray suit with a floral pocket square.

"I don't understand why you insist on being difficult," her mother said, her heels clicking on their way out. "You never used to be like this."

Mina kept her mouth shut, not wanting to make things worse. Of course she hadn't been like this as a kid. Back then, she hadn't realized she could stand up for herself, that she could make her own decisions and be happy with them. She'd been fighting her entire life to be the person she wanted to be while pleasing her parents, and even as an adult it wasn't coming easy.

She could see that more clearly now that Christian was gone. She'd been stifling herself for her family and then for him.

It baffled her that the previous night she'd somehow been enjoying herself, and now she couldn't wait to fly home in a few days. Typical.

She managed to keep to herself that afternoon and the following day in the flurry of decorating, finding small tasks to help with that kept her away from her mother. She wanted to help in the kitchen, but her mother had hired caterers and made clear that Mina was not to "interfere with their work." That didn't stop her from sneaking into the kitchen a couple of times to steal a piece of halva, savoring the texture and bite of the added pistachios.

As she got dressed for the party, she wished she had someone with her to act as a buffer. Someone like Zoey. Zoey was charming and tactful and always made Mina feel better simply by being in the same room.

Mina checked her phone. She hadn't heard from Zoey since the first night, and that was probably a good thing. But Mina missed her.

A knock on the door made Mina smudge the eyeliner she'd been applying, and she groaned. Yasmin poked her head in. "Shit, sorry!" she said, grimacing when she saw the black line across Mina's face. "I was just coming to say hi."

Mina hadn't seen Yasmin yet since her eldest sister had been busy at work, so she couldn't exactly get upset. "Hi," she said, hugging her. Yasmin looked beautiful in a long green sleeveless dress with gold embroidery on the neckline and hem.

"Farrah told me Maman's been getting on your case already." Yasmin brushed a thread off Mina's suit jacket.

Mina shrugged. "You know what she's like."

With a sigh, Yasmin brought her gaze to meet Mina's. "I do, but I also know what you can be like. You're both stubborn."

Mina didn't think wanting something different from her mother made her stubborn, but she didn't want to fight with her sister too, so all she said was "Maybe."

"Here, let me do that for you." Yasmin took her eyeliner and waited as Mina wiped off the errant line. Trying not to blink, Mina let her sister line her eye, once again feeling like a teenager. It was nice, though, to have someone help her. "There. What do you think?"

Mina looked in the mirror. The lines were thicker than she would have done them, but she looked good. "Perfect. Thank you."

"Of course. Now, let's go out there and have a good time, hm?"

Once more, Mina checked her phone. No texts from Zoey. She slid it into her pocket then linked arms with Yasmin, willing herself to paste a smile on her face and be amiable. It was only one evening.

THE PARTY WAS IN FULL SWING WITH PEOPLE DRESSED in formal wear mingling and laughing with drinks in their hands. The house had been transformed into a winter wonderland, white-and-silver garlands adorning the railings, pearl-white candlesticks with flickering flames on various surfaces, a giant tree with white and silver decorations standing tall in the foyer. Mina had seen most of it being set up, but it was an entirely different experience to see the house finished and full of guests.

Waiters walked around with hors d'oeuvres on silver trays, and someone was playing Christmas carols on the piano. Mina snagged a glass of champagne from a waiter as Yasmin floated off to find her husband. The likelihood that Mina knew anyone here was slim. Well, she knew a few of her parents' colleagues in passing, but not enough to want to talk to them. She kept a smile on her face, nonetheless, and tried to give off the air that she hadn't a care in the world.

At least when she'd been a kid, she could be forgiven for running off with the excuse that she was bored. A few times, she'd even snuck away with other kids at the party to play video games upstairs. It was easier to avoid punishment when she had accomplices.

She wasn't a kid now, though, and she couldn't hide from the party without upsetting her mother. So she wandered around until she found Farrah and Cyrus sitting by the fireplace in the living room. "Mina!" Farrah waved her over. "These are my colleagues from the clinic." She introduced them all, and Mina nodded at them politely, shaking hands when necessary.

At eight o'clock on the dot, Mina's mother took her place in the foyer on the landing and clinked a spoon against her glass for everyone's attention. Time for her annual speech. Mina wondered what she'd say this year. Usually, she reflected on the past year and what she was grateful for, which was essentially an excuse for her to brag about everything that had gone right in their lives.

Mina understood it, to some extent. Her parents had worked their asses off to get where they were. She knew that's why they had such high standards for her and her sisters. But wanting the best for someone didn't mean ignoring what they wanted, and that's where Mina drew the line.

"Thank you all for coming to this party," her mother said, beaming at the guests. Mina's father stood behind her, his hand resting lightly on her mother's waist, the perfect picture of support. "As you know, we host this party every year, but this year feels special because it's the first time my entire family has been together since last Christmas." She locked eyes with her daughters, gesturing for them to join her.

Mina gritted her teeth but followed her sisters to the stairs. She tried to school her face, to not grimace too much at everyone looking at her.

"My daughters are talented and beautiful young women, and it makes me proud to stand here with them." Once again, Mina struggled to keep her expression neutral. "Yasmin is one of the top neurosurgeons in the country, and earlier this year she received funding for a research project that could change the face of medicine." She put a finger over her lips to indicate that she couldn't reveal more, but everyone clapped, and Mina knew her sister would be fending people off later as they tried to dig the details from her. "Two years ago, Farrah opened her own dental clinic, and this year she's been busier than ever with a full load of clients." More applause, and Farrah's cheeks pinked. "And Mina, my youngest . . . Mina is finding her way." More applause, although not as enthusiastic as it had been for her sisters.

As her mother continued the speech, Mina clenched her jaw. It was unlikely that anyone else noticed that pause in her mother's words, but Mina sure did. And she knew exactly what it meant. It meant that her mother had struggled to come up with something about Mina that people could praise. That her mother was truly proud of. And even if people hadn't noticed the pause, they surely noticed that "finding her way" didn't sound nearly as impressive as Farrah's and Yasmin's achievements. It wasn't an achievement at all.

When her mother finished the speech and gave a toast to her family and guests, Mina downed the rest of her champagne. She set the empty glass on a side table harder than necessary, then she walked up the stairs, right past her parents. Her mother looked at her, her eyes narrowing, but Mina said nothing. She kept walking until she was in her room, then she locked the door behind her.

Before she knew it, she was on her bed with her phone in hand, calling Zoey.

"Hello?"

Zoey's voice calmed her immediately, and she sagged into the cushions. "Hey."

"Is everything okay?"

For a moment, Mina couldn't say anything. She squeezed her eyes shut then sighed. "Remember when I said things were going well so far?"

"Yeah. I take it they're not going so well anymore?"

"*So far* has come and gone. It's long gone now." She looked around her room, for the first time taking in how bland it was since her parents had renovated it. All the posters she'd had were gone, and even the colorful bedspread had been replaced with one that was white and refined.

The sound of something clanging came from the other end— a plate maybe, or a bowl. "I'm sorry. Do you want to talk about it?"

Mina hadn't thought beyond calling Zoey, but she realized now that she did want to talk about it. "I think I do. But are you eating dinner? I'm sorry, I forgot about the time difference." Then she remembered the date. "Oh my god, and it's Christmas Eve! Are your mom and aunt over?"

"Yeah, but don't worry about it. We'll probably eat in an hour or so. Tell me what's going on." It wasn't a command really, more of an invitation.

And Mina needed that.

Once she started telling Zoey about the party, she couldn't stop. She told her about how her parents hosted the event every year, how her mother would give a speech, and how tonight's contained all the veiled disappointment Mina had been anticipating since she walked through the front door two days ago.

"I can't believe she said that," Zoey said, her voice filled with outrage. Her anger warmed Mina's heart. "She couldn't even try to come up with something better?"

"Right? She prepares these speeches ahead of time, even practices them. Which means she either revealed what she truly thought in the moment, or that's all she wrote about me. I'm *finding my way*. I don't even know if she really understands what I do. She's never made the effort to find out."

To Mina's horror, tears rose in her eyes, making her vision blurry. She swiped the back of her hand across them and blinked at the makeup now streaked on her skin.

"Ugh. I wish I could be there with you," Zoey said, which set Mina's heart pounding. She wished Zoey were there too. "You deserve so much better than that, Mina. I told you before that what you do is meaningful, and the fact that your parents don't seem to care about it . . . that's not cool."

Mina swallowed thickly. "I don't even know what my dad really thinks. He goes along with whatever my mom says. Sometimes, when it's just the two of us in the kitchen, I get the feeling that he's happy I'm happy. He at least asks me about my life rather than making assumptions or judgments. But with my mom in the room, it's like he has to agree with her."

"Yeah, and that's not really showing support. I'm so sorry you're dealing with this. Have they mentioned Christian yet?"

Switching to speakerphone, Mina flipped onto her side to stare out her window. "No, thank god. They will, though. I'd bet a million dollars, which I don't even have. Christian's name has been suspiciously absent from every conversation." She gritted her teeth. "Anyway, enough about my crappy night. How are things at home?"

Home. Juniper Creek had become home for her in the last few years, and that felt true now more than it ever had before. This house wasn't hers. It wasn't her home anymore. She didn't even feel welcome here. Not really.

"Things are fine here. Nothing to report."

"How was work today?"

"Slow, besides a couple of people who bought wreaths last-minute."

The two of them continued to talk until Zoey had to go for dinner. Mina didn't want to hang up, but she didn't want to take more of Zoey's time either.

"Okay, well, I hope you have a good dinner," Mina said, stifling a yawn. "Say hi to your mom and your aunt for me, and give Zelda a hug."

"Will do. If you need to talk again, you know where to find me."

TWENTY-FOUR

MINA

Mina somehow plastered a smile on her face for Christmas morning. She smiled through breakfast and as everyone prepared to open gifts. Her entire family, including her sisters and their spouses, sat in a loose circle on the various couches and chairs in the expansive living room, Christmas carols playing softly in the background and a fire crackling merrily in the electric fireplace.

Mina sat on the floor near the tree, handing out gifts to everyone—her duty as the youngest.

She kept that smile on her face when her parents opened her gift to them—a basket of homemade jams made from berries in the Juniper Creek area. Mina had seen it at Juniper Foods and thought it was sweet. Baba hugged her and seemed to enjoy the gift, and her mother even smiled, although it didn't quite reach her eyes.

Farrah unwrapped the scrapbook Mina had made her, inspired by Zoey's scrapbook for Wren. "Mina, I love this!" She put a hand on Mina's knee and squeezed, her eyes glossy.

"Aw, I got one too!" Yasmin said, holding her own personalized scrapbook. She flipped it open. "Oh my gosh, look at how little we were!"

Baba had answered her request for family photos, and she'd picked out different ones for each of her sisters. She'd considered making a scrapbook for her parents too, but she didn't think she could stomach yet another loved one brushing off something she'd spent hours on. She could have made one for Baba and then given her mother the jam, but . . . that wouldn't go over well.

Mina had to accept that her mother didn't love her as much as her sisters no matter what she did.

Her parents gave her money as her gift, which she was genuinely grateful for. It gave her more time to find a job with a video game developer.

And Christian's name had yet to tarnish the holiday spirit, which was a gift as well.

While some people's families lounged around in pajamas on Christmas Day, Mina's mother made sure everyone got dressed before they hung around with their respective gifts. The scrapbooks were a hit with her sisters and their husbands, all four of them poring over the photos and laughing. Mina sat with them, loving that at least some people found joy in her contributions to the day.

She wondered what Zoey was doing and if she was enjoying her holidays. From what she'd seen of Zoey's mom, Mina imagined Zoey was having a wonderful day. She, Mandy, and her aunt Shannon probably loved each other's gifts and had fun holiday traditions that didn't require wearing dress clothes to dinner.

Farrah went for a nap, Yasmin put her nose in a book, and the husbands were on their best behavior, playing Rook with Mina's parents. Mina thought of grabbing her Steam Deck to play a few games, but she could imagine the look on her mother's face if she spent the day absorbed in video games.

Instead, she went to the washroom and pulled out her phone.

MINA

Merry Christmas! How's your day going?

To her surprise, the three dots that indicated Zoey was answering showed up almost immediately. Her mood lifted.

ZOEY

Happy Holidays! My day is going really well 😊 we're playing board games and drinking spiked eggnog

MINA

Sounds fun! Can you give Zelda extra treats from me tonight? For her Christmas present

ZOEY

Of course. I might have bought her a few new toys too . . . hope you don't mind

The fact that Zoey cared enough about Mina's cat to get her toys for Christmas made Mina's heart melt.

MINA

Aww, thank you. I love that

ZOEY

How are things going for you?

MINA

Okay so far. No explicit digs at me, anyway

ZOEY

Good. You know where to find me if you need me

Blood rushed to Mina's cheeks, and she had to remind herself that Zoey wasn't interested in being more than friends. She was just being friendly. A good friend. A good neighbor. Nothing more.

A knock at the door startled Mina, and she almost dropped her phone. "Mina, are you okay in there?"

Her mom.

"Yeah, I'll be out in a minute." Mina stuck her phone in her pocket, flushed the toilet even though she hadn't used it, then washed her hands. Her mom would probably notice if Mina opened the door and there was no whiff of overly strong lavender hand soap.

Her mom stood there in her green blouse and black slacks, her hands on her hips and her severely plucked eyebrows raised. She didn't say anything, just turned and walked back to the dining room.

Great. So she was checking in on Mina.

Once upon a time, Mina would have appreciated her mother's attention. Now, though, she knew that that attention usually led to scolding. But she couldn't exactly scold Mina for taking too long in the bathroom. Even Ava Hasanza had limits.

To make the rest of the afternoon pass more quickly, Mina joined the card game. She didn't really care if she won or lost, but she needed something to do that kept her from stewing in her anxiety.

Only one more family dinner to get through, then she would visit Declan the next morning and fly out in the evening. She could do this.

By the time dinner came around at eight thirty, she'd relaxed a bit. She helped Baba finish dinner preparations in the kitchen, and Farrah and Yasmin set the table. Their mother carried out the wineglasses. Everyone was laughing and joking with each other, including her mom. There was no tension in the air for once, and Mina basked in it.

She should have known it couldn't last.

After they sat around the table, Baba poured them all wine. "There's an extra glass," he said, frowning.

"Ah." Mina's mother pressed her fingers to her temple briefly, closing her eyes. "Sorry, that was my fault. When I brought out the glasses, I was thinking about dinner last year, when Christian was here."

Mina's fingers clenched, her nails digging into her palms.

"It's a shame he's not here this year. I liked that boy. Mina, you never told us exactly what happened."

All eyes turned to her, and she wanted the ability to shrink like Link could in *The Legend of Zelda: The Minish Cap.*

She took a gulp of wine to fortify herself. "He left."

Her mom tilted her head. "Why would he do that?"

Farrah bit her lip. "Mom—"

Her mother held out a hand. "Farrah, please. I just want to know."

"I guess things just weren't working." Mina held her wine glass so tightly, she was afraid it might shatter. "I got home from work one day, and he was gone. All he left was a note."

Farrah gasped, and Yasmin said, "Oh my god, Mina."

Baba said nothing.

Her mother, on the other hand, frowned. Her dark eyebrows drew together. "Was it your job?"

"What?" The word escaped Mina's mouth with barely any sound to it.

"Your business degree," her mother stated. "You have it, but you're still working at a grocery store."

Why did it *always* come down to Mina's job?

Mina closed her eyes, willing herself not to snap. She breathed deeply through her nose and focused on the feeling of her chair supporting her body, her feet firm on the floor. When she opened her eyes again, Farrah looked shell-shocked, her eyes wide as she clutched Cyrus's hand. Yasmin had her hand on her mouth, her gaze on the table.

"Well, there had to be a reason," their mother said, her gaze severe. "People don't leave for nothing."

Words had fled Mina's mind, and they seemed to have fled everyone else's too since no one replied. Her father put his hand gently on her mother's arm. Mina willed him to stand up for her, but all he did was shake his head slightly.

Mina's stomach roiled.

"I don't feel well," she said quietly. That was all she could get out before she slid back her chair and left the room.

No one followed her.

Things had been going so well. She'd let herself be lulled into believing that this visit wouldn't be that bad, that maybe she'd imagined how things had been in the past.

But, of course, her mother had to prove her wrong.

Half an hour later, a soft knock sounded at Mina's bedroom door. Farrah opened it gently. "Can I come in?"

Mina had changed into her pajamas and was in bed, playing *Slay the Spire* on her Steam Deck. Beating one monster after the other helped take her mind off her mother's comments. "Yeah, I guess."

Farrah came in and stood at Mina's bedside, wringing her hands. "Mina, I am so sorry. What Maman said was totally uncalled for."

"Yeah, it was," Mina said. "But it wasn't entirely unexpected, was it?"

Farrah reached out but didn't touch Mina, as if afraid Mina's anger would burn her. "I think she's worried about you. She wants the best for you."

Mina scoffed. "She has a shitty way of showing it." Her entire life, she'd faced her mother's disappointment. Nothing she did was ever good enough.

"I know." Farrah's eyes were glossy with tears. She sniffed and rubbed her nose. "Did Maman ever tell you about when she first moved to Canada?"

"Not really. She doesn't share that stuff with me."

Farrah nodded ruefully. "Yeah. I wish she would share more with us. But I think she doesn't because she wants to shield us or something." She paused and smoothed a hand over the quilt. "She had to retake a bunch of high school courses because they wouldn't let her graduate, and Baba told me that she had to fight to be taken seriously in law school."

Mina raised her eyebrows. "So? That doesn't mean she gets to judge me for working at a grocery store. If anything, she should be more sympathetic about the struggles of getting the job you want."

"Maybe. But I don't think that's how she sees it. I think she's always pushed us because she wants us to find success without struggling like she did. She wants us to be financially stable and be 'high enough' in society"—she made air quotes with her fingers—"that people can't question us, you know?"

Mina chewed on that for a minute. She knew neither of her parents had had it easy when they'd moved to Canada. No immigrants did, really. She understood that. She respected how hard her parents had worked to get to where they were. But her life was different from her mother's, and she didn't want the so-called protection of a corporate job or a medical license.

"Anyway"—Farrah squeezed Mina's hand—"will you join us for dessert? Yasmin and I are leaving soon, and we won't be back tomorrow before you go to Declan's."

Mina considered it, but the thought of facing her mother made her feel terribly small. Even if Ava had good intentions, her actions tore Mina down time and time again. "I can't. I'm sorry." She pushed herself up and opened her arms, pulling her sister into a quick hug. "It was good to see you. Give Yasmin a hug from me too."

After Farrah left, Mina stared at the closed door, wishing she knew the magic spell that would help her mother understand her. She didn't know if it even existed, and looking for it was getting exhausting.

TWENTY-FIVE

ZOEY

J ust as Zoey was sitting down for Christmas dinner with her mom and her aunt, she received a few texts from Mina about how she was spending the rest of the evening alone in her room.

ZOEY

Oh no, what happened?

MINA

My mom finally brought up Christian and how
I have yet to use my business degree

ZOEY

Well shit

Want to call to talk about it?

MINA

No, it's okay. Just gonna sleep, I think

ZOEY

Okay. Sending you a virtual hug 🤍

MINA

Thank you 🤍

Zoey frowned but set down her phone. She hoped Mina was okay.

"What's got you looking so troubled?" Aunt Shannon asked, nudging her elbow.

The two of them sat kitty corner to each other at the dining table, with Mom on the other side. They'd popped Christmas crackers a few minutes ago, and each of them wore a flimsy paper crown. Christmas dinner was spread out on the counter since it wouldn't fit on the table, and Zoey had piled her plate full of turkey, mashed potatoes, green bean casserole, stuffing, cranberry sauce, and gravy.

"Mina isn't having a great Christmas," she said, sticking her fork in her potatoes.

"Oh, I'm sorry to hear that," Mom said, frowning. "Is she unwell?"

Zoey waved a hand. "Family stuff." Even if she knew the details, they weren't hers to share.

Aunt Shannon pursed her lips, and Mom set down her cutlery, looking at Zoey intently.

"You know," she said, "we have it pretty good. We've had our share of struggles, but the three of us are here together, and we love each other. I'm so grateful for you two. I'm glad I can spend the holidays with you and not worry about us fighting."

Zoey wondered if that was a jab at her dad, or a comment in relation to what Mina was going through.

Zoey's memories of holidays with both her parents were fuzzy. The holidays that stuck out the most to her were the ones when Mom hadn't had the energy to do much. Zoey had tried her best to celebrate and cheer her mother up on those days, but they'd been hard.

The Christmas after her father left had been the worst. Mom hadn't seen a doctor for her depression yet. She'd been in bed for most of December, and Zoey hadn't known if they would even have a Christmas. She'd struggled to put up the fake tree by herself, and she'd put on music while she decorated it. But it had felt so lonely. She'd wished more than once that her father had been there, but he'd never even called. He didn't send a card or a gift.

It was as if he'd never existed. Except that he had, and Zoey had to figure out how to put her family back together without him.

Thank god Wren's parents had invited them over for Christmas Eve dinner, and they'd asked Zoey to spend the night. After they had opened gifts the next morning, Zoey had walked back to her house down the street to bring Mom breakfast, and they'd exchanged gifts.

The thought of it brought tears to Zoey's eyes.

Mom held out her hands, and Zoey and Aunt Shannon each grabbed one, their arms making an awkward triangle over their plates.

"I love you too, Mom," Zoey said, squeezing her mother's fingers.

"And I love both of you," Aunt Shannon echoed, "even when you insist on making the rolls instead of buying them from the store."

Mom grabbed one of said rolls and took a big bite. "They're better this way," she said, her mouth full, and Zoey snorted.

As Zoey ate, she turned over her mother's little speech. They had gone through a lot to get here, and Zoey was proud of all of them. They were a family of three single women who all managed to support themselves and each other against the odds.

If only Zoey could get going with her plans to expand her business, she could feel more confident about her ability to support herself. But she hadn't finished the proposal yet. She hadn't even touched it since she had worked on it with Mina.

Instead, she'd told herself she had to focus on preparing for the Christmas market earlier that week, which had gone well. People loved gifting candles for Christmas, which worked in Zoey's favor.

What didn't work in her favor was letting herself get distracted constantly from her plans to grow her business.

She was starting to wonder if she really wanted to expand in the first place. It didn't make sense that she kept putting it off when making more money would help her pay Aunt Shannon full rent and start saving for bigger things. But that was a problem for another day.

After dinner, the three of them moved to the living room to watch holiday movies. Zoey absently checked her phone. No messages.

She wondered what Mina was doing. Probably playing video games, which seemed to be her comfort activity, or sleeping like she'd said she would. She hoped Mina could shake off whatever negativity her mother had heaped on her. She'd probably need to decompress once she got home the following evening.

Which gave Zoey an idea. It was a small idea, but it was something.

If Mina's holiday had been stressful, Zoey would make sure her return from that holiday was as relaxing as possible.

TWENTY-SIX

MINA

The next morning, Mina was exhausted. She'd been exhausted since dinner the night before, even though she'd done nothing but play video games and sleep. She tiptoed downstairs with her packed suitcase, managing to catch Baba for a quick goodbye before she snuck out early to Declan's.

"Hey, stranger," Declan said when he opened his apartment door. He pulled her into a hug. "You're right on time for breakfast."

"Hi, Mina!" Declan's girlfriend, Lila, stuck her head out of the kitchen and waved. She wore a pink frilly apron, and she had flour streaked across her cheek. "It's good to see you!"

"So how bad was it this time?" Declan asked as Mina followed him into the kitchen.

"Oh, you know. I didn't even get through dinner last night."

"Ugh, I'm sorry," Lila said, wincing. Mina knew Lila hadn't talked to her parents in years because they had extreme differences in their personal beliefs, so Lila knew how Mina felt. "At least you get to end your visit on a high note. I made cinnamon French toast and caramel sauce, plus eggs and bacon!"

"Thank god for good food," Mina said, plopping into a chair at the round four-person table.

As they dug in, Declan switched the topic to something more palatable. "How's your portfolio work going?"

"Really well, actually. I think I finally have enough models to start applying for jobs. Would you mind looking at it for me?"

"Nope. Send me the link, and I'll look after breakfast."

Once the table was cleared, Declan got his laptop and opened Mina's portfolio. "Dude, this looks fantastic! Lila, look at this one." He tilted the screen so his girlfriend could see. "This is the dragon I was telling you about, the one with flowers growing down its back. Isn't it sick?"

Lila's eyes lit up. "Oh my gosh! I want one."

Blood rushed to the tips of Mina's ears. "Thanks. Do you think there's enough there to get me a job?"

"I mean, I can't say for sure, but this definitely showcases your skills." He crossed his arms over his chest and scrutinized the screen again. "I think you've got a good chance of getting the job you want with this."

"Yeah?" Mina's anxiety quietened. "Awesome."

After breakfast, they moved to the living room with mugs of tea and coffee. Declan and Lila curled up together on the loveseat, almost sickeningly cute together, while Mina perched in a lounger.

"How's Zelda these days?" Declan asked, his hand on Lila's knee.

"Good, I think. My neighbor is watching her for me until I get home tonight." The thought of Zoey warmed her more than her tea did.

He raised his eyebrows. "The neighbor with the candle company? You work with her now at that plant place, right?"

"Yeah. She's really nice." Mina hadn't told Declan about her feelings for Zoey yet, and she wasn't sure if now was the right time. Or if *ever* was the right time, considering Zoey didn't return those feelings. Work was a safer, less complicated subject. "And the flower shop is more fun to work at than I expected. Eleanor, my employer, is fantastic."

"That's cool," Lila said. "Do you get to make bouquets and stuff?"

They talked about work for a while then played *Super Smash Bros.* until Mina had to head to the airport. Leaving Declan's place hurt almost more than leaving her parents'.

HER MOOD HAD BRIGHTENED CONSIDERABLY AFTER visiting Declan and Lila, but it started to fall again on her flight home.

No matter what her mother did or said, Mina always visited hoping things would be different. She loved her family, including her mom, but it hurt a little more every time they failed to stand up for her or understand her. Especially Baba.

She caught a cab home, wincing at the cost. She could have called Vera or maybe Zoey, but she didn't want to trouble anyone. When she got out of the cab in front of her house, Mina's eyes flicked over to Zoey's. The downstairs lights were off, but one upstairs light was on.

Then she turned to her place, which she'd missed more than she expected. She couldn't wait to get inside and snuggle with Zelda, and she struggled to get the front door open in her excitement.

"There we go," she said, finally stepping inside.

Soft music reached her ears. "True Blue" by boygenius, one of her favorite songs. Mina slowly slipped her shoes off and followed the sound to the kitchen, wondering if Zoey had stuck around for some reason.

Her stomach flipped at the idea.

Zoey was nowhere to be seen. The music played from Mina's portable speaker on the counter. A notecard showing her name was tented on the table beside a bag of bath salts and a Bell Lights candle called A Perfect Cup of Hot Chocolate. Mina unscrewed the lid and inhaled the scent of fudge with a hint of marshmallow. It made her mouth water. Smiling, she picked up the notecard.

It was written in Zoey's writing. Mina recognized her swirly style from when she'd made Wren's scrapbook.

Mina,

I know nothing will make up for a holiday trip gone wrong, but I hope this helps.

Love,
Zoey

A half-confused, half-pleased noise escaped Mina's throat. The word *love* before Zoey's name made her face flush.

She knew it didn't really mean anything, but still.

She shook her head, amused, and took the candle and salts upstairs. She was too tired for a bath, but she lit the candle while she got ready for bed. She opened her suitcase but didn't bother unpacking, and Zelda seemed happy with that as she made biscuits on Mina's dirty clothes.

No one had ever welcomed Mina home like this before, and she wasn't exactly sure how to react. Saying thank you was probably a good start.

MINA

This candle smells AMAZING. And I'm excited to use the bath salts! Thank you 🤍

ZOEY

Hehe. Thought you'd like it

Feel better now that you're home?

MINA

Definitely

ZOEY

Good. I'm excited to see you at work
tomorrow

MINA

I'm excited to see you too

ZOEY

Mina's heart jolted at the sight Zoey's emoji, and she put her phone down for the night.

She didn't know what to do when it came to Zoey. Her feelings had strengthened while she'd been gone, and Zoey wasn't helping with her note or her candle or the bath salts or how she'd put on Mina's favorite music. Mina didn't know if she could see Zoey at work and not turn into a melted pile of lovesick goo.

But she'd have to manage somehow. It was either that or stop working at Thistles and Stems.

Feeling both exasperated and immensely grateful, Mina fell asleep to the warm, soothing smell of chocolate.

TWENTY-SEVEN

ZOEY

Zoey woke the next morning feeling pleased with herself. Mina had loved her gift, and they were going to see each other that morning as they picked up a new pot collection Eleanor had ordered from an artist in Chilliwack. It didn't seem like the job required two people, but Zoey wasn't going to mention it.

She was about to leave when a knock sounded on her door. She opened it to reveal Mina in her winter jacket with her backpack slung over her shoulder.

"Good morning." She smiled, and Zoey's heart did a somersault.

"Hey. You seem chipper this morning."

"Yeah, I feel pretty good, surprisingly. I think that candle might have helped."

Zoey beamed and grabbed her bag. "I'm happy you like it."

"I love it. It made me want chocolate for breakfast, though, which I hear isn't the healthiest way to start a day."

"Where'd you hear that? I wouldn't trust that source."

Mina laughed, and Zoey was sure her smile was about to grow right off her face. "Whose car do you want to take for our little road trip?"

"Yours? If you want. Doesn't matter to me."

"Mine it is."

Being in a car with Mina forced Zoey to face her feelings head-on. She couldn't avoid them when Mina was sitting *right there*, her lips bright red, her thigh within easy reaching distance.

Zoey had tried to see Mina only as a friend. That had failed, obviously, and she had tried to create more distance after they'd kissed.

But she wanted to do more than kiss Mina. Even as they drove to work to clock in before going to Chilliwack and Mina talked about the better parts of her visit, Zoey wanted to hold Mina's hand and run her thumb over the sensitive part of Mina's wrist. She wanted to know Mina as more than a friend.

They arrived at Thistles and Stems in no time, clocked in, grabbed the receipt for the order from Eleanor, and got back in the car.

"Do you mind if I play music?" Mina asked before they drove off.

"Nope. Go for it." Zoey connected Mina's phone to her car's Bluetooth, curious about what she'd play.

She put on a song called "Red Wine Supernova" by Chappell Roan, which Zoey hadn't heard before. It was catchy.

"So," Mina started, "I don't think I've asked you this before. Why did you start a candle business?"

Zoey hummed thoughtfully. She wasn't sure she'd ever told anyone—other than Wren—why she'd started her business. "It's sappy."

"That's okay. I want to know anyway, as long as you're comfortable sharing."

Zoey shrugged. "When my mom has low days, she likes to light candles. It was an easy thing I could do to cheer her up when she was at her lowest, you know? I used to collect candles at markets and say they were for me, but really they were for her. And I couldn't bear to throw away the remaining wax at the bottom when the wick burned out, so I started re-melting the leftovers and making them into new candles, which gave me the idea to start my own business. If I can bring some light—literally—to someone's day, then I want to do that."

"Wow," Mina said. "That is sappy, but I love it." Her voice was filled with such tenderness that Zoey glanced over at her.

Mina's expression made heat flare from Zoey's head to her toes. She bit her lip. *Eyes on the road, Zoey.* "Thanks."

They parked in front of a pottery studio in Chilliwack called Mud & Glaze, which had hippie-style flowers painted in bright colors all over the door. Zoey liked the place immediately.

"Whoa," Mina said as they walked inside. The interior was just as colorful as the front door. Abstract shapes covered the walls, all the tables and chairs shouting at them in primary colors. The least colorful thing in the room was a shelf of pots and various sculptures waiting to be painted along the far wall.

"Someone likes color," Zoey muttered.

A White woman with short pink hair emerged from the back room, her hands full of paintbrushes. "Hello!" she chirped. "What can I help you with?"

"We're here to pick up an order for Thistles and Stems," Zoey said as Mina held up the receipt.

"Oh, for sure. The boxes are in the back. I'm Kizzy, by the way." She didn't bother with the receipt, waving it off when Mina tried to hand it to her.

Mina and Zoey introduced themselves and followed Kizzy to the back room, which was much larger than Zoey had expected and not nearly as colorful as the rest of the shop. The walls were white, and art supplies of all kinds filled the rows of wooden shelves. Kizzy gestured to three boxes pushed against the side wall. "I can help you carry them out. I packed everything in bubble wrap, so no matter how chaotically you drive, they should survive."

Eleanor hadn't shown Zoey or Mina what type of pots she'd ordered, and Zoey was curious to see them—even more so now that she'd met the artist behind them.

Putting the boxes in the trunk didn't take long, and she and Mina were back in the car before Zoey could catch her breath.

"Kizzy is certainly a character," Mina said, sounding impressed. "Her studio is . . . bright."

Zoey laughed. "You can say that again. What do you think the pots will look like?"

"Honestly, I have no idea. Something with polka dots, maybe? Or a Picasso-style face pot? What do you think?"

"I can definitely see Kizzy dabbling in cubism."

"Or pop art. Something colorful."

"And maybe glittery."

"Like a disco ball! We don't have a disco ball pot yet."

The ride back felt more relaxed as they chatted. Mina had a shift at Juniper Foods later that afternoon and Zoey was working until five, but neither of them were in a rush to return to town.

Zoey laid her hand on the center console as she usually did when she drove, and she almost jumped when Mina put her hand beside it. Their pinkies touched, just a brush at first. Then Mina slid her hand closer until it was partially on top of Zoey's.

There was no way that was a mistake.

They stayed like that the entire ride to the shop, Zoey's heart galloping the whole time. This had to mean Mina wanted her too, despite what she'd said a few weeks ago.

Neither of them spoke when they got out of the car. As they unloaded the boxes, Mina caught Zoey's eye a few times, and blood rushed to Zoey's cheeks. She tried to play it cool as they brought the boxes inside, but she didn't think she was successful.

"Did everything go alright?" Eleanor asked, hands on her hips as she surveyed her new stock.

"Yeah. I don't think we broke anything," Zoey said.

"Can we see the pots?" Mina asked.

Eleanor nodded. "Of course. I'd like to get a few of them out today anyway." She grabbed a knife and sliced through the tape on top of the boxes, then she lifted the cardboard flaps. "Here they are!"

Just like Kizzy's studio, the pots were colorful and chaotic. There didn't seem to be a theme for them other than *bright*. There were mushroom cottages, a fox, an octopus, a few galaxy pots that glittered, multiple rounded pots with bright floral designs, fish pots complete with fins and a tail, and a few that didn't resemble anything at all but were somehow pleasing to look at.

"These are interesting," Mina said, holding up one that was very clearly boobs with bright purple areolas and wine-colored nipples.

"That's exactly why I got them," Eleanor said, her eyes sparkling. "Let's put that one in the window."

Zoey locked eyes with Mina, stifling her laughter. Mina shrugged and took the pot out front. They worked on a display for the new goods until Mina needed to leave for her shift at Juniper Foods.

"I'll see you later?" Zoey asked. Her question implied more than simply seeing Mina later, and she wasn't sure if Mina would pick up on it.

But Mina's answering smile was more of a smirk, as if she knew exactly what Zoey was thinking. And maybe she was thinking the same thing. "Yeah. You know where to find me."

A split second after Mina left, Zoey rushed to the door and called after her, "Do you want me to pick you up later? To drive you home?"

Mina had barely made it a few steps. She raised her eyebrows. "Are you sure? I can walk like I always do."

"But . . . it's slushy. You'll ruin your shoes." Zoey knew it was a shitty excuse, but she couldn't help herself. She had to see Mina again as soon as possible.

Mina shrugged. "Okay, sure. Thanks."

When Zoey went back inside, she couldn't help her little skip of happiness.

TWENTY-EIGHT

ZOEY

Waiting to pick up Mina from her shift was agony—she wasn't off until ten thirty. Zoey kept running through everything that had happened between them that day. Every glance, every touch, every word they'd said.

Zoey poured a few candles to keep herself busy, but her hands were too shaky to apply labels to the jars. She was more nervous than she'd been in ages.

Finally, the time came for her to drive to Juniper Foods. She turned on a podcast in the car, listening to the host recount the Black Dahlia case as she sat parked in front of the store, waiting for Mina. It wasn't the most cheerful topic, but it kept her mind occupied.

Mina and Vera exited the shop a few minutes later, laughing. They waved at each other, and Vera waved at Zoey then headed to her car.

Mina slid into the passenger seat as the podcast host talked about how Elizabeth Short had been found.

"Jesus Christ," Mina said, her jaw dropping.

Zoey quickly turned off the podcast. "Sorry! That probably wasn't what you wanted to hear right after work."

Mina's eyes were wide with horror. "That's not what I want

to hear *ever*. How can you listen to this stuff? Do I need to be worried about you?"

Zoey huffed a laugh. "No. If anything, you should be glad I have so much knowledge about murder. I know how to avoid it."

"That, and you probably know exactly how to dismember someone."

"I can neither confirm nor deny that."

"How comforting."

To lighten the mood, Zoey put on "The Edge of the Earth" by The Beaches. Mina relaxed against the seat as Zoey pulled out of the parking lot.

"How was your shift?" Zoey asked.

"Good. Vera brought me a cupcake after dinner."

"She's just like her mother," Zoey said with a smile.

"Yeah. I'm pretty lucky to work for both of them."

They didn't say anything else for the last minute of the ride, and something grew in the air between them. Something electric.

"I'll walk you to your door," Zoey said when they arrived. "As is chivalrous." And selfish, since she hoped Mina would let her kiss her like she'd been wanting to do all day.

Mina laughed softly, and Zoey tried not to read too much into it.

They strolled up Mina's walkway, Zoey fighting the urge to hold Mina's hand. "Well, this is me," Mina said. She unlocked the door and opened it a crack but didn't go in.

Zoey hadn't moved to go to her own house, standing far enough from Mina's door that it wouldn't seem weird.

"Do you want to come in?" Mina asked.

She didn't give a reason, but Zoey's hope soared. She couldn't keep it away from the sun, no matter how hard she tried. And she also didn't really want to.

Her voice was breathy when she said, "Yes, please."

They both stepped inside. Mina let her backpack slide off her arm onto the floor as she toed off her shoes, then she shrugged out of her jacket and hung it up. Zoey put her purse on the floor and slipped her own shoes off, placing them neatly on the shoe rack against the wall. Every movement felt charged, the air between them crackling with a tension that was impossible to ignore.

Mina turned around, leaving only inches between her and Zoey. She licked her lips, and Zoey's eyes followed the movement. Her breath hitched.

Heat melted through Zoey's core and between her thighs.

She wasn't supposed to feel this way about her neighbor. She wasn't supposed to feel this way about *anyone*. She had seen what love could do to someone. Loving someone meant giving yourself to them, opening yourself to them, and making them part of your life. It could bring you to the top of the world, and it gave you no protection when you plummeted back down.

But she didn't want to resist it anymore. She didn't want to resist Mina.

Mina's brown eyes widened as Zoey stepped closer, lifting her hands slowly so her fingertips hovered over Mina's bare forearms. Zoey's skin tingled in anticipation.

"Mina," Zoey said, her voice barely above a whisper.

Mina matched her volume when she replied, "Yeah?"

Words fled her mind and made it impossible to answer, so Zoey did the next best thing. She closed the remaining space between them, sliding her hands up Mina's arms, one to her shoulder and one around her waist, drawing her close. The contact was electrifying, each touch fueling the fire within her.

"Can I kiss you?" Her gaze lingered on Mina's lips, her red lipstick inviting.

Those lips parted and Mina nodded, her breath coming faster.

When they came together, Zoey gasped. Mina's lips were so, so soft. The kiss was gentle, tender, a perfect blend of hunger and sweetness.

Mina pulled back for a breath, her eyes a darkened bronze that made heat pool low in Zoey's stomach. They looked at each other for a moment, both panting quietly.

Then Zoey couldn't keep her hands off Mina. She slid her

fingers up the back of Mina's neck and into her hair, pulling their lips together again, tugging Mina firmly against her. A noise escaped Mina's throat, the sound making Zoey grin against Mina's mouth.

She'd ached for this while Mina was gone, hoping that their first kiss weeks ago hadn't been their last. And now that Mina's lips yielded against hers, their tongues sliding deliciously against each other, Zoey didn't want this to end.

"Zoey," Mina said breathlessly as Zoey moved her mouth to Mina's neck, kissing the soft skin just under her ear.

"Mm?" Zoey's mouth was too occupied for her to answer. Without consciously deciding to do so, she pushed Mina gently against the wall, sliding her thigh between Mina's legs, grinding against her. Mina made that noise again, pitched higher this time.

"Coat," Mina said, tugging on Zoey's sleeve.

With a groan, Zoey took a step away to shuck off her coat, dropping it to the floor. Any time away from Mina was too much.

They crashed together again, a moan rising from Zoey now. "You taste so good," she said, her eyes on Mina's full lower lip. She wanted to see those lips kiss-swollen from her own mouth.

"So do you." They stopped for a breath, and Mina laughed as she looked at Zoey in awe, as if she couldn't believe what was happening. "You're gorgeous."

Zoey quirked an eyebrow and ran her thumb over Mina's lip. Kissing Mina filled her to the brim with confidence, and she wasn't about to squander it. "Am I?"

Mina's eyes narrowed playfully. "You know you are." She nipped at Zoey's thumb, then they were kissing again, Mina pushing her backward toward the stairs. "Upstairs," she said, turning and grabbing Zoey's hand.

They ran up to Mina's room, their lips locking once more before they'd even passed the threshold. Zoey wanted to inhale Mina, to feel every inch of her. She pushed Mina back onto the bed, her chest heaving. "Is this okay?"

Mina nodded, her eyes heavy lidded with want. Zoey

suspected she looked the same. At the very least, she knew she was flushed, heat washing over her skin.

"Are you sure about this?" Mina asked, propping herself on her elbows. Mina had called Zoey gorgeous, but Mina was truly the gorgeous one, lying back on the bed with her hair mussed and her breaths ragged.

"Yes. Absolutely sure." Anticipation flowed through Zoey, her clit pulsing with need.

"Then get over here." The expression on Mina's face was positively wicked, and Zoey loved it. She clambered onto the bed, hovering over Mina. "Clothes off?" Mina asked, pausing with her hands at the hem of Zoey's dress. Her fingernails lightly scratched Zoey's thigh, and even through her leggings the touch lit Zoey's skin on fire.

She wanted more. She wanted to burn.

"Yes, please."

Zoey tugged her dress off over her head in one smooth motion, but when she reached to undo her bra, Mina grabbed her wrists. "Let me."

Scooching to the edge of the bed, Mina sat with Zoey between her thighs, looking at her, her eyes bright with desire. She bit her lip, and Zoey caught her breath at the sight, resisting the urge to push Mina against the bed and kiss her feverishly.

Mina leaned forward, placing her lips along the top edge of Zoey's bra, kissing her sweetly. Zoey groaned, not even trying to hide how good that felt. Mina's hands were warm on Zoey's waist, holding her still while Mina kissed and licked along Zoey's bra line until Zoey thought she might come just from that.

Finally, Mina unclasped Zoey's bra, pulling it slowly down her arms, her eyes on Zoey's own. She dropped the bra to the floor, leaving Zoey standing there in her leggings, her underwear starting to soak through. Then Mina's hands were on her waist again, and she took one of Zoey's nipples in her mouth, sucking lightly.

Zoey threw her head back and closed her eyes, her legs trembling.

Mina moved to the other nipple, making a satisfied humming noise.

It was too much. Zoey pushed Mina onto her back, diving down to kiss her. She felt Mina's fingers glide under the elastic at the top of her leggings, then Mina was pulling them down. Zoey stepped out of them and her underwear, kicking them to the side.

"What about you?" she said into Mina's mouth. "Clothes off."

Mina laughed, and Zoey felt the rumble of it all the way to her toes.

"Impatient, are we?" Mina asked. She leaned back once more as Zoey stood, and her eyes took in Zoey's naked body slowly, drinking her in. "Wow. You're beautiful."

Many people had seen Zoey naked in the last few years and had admired her both verbally and physically, but the look on Mina's face was different. It made Zoey stand straighter, made her feel better about herself than she'd felt in ages.

If only she could see Mina's body in return.

With her lips parted, Mina began unbuttoning her black button-up shirt, her gaze on Zoey's the entire time. Zoey stood back and watched her, content to enjoy the show. "That's it," she said, her voice low. "Strip for me."

Mina's hands trembled as she finished unbuttoning her shirt and pulled it off. Her bra was black and lacey, somehow turning Zoey on even more. Moving slowly, Zoey straddled Mina's lap, running her hands down Mina's shoulders to her back and up again. She reached between her legs, struggling for a moment with the button on Mina's jeans then grinning when she finally got it open.

"You'll have to stand if you want these off," Mina said, her voice breathy.

"Oh, I do." Zoey stood and helped Mina pull her jeans off,

revealing pink briefs with cat paws on them. "Oh my gosh." A laugh bubbled out of her. "Those are adorable."

Mina pushed her shoulder lightly. "Shut up. I wasn't exactly expecting this today."

Zoey smirked. "And what's this?" she asked, running her fingers over a tattoo on Mina's thigh. It looked like an anchor with three concentric circles over it.

"It's the Elden Ring." Mina ducked her head. "It's from a video game, and it's hard to explain."

"One of your favorite games?"

"Yeah. It's pretty lore heavy."

Zoey leaned down and kissed the tattoo, tracing the lines with her tongue. "I'll have to watch you play sometime."

Mina shivered. "You have no idea how hot that is."

With a snort, Zoey lowered herself over Mina, the two of them kissing as they shuffled across the bed so they could stretch out. Zoey leaned on her elbows, her nose touching Mina's.

Mina placed her palm against Zoey's cheek. "I, um . . . I haven't done this before. With a woman. But I think I have a pretty good idea of how."

The tenderness on Mina's face made Zoey's heart squeeze. "We don't have to, if you don't want to."

One side of Mina's mouth ticked up. "Oh no, I do. I've been tested since Christian, and I'm good to go."

With that reassurance, Zoey lowered her mouth to Mina's once more. She ran her tongue along Mina's bottom lip. "I'm also clear. Just let me know if anything is too much, okay? We can stop at any time."

Mina swallowed audibly and surged up to kiss Zoey as if she couldn't hold herself back anymore.

Zoey hummed contentedly and gently pushed Mina flat on the bed. She worked her way over Mina's body with relish, removing her bra and sucking lightly at each of Mina's breasts, loving how Mina squirmed underneath her. Kissing down the smooth plane of Mina's stomach, Zoey relished how soft she was.

She grasped either side of Mina's underwear and slid them off while she marveled at Mina's bare legs.

Without prompting, Mina spread them so Zoey could fit between them. A smile spread over Zoey's face. "Is this what you want?"

"Yes," Mina said in barely more than a whisper.

Zoey made herself comfortable on her stomach, tracing circles on Mina's inner thighs with her fingers. She kissed Mina's lower stomach then lightly dragged her teeth over Mina's hip bone. Mina made a soft mewing noise, and Zoey's smile grew. She'd barely touched Mina yet.

"Zoey," Mina said, her voice strained, "please."

"Please, what?" Zoey asked, enjoying herself far too much.

When Mina looked at her, her eyes were pleading. "Please touch me."

"Isn't that what I'm doing?"

Mina scowled, and Zoey laughed. She brought her face down, kissing Mina right above her clit and making her groan. She slicked a finger through Mina's folds, loving how wet Mina was for her. When Mina thrusted into her hand, Zoey laughed again with satisfaction.

"Tell me what you want," she said, licking Mina gently. She tasted salty and a bit sweet, and Zoey basked in it.

"I want your tongue on my clit," Mina said, raising her arms to frame her head where she lay on the pillow, her dark hair splayed around her. "I want you to make me come."

"How can I deny you anything?" Zoey whispered.

There was no more holding back.

TWENTY-NINE

MINA

Mina quivered under Zoey's ministrations, her hand twining in Zoey's hair as Zoey licked and sucked at her clit. Zoey knew what she was doing.

"Every bit of you tastes amazing," Zoey said, the cool air of her breath on Mina's clit making her twitch in pleasure.

It wasn't long before Mina's feet were tingling, a sure sign of her orgasm approaching. She threw her head back, her eyes squeezed shut as Zoey pushed into her, her tongue delving deep.

"Zoey, I'm going to—"

She unraveled, waves of pleasure rolling over her as her thighs tightened around Zoey's head. Zoey grasped Mina's thighs, her fingers digging in just enough to push Mina's pleasure that much higher, and Mina couldn't stop the cry that escaped her throat even if she wanted to.

"Okay, okay, okay," she gritted out, pushing lightly on Zoey's forehead. Zoey backed off and Mina's body continued to spasm. As she rode it out, she felt Zoey shift beside her on the bed, trailing her fingers lightly up and down Mina's arm.

"Oh my god," Mina said, gasping. Her eyelids fluttered open. Zoey wiped the back of her hand across her mouth, pressing her lips together over a smile.

"How was that?" Zoey asked.

"That was . . . wow." A pleasant feeling of release settled over Mina's body, and she melted into her bed, her head so heavy that she couldn't lift it.

Zoey laughed. "I'll take that as a compliment."

"Mm, you should." Mina lay still for another moment in bliss, then she rolled onto her side to face Zoey. "That was amazing."

"Good." Zoey moved closer to Mina, gently shifting her leg so it was slightly on top of one of Mina's. Their breasts pressed together, the feeling comforting and erotic at the same time.

"Can I return the favor?" Mina asked, stroking Zoey's side and watching as goosebumps erupted on her skin. She moved her hand to Zoey's ass, cupping it and pulling Zoey closer.

Zoey's eyes narrowed in pleasure. "You can do whatever you like," she said, bringing her lips to Mina's. Mina tasted herself on Zoey's tongue, and she loved it. She took her time exploring Zoey's mouth, palming Zoey's breasts as she did so.

"I love how you're touching me," Zoey murmured, and her praise turned Mina on even more.

Mina pushed herself to her knees and moved to Zoey's feet. She didn't know if she could eat Zoey out with the same skill Zoey had, but there were other ways to make someone feel good.

Starting at Zoey's ankle, she kissed her way up Zoey's body, rubbing her hands over Zoey's skin as she went. Zoey was dotted with freckles, and Mina tried her best to kiss every single one.

"Mmm." A grin spread over Zoey's face.

Mina planted a kiss on Zoey's clit and moved her hand along Zoey's bare thigh. "That tickles." Zoey giggled.

Mina smiled. She shifted her hand to where her mouth had been, feeling how soaked Zoey was, and she moved to cover Zoey's mouth with her own. She left enough space between them so she could keep her hand right where Zoey needed it.

"Let me know what feels good," Mina said, moving her fingers slowly in circles. Although she hadn't done this before, she knew what felt good for her, and she hoped it'd feel good for Zoey too.

Everything around her faded away until the only thing on her mind was Zoey's pleasure.

"That's good, right there," Zoey murmured. She looked at Mina from beneath her lashes, and Mina brushed a kiss over her eyebrows.

Zoey made a satisfied noise that brought Mina higher. She increased her pace, paying careful attention to how Zoey reacted. "Down a bit," Zoey said. "Yes, right there. God, you're so good at this, Mina."

Mina kept her fingers moving over Zoey's clit as her lips pressed against Zoey's, and Zoey twined her fingers in Mina's hair, moaning into Mina's mouth. Never in her life had Mina experienced something so hot. She felt like she would burst with the sheer joy of it.

"I'm almost there," Zoey said, her breaths coming faster now.

"Good." Mina's voice was low. She wanted to make Zoey feel as amazing as she felt. She wanted Zoey to see stars, to leave the planet altogether and travel galaxies.

Zoey's breath hitched and she cried out, her body shaking. Mina watched her face, watched how Zoey's mouth fell open as she came on Mina's hand, clenching around her fingers. Mina stilled, allowing Zoey to relax.

She melted like Mina had earlier, and after a few moments she rolled onto her back with a satisfied sigh.

Mina snuggled into her side, and Zoey drew her in, her arm warm around Mina's shoulders. Mina rested her head against Zoey's chest, baffled at what had just happened now that she could think clearly again.

Well, somewhat clearly.

The sound of Zoey's heartbeat under her ear grounded her, but the more she listened to it and the more comfortable she became, the more a feeling she couldn't quite name rose in her chest. It overwhelmed her and tears sprang to her eyes, running down the side of her face onto Zoey's slightly sweaty skin.

"Hey, what's wrong?" Zoey shifted, lifting her head, clearly trying to see Mina better.

Mina wiped away her tears. "Nothing," she said, her voice thick. "I'm just . . ." She grasped at words, none of them seeming adequate to express what she was feeling. Sitting, she pulled a pillow to her chest, hugging it.

Zoey sat up too, holding Mina's hands. Her gaze was attentive, and that made Mina's chest feel even bigger, lighter. It brought more tears to her eyes.

"Sorry," she said, laughing. "I swear I don't usually cry after sex."

Zoey squeezed Mina's hands. "I wouldn't mind even if you did."

With a deep breath, Mina tried to compose herself and put together an explanation that would make sense. "It's been so long since I've felt this . . ." She wanted to say *loved*, but the word seemed so strong even if it was accurate, and she didn't want to scare Zoey away. She swallowed and tried again. "It's been so long since I've felt this cared for. The last couple years that Christian and I were together . . . it felt like he never really saw me. Like I just existed in his space. I tried to repair what we had so many times, but he didn't put in the same effort. I didn't realize until after he left that I was clinging to our relationship because it felt safe."

She paused and took a shuddering breath. "You know that my parents liked him, and I thought being with him—with his stable job and his ambitions to save the world—was what success looked like. Even if I didn't have a high-paying career that my parents approved of, at least I had a relationship that looked good on the page. But it didn't feel good at all."

Zoey shifted closer to Mina so their knees touched, and Mina kept her eyes on their joined hands as she spoke.

"I guess what I'm saying is, I've never felt seen or appreciated.

Not by my family, not by Christian." She met Zoey's gaze, noticing the flecks of darker blue in Zoey's eyes for the first time. "But you don't make me feel like a burden. You make me feel like I'm worth something."

Zoey leaned forward and kissed Mina's lips then kissed the tears from her cheeks. "You *are* worth something. You're worth so much, Mina." She shifted against the headboard, drawing Mina to her. Without hesitation, Mina leaned into Zoey, her head on Zoey's shoulder. Zoey rubbed her hand up and down Mina's arm, and Mina sighed, warm and content.

She could get used to this.

THIRTY

ZOEY

Mina's tears were salty on Zoey's lips, and she wrapped her arm around Mina's waist, pulling a pillow onto both of their laps. Mina's head was warm on her shoulder, and she tilted her own head to lean lightly against Mina's. What Mina had said shot straight to her heart, and she never wanted to let go of her. She wanted to do whatever she could to make Mina feel appreciated, to make her feel loved.

"Why are our relationships with our parents so complicated?" she said with a small laugh.

Mina made an inquisitive noise, reaching for Zoey's fingers on top of the pillow.

"You know my dad left when I was thirteen, right? I've told you how hard that was on my mom. She had one of the worst depressive episodes she's ever had, and my aunt was teaching at the time, so she couldn't stay with us. She visited on weekends when she could, and I'm grateful for that. But the rest of the time it was just me. Me and Wren. I hated my father for that, and I'm still angry at him. Mom's depression isn't her fault, but she was struggling, and he left us to handle that without him when he'd been the one to take care of us before. He left us, full stop. I shouldn't have had to cook for us and clean our house and have Wren's parents drive me to school. And Mom wouldn't accept help at the time, either, which made the whole thing worse."

Her gaze unfocused as she thought about how many times she'd opened her mother's bedroom door, hoping to see Mom sitting up and looking somewhat put together, only to see her sleeping form as always. Her side rising and falling slowly as she breathed, her hair a tangled halo on the pillow.

"She eventually came out of it, but it really hurt at the time. I had lost one parent and didn't know how to bring the other back."

"I'm sorry," Mina said, and Zoey shrugged the shoulder Mina wasn't leaning on.

"It's why I can't understand why my mom puts so much effort into pushing me to date. It's like she's obsessed with finding me someone. Every time I tell her I'm not interested, she gets this look on her face like it's the biggest disappointment. Like *I'm* disappointing her because I don't want to become so dependent on someone again." The irony of this situation wasn't lost on Zoey—how she was currently in bed with someone she cared deeply for.

Mina shifted. "So . . . you don't want to date anyone?" Her words were tentative, as if she was scared to hear Zoey's answer, and Zoey realized how what she said could have sounded.

"No, I . . ." She turned to look at Mina, needing to see her face as she said, "It's different with you. I think I would have been interested in dating earlier if my mom hadn't been pushing it so hard. I think . . . I think I started to avoid dating, to ignore any feelings I had about anyone, partly to spite my mother. I don't even know if that makes sense." She shook her head and laughed ruefully. "I don't know anymore."

Mina nodded, looking thoughtful. "It makes sense, in a way. She was pushing you into something you were already wary about, which made you even less inclined to do that thing."

"Exactly."

"But . . . now you're willing to try it?" Mina bit her lip, her gaze flicking away from Zoey's.

Zoey let go of Mina's hands to place hers on Mina's cheeks. "Mina Hasanza, I care about you." She needed Mina to know that, to feel it right to her toes. "I care about you so much."

One corner of Mina's mouth lifted. "But? I can feel a *but* coming."

"There is no *but*. I care about you. I just don't want to put a label on this"—she waved a hand over the two of them—"yet. If that's okay."

Mina's eyes darted between hers, and Zoey held her breath. She wanted to be with Mina, badly. But the thought of naming what they had, calling Mina her girlfriend or her partner, made her uncomfortable. Labelling it would mean she had put part of herself in someone else's hands, and she couldn't do that again. It made her want to run and hide.

And she didn't want to move from this spot.

Finally, Mina said, "That's totally okay." Her eyelids lowered, giving her that sultry look once again. "Can I still kiss you, though?"

The relief that shot through Zoey almost made her collapse.

"Yes, you goof." Zoey surged forward to kiss Mina, losing herself once more in the taste of Mina's lips and the feeling of Mina's hands on her bare skin.

MINA

Mina woke the next morning with her face pressed to Zoey's back, Zoey's hair in her eyes. She shut off her alarm and groaned, loath to leave this beautiful woman in bed.

Zoey echoed her groan and rolled over. "Is it morning already?"

The two of them had stayed up long into the night, exploring each other's bodies and learning what each other liked.

"I hate it too." Mina planted a kiss on Zoey's collarbone. "But I have to go to work." She swung her legs out of bed.

"Nooo, don't leave me," Zoey said, rolling to wrap her arms around Mina's waist. "Tell Vera you're sick and stay in bed with me."

Mina laughed. "Since when are you a rule breaker?"

"Since I discovered how good you are in bed."

"Oh, I'm that good, am I?" Mina shifted out of Zoey's arms but turned to lean over her. Zoey's hair was a mess, either from sleeping or sex or both, and Mina loved it. She loved seeing Zoey undone in the best way, sleepy in her bed.

"Now you're just fishing for compliments." Zoey's grin was sly.

Mina kissed her, sliding a hand along Zoey's arm. "Maybe." Before Zoey could pull her back into bed, which wouldn't be hard considering Mina wanted to be there, Mina headed for the bathroom.

The sound of disappointment Zoey made behind her gave her an extra boost of energy.

That energy coursed through her as she dressed and put on makeup. She emerged from the bathroom to see her bed neatly made, the clothes she'd discarded the night before now in her laundry basket. Zoey was nowhere to be seen, but Mina could hear water boiling downstairs.

She followed the sound. Zoey stood at the kitchen counter in yesterday's dress but no leggings, her hair in a messy bun. "I'm making waffles," she said, gesturing at the toaster in front of her. "The easy way."

"I love waffles made the easy way," Mina replied, kissing her on the cheek. She scrounged in the fridge for something to bring for lunch, but she hadn't gone shopping yet since she'd returned home.

"Why don't I bring you something for lunch?" Zoey must have deduced what Mina was doing. "I have the afternoon shift at Thistles and Stems, so I can drop it off for you before that."

"You'd do that for me?"

Zoey's cheeks flushed. "Yeah, if you want me to."

"Zoey Bell, I would love it if you'd bring me lunch." She pulled Zoey in for a kiss, and they only disengaged when the toaster popped. "Why don't you come over after your shift, and I'll make dinner to repay you?"

"Mm, I like this arrangement."

"By the way, have you given Eleanor your proposal yet? I was thinking about it the other day." She hadn't recalled Zoey saying anything about it since they'd worked on it.

Zoey ducked her head. "No. I haven't exactly finished it. I was sort of hoping you'd help me with it again."

"Do you want to do that tonight? It shouldn't take that long."

"You're going to make me dinner *and* help me finish my proposal? But only one of those is in repayment for lunch." Her open expression shifted, her eyes filling with mischief. "How can I thank you for helping with my business?"

Mina smirked. "I'm sure you can come up with something."

They sat close to one another as they ate their waffles, which was the ideal way to start the day in Mina's opinion. Zoey seemed happy with their morning together too, pulling Mina in for a long kiss when she left for work.

Mina would happily make this her new normal.

MINA THOUGHT ABOUT ZOEY ALL DAY. HER WAVY brown hair that shone golden in the light of the sun. Her blue-green eyes that reminded Mina of the ocean. The salty taste of her smooth skin, the softness of her stomach and the curves of her hips, the way her mouth formed an *o* when she threw her head back in ecstasy, her perfect pink lips kiss swollen.

When Zoey dropped off an individual-sized homemade charcuterie board at Juniper Foods for Mina's lunch, Mina snuck in a kiss, which Zoey readily returned. "See you later tonight," Zoey whispered against Mina's lips.

"You know where you'll find me," Mina murmured back.

She watched Zoey leave through the sliding glass doors, and when she turned around, Vera was smirking at her.

Mina waited for her to say something, but she didn't. She rolled her eyes. "Yes, I am sort of seeing Zoey now."

"Sort of?"

"We're not official or anything." Which was fine with her. At least, she thought it was. Less pressure.

Vera grinned cheekily. "I see."

"I'm glad you see." Mina gave her an exaggerated nod then went to the break room to eat the lunch Zoey had so thoughtfully made for her.

The glass container Zoey had put together contained crackers fanned out neatly beside evenly sliced pepper salami and cheddar cheese. A cluster of grapes filled the corner of the container with a few apple slices, the whole thing rounded out with a nest of pistachios. Mina popped a grape in her mouth and closed her eyes with happiness. Only Zoey could make such an adorable and classy lunch, and she'd included Mina's favorite nuts.

She knew she shouldn't compare Zoey to Christian, but her brain kept going there. At least Christian never won in her memories. She couldn't recall a time when he'd made her lunch like this, much less brought it to work for her. And without prompting.

She'd made him meals more times than she could count. Although she enjoyed cooking, it got tedious when the person you were cooking for didn't acknowledge the food aside from shoving it in their mouth. He used to show his gratitude in the early days of their relationship, but that had stopped at some point. She hadn't really noticed until it had been grating on her nerves for months.

There was every possibility that the same thing could happen with Zoey, but for some reason Mina didn't think it would. She didn't feel the same unsteadiness around Zoey, as if at any moment she could take a wrong step and fall off a cliff. Zoey made her feel solid, secure.

Her good mood lasted for the rest of her shift, and she bought a few things to make dinner with before she walked home.

By the time Zoey arrived shortly after six, Mina had two plates of fettucine alfredo steaming on the table beside slices of fresh bread, a dish of olive oil, and the salt shaker. She'd also prepared a small plate of caprese salad for an appetizer. She'd been craving Italian food, and she hoped Zoey would like it.

Before Zoey even stepped through the door, she wound a hand into Mina's hair and pulled their bodies together, kissing

Mina tenderly. Mina had to ignore the urge to guide Zoey to the couch, reminding herself that dinner was cooling.

"It smells amazing in here," Zoey said as she slipped off her shoes. "What did you make?"

Mina filled her in on the evening's menu, relieved at Zoey's excitement for pasta.

"I used to make pasta dishes all the time for my mom because they were easier than other things," Zoey said. "It was never this fancy, though. Usually mac and cheese or something with a premade sauce."

"Those sound like good meals to me." Mina pictured a teenage Zoey standing over a stovetop, draining pasta. She'd been so independent from such a young age. She'd had to be. Mina resented her parents for a lot of things, but at least she'd always been taken care of.

The two of them dug in, both hungry after work.

Zoey moaned after the first bite of pasta. "You can cook for me more often if you'd like," she said, licking her lips.

"I'd be happy to. Especially when you make that noise."

"What noise? This one?" Zoey replicated her moan, exaggerating her expression of pleasure.

Mina laughed. "Yes, that one."

"If you like that noise so much, I can make it more often. In exchange for good food, that is. Or good sex. Either works."

Mina tapped a finger against her lips. "You know, that seems fair to me. I accept the deal."

"I thought you might." Zoey slid a forkful of pasta into her mouth, her expression positively wicked.

Heat flooded Mina's stomach, and she squeezed her thighs together. "We are not going to get your proposal done tonight if we keep talking like this."

Zoey shrugged. "We could move the proposal work to a different day. Do more fun things this evening."

"Zoey." Mina gave her a look. "How long have you been working on this?"

"I know, I know. And I wanted to give it to Eleanor before the end of the year. Ugh, fine. But only if we can reward ourselves with ice cream after."

"That's reasonable."

Zoey nodded decisively.

They finished dinner then cleared the table to use as their workspace. Mina fed Zelda while Zoey went back to her place for her laptop.

"Let's get this over with," she said a few minutes later, the laptop set in front of her. Dread lined her face as if she were walking to the gallows rather than working on a business plan.

Mina leaned over, her mouth close to Zoey's ear. "The faster we get this done, the sooner we can have ice cream. And other nice things."

Zoey glared at her. "Now I want to work on this even less."

Sliding her chair a few feet away, Mina said, "I'm staying over here until it's done. How's that?"

"Can you slide a few inches closer whenever I finish one of the template sections? It's like a reward."

Mina considered the idea. "Okay."

Zoey gave her a huge cheesy grin, all teeth, and got to work.

As Mina helped her—from a distance to start, of course—she marveled at their situation. Zoey wanted her to be there, not just to help her, but because she enjoyed Mina's company. She wanted Mina to move closer to her *as a reward*. Mina had never felt valued like that before. It made her sit a bit straighter.

The two of them eventually completed the business proposal, with Mina inching closer to Zoey as the Word document filled. By the end, she was motivating Zoey with light kisses to her neck, her jaw, her shoulder.

Zoey was squirming by the time she said, "It's done!" triumphantly.

She hopped out of her chair and pushed it aside, straddling Mina. "Now I get my *real* reward."

"What about ice cream?" Mina asked, sliding her hands along

Zoey's thighs under her dress. She would never get enough of Zoey in dresses.

"Screw ice cream. This is better."

She devoured Mina's mouth, and Mina had to agree that kissing Zoey was far better than any dessert.

THIRTY-TWO

ZOEY

Eleanor agreed to meet Zoey at the bakery after work the next day to discuss Zoey's proposal. They were both off at five, so they walked there together. Although this was her first time pitching her idea to another business owner, it felt much more casual than it would with someone she didn't know well.

The actual pitch didn't take long, and Zoey slid over the official proposal in all its glory. "You'll find everything you need to know in here," she said, tapping the cover page. "Including a list of my products, a marketing strategy, and plans for distribution."

Eleanor raised her eyebrows and picked up the document, flipping through it. "Thank you for being so thorough. I'll admit, I never considered selling other products at Thistles and Stems, but you've made a good case for Bell Lights. I'll have a think and get back to you soon."

Zoey beamed but restrained herself from wiggling excitedly. This was a business meeting, after all.

Mina had the closing shift at Thistles and Stems that day, but Zoey couldn't wait to tell her how the meeting had gone. She walked straight there after saying goodbye to Eleanor, her chest swelling with pride as she walked through the front door.

Mina was at the cash register, currently talking with Evvie

Adler, one of Eleanor's good friends. Zoey had some acquaintance with Evvie since she came into the shop often.

Zoey slid behind the counter. "Do you mind if I snag Mina's attention for a second?" she asked Evvie.

Evvie shook her head. "Not at all. I'll browse the new pots."

Mina looked at Zoey, her eyes widening in question.

"The pitch went really well!" Zoey said, radiating confidence. "Eleanor loved the proposal, and I have a good feeling about how she'll respond."

Mina's eyes lit up and she threw her arms around Zoey. "Congrats," she said in Zoey's ear. "I knew it would go well. There's no way she'll say no." When she dropped the hug, she put her hands on either side of Zoey's face and kissed her gently.

"Ooh."

They broke apart to see Evvie grinning slyly at them. "I don't know what you're celebrating, but it must be good. Congrats, Zoey."

Zoey laughed. "Thanks, Evvie. I'm sure you'll find out if the idea goes through." She turned back to Mina, energy fizzing inside her. "Anyway, I just wanted to tell you that. I couldn't have done it without you."

"You would have figured it out eventually."

"But I'm glad I didn't have to. You're the best."

Mina kissed her again. "You are, actually, but we can argue about that later. I'll see you tonight," she said, her voice low enough so only Zoey could hear.

Zoey grinned, Mina's tone sending a thrill through her. They'd be celebrating more tonight, and she looked forward to it.

ALL THE SHOPS ON MAIN STREET, EXCEPT THE DINER, closed early on New Year's Eve for Creekfest. A stage was erected in the park for regional bands to play, and a few businesses set up booths selling merchandise, food, and drinks.

Zoey had considered selling her candles there this year, but she and Wren had gone as patrons for the past two years, and they weren't about to break tradition. Except this year, the two of them were attending the one-night festival with Mina.

"Finally! Geez, you can be so fucking stubborn sometimes," Wren had said on the phone when Zoey told her she and Mina had slept together.

Zoey had rolled her eyes. "Yes, okay, you're always right and I should always listen to you."

"Yes, you should. Thank you for finally admitting it."

Now, the two of them were in Zoey's bedroom getting ready for the festival.

"How do I look?" Zoey asked, twirling for Wren in her bedroom. She'd donned a short black dress and burgundy leggings for the evening, and she'd added a sparkly black ribbon to her ponytail. She'd paired the ensemble with black combat boots, going for an edgier vibe.

Wren appraised her from her spot on the bed. "Like you're going to a rock concert and not a small-town New Year's Eve concert that showcases mostly country bands."

"Perfect. That's what I'm going for."

"Hoping to impress a certain neighbor even more?" Wren asked, waggling her eyebrows. She got up to finish her makeup, her blue jeans and sweater much more casual than Zoey's outfit. She'd argued that they didn't need to dress up since they'd be wearing winter jackets anyway.

Zoey begged to differ. Tonight was an occasion, and one should always dress up for occasions.

They met Mina out front a few minutes later. Mina wore black jeans and her puffy jacket with floral stripes, and she'd added silver sparkles to the corners of her eyes. "Ready to go?" she asked. She leaned over to peck Zoey's cheek, and Zoey slid an arm around Mina's waist.

"Yes," Wren said. "Let's party!" She shimmied, making them laugh.

As they sauntered toward the festival, Zoey and Mina let Wren walk ahead of them.

"Excited for tonight?" Zoey asked, her arm linked with Mina's.

"Sure." She didn't sound very excited.

"You're not? I thought you wanted to go to Creekfest."

"I do. I think it'll be fun. It's just crowded. And loud."

Zoey looked at her, examining her expression. Her jaw was a bit tight, but she didn't seem overly upset. "Can I do anything to help? Do you need your extra anxiety meds?"

Mina shook her head. "I brought my Loops, which should help."

"Loops?"

"They're basically ear plugs. They allow me to hear still, but they make everything quieter."

"I've heard of those," Wren said over her shoulder. "I see ads for them online all the time."

"Oh. That's cool." Zoey made a mental note to get a pair for her mom. "Okay, well let me know if we need to leave early. I totally don't mind if we do."

Mina squeezed Zoey's arm to her side. "Thank you. I will."

The murmur of people talking and laughing grew louder as they approached the park. The sun had gone down, but the park was lit with stage lights, glow sticks, and car headlights as people tried to find parking along Main Street. Zoey could smell beer, popcorn, and hot dogs, and her mouth watered. She hadn't eaten dinner specifically so she could stuff herself with mini donuts.

"Drinks first?" Wren asked.

"And food, please!" Zoey said.

The three of them bought drinks and snacks then found a spot to stand at the back of the crowd where it wasn't too claustrophobic. Zoey and Wren would usually be in the thick of things, but there was an unspoken agreement to respect Mina's comfort levels.

They were already attracting attention that Zoey hadn't

expected. She caught more than one person not-so-secretly eyeing her and Mina as they walked together, and a few gave Zoey knowing smiles. She returned their smiles awkwardly, glad that at least they hadn't said anything.

Mina leaned close to Zoey's ear. "You seeing the weird looks too?"

"Yep."

Mina sighed. "Nothing in this town stays secret for long."

Doing their best to ignore their nosy neighbors, they chatted and bobbed their heads to the music, enjoying the atmosphere.

"Remember when that famous drummer came a couple years ago?" Wren asked, sipping her hot cider. "And he declared his love for Evvie! Whatever happened with them? Are they still together?"

Zoey grinned, jerking her head to an older crowd sitting at a picnic table nearby. Wearing her usual rainbow scarf, Evvie sat next to a gray-bearded man with a cane. They gazed at each other with the gooiest expressions, and Wren let out a snort.

"Ah. Clearly still together. And so damn cute!"

An hour or so after they finished their snacks, they decided to get hot chocolate.

While they were standing in line, Zoey's gaze landed on the black Loops in Mina's ears. "How are you feeling so far? Everything alright?"

Mina nodded. "It's not too overwhelming, if that's what you're asking. I'm having fun."

"Good." Zoey leaned her head on Mina's shoulder, sighing in contentment. She'd never been *with* someone on New Year's Eve before, and she was excited to have a person to kiss when the clock struck midnight. Not that she bought into all that romantic stuff, but then she could say she'd done it at least once.

Once they had their hot chocolate, they walked across the street to get a better view of the fireworks. Many people had the same idea, and the sidewalks by the diner and at the library were crowded.

"Let's go somewhere more open," Mina said, and they followed her to the grocery store parking lot. A few people were hanging out there too, but not as many.

Lorelai, the town's mayor, started the countdown from the stage. The speakers placed around the park ensured everyone in the area could hear.

"Five, four, three, two . . ."

Zoey grinned at Wren then turned to look at Mina, the streetlights reflecting in her eyes. They yelled "Happy New Year!" at the same time then kissed, laughing as they did.

A feeling rose in Zoey's chest, warm and light. Something more than joy. She couldn't quite name it, and she didn't know if she wanted to. The feeling grew as she saw the happiness on Mina's face, the way her lipstick had smudged slightly on her bottom lip.

Zoey kissed Mina again and let her emotions wash over her. They didn't need to be labelled. Not in that moment.

All Zoey needed was the feeling of Mina's lips on hers, the sound of fireworks exploding overhead, and the taste of hot chocolate in her mouth.

THIRTY-THREE

MINA

Mina enjoyed New Year's Eve more than she'd expected. She didn't find the crowds or the noise as overwhelming as usual, and she was with her favorite person: Zoey. Wren was growing on her too, especially as they learned more about each other. Wren played quite a few video games, so she and Mina always had something to talk about.

The only part of New Year's Eve that she didn't enjoy was going back home. Wren was staying at Zoey's, which meant Mina was not.

She wouldn't mind being by herself except all she wanted to do was snuggle in bed with Zoey. Maybe eat her out first and give her an incredible orgasm to start off the year, but then snuggle. All night.

Since she couldn't do that, she settled for snuggling with Zelda.

"Happy New Year," she said softly, kissing the cat on her head. Zelda purred and nudged Mina's hand for more pets. "Just you and me tonight."

Since Christian had left, she couldn't get enough of the extra room in bed, starfishing every night simply because she could. But after Mina spent a mere four nights with Zoey, the bed seemed massive. And cold.

The two of them hadn't discussed what they were to each other yet. Mina got the feeling that Zoey was avoiding it. Zoey had said their first kiss was impulsive, but there was no denying there was something more between them now. Mina couldn't be the only one who felt it.

She'd been trying to tell herself that keeping things casual was better because she didn't want a repeat of what had happened with Christian.

But Zoey had already proven herself better than Christian in so many ways. Mina never felt stifled around her. She never felt like she had to act a certain way or do things for Zoey to make Zoey like her.

For some reason, Zoey seemed to like Mina simply for who she was. And she'd only really known Mina while she was struggling. Struggling to pay bills, struggling to find a job, struggling with her family. None of it was easy, and Zoey didn't seem to care. Even though Zoey strived for perfection for herself, she never seemed to hold Mina to that standard.

Zoey was fresh mountain air in the uphill trek of Mina's life, and Mina couldn't breathe enough of her.

OVER THE FOLLOWING WEEKS, MINA AND ZOEY SETTLED into a routine. Depending on their work schedules, they brought each other lunch and made each other dinner. They spent nights at each other's houses, sometimes at Zoey's if she was working late on her candle business, sometimes at Mina's to keep Zelda company.

Eleanor had accepted Zoey's business proposal, so they brought candles into Thistles & Stems, placing them artfully on the shelf with the succulents. Zoey had started working on a new collection specifically for the shop that smelled like different flowers. Eleanor had given her a book she had published years ago called *The Symbology of Flowers* so Zoey could create candle titles from the flower meanings.

Mina had had no idea Eleanor was an author in addition to a florist and a business owner, and she was impressed. She strived to achieve that level of success one day.

Often, while Zoey worked on her business—packing orders, pouring wax, trimming wicks, applying labels—Mina researched companies to apply to for 3D modelling. She felt much better about her work these days, and she sent out resumes for every job she felt qualified for.

Everything with Zoey was flexible and easy, and Mina couldn't remember the last time she'd felt this happy. Declan was thrilled for her too when she finally told him what was going on with her and Zoey.

"I knew you were hiding something at Christmas!" he said.

"I wasn't really *hiding* it. I mean, our first kiss had been a few weeks before that, but I wasn't sure where it was going." If anywhere.

"Well, I approve."

Mina laughed. "You haven't even met her!"

Declan grunted dismissively. "Doesn't matter. She's not Christian, and you seem genuinely happy with her. That's enough for me. For now."

Despite his proclaimed approval, he grumbled at her for not playing video games with him as much. But he could live. He'd acted the same way when he first started dating Lila.

Of course, Mina hadn't told her family about Zoey yet. Since they hadn't put a label on their relationship, she didn't want to say anything. As comfortable as she was with it all, she didn't want to take it too seriously. And telling her family would make it serious. Not to mention she hadn't had a girlfriend before, and she wasn't entirely sure how her parents would react to that.

Part of her was afraid that if she got too attached, everything would be snatched away. And yet she couldn't stop her feelings from growing.

She couldn't stop herself from picturing a future with Zoey, one where they lived in the same house. One where they were clearly dedicated to each other, where they agreed to be exclusive and made this into something Mina could trust wholeheartedly. One where Zoey was her girlfriend.

She remembered what Vera had told her in November, when Mina had wanted to know what her first kiss with Zoey had meant. Sooner rather than later, she needed to talk to Zoey about what she wanted.

But she didn't want to scare Zoey away.

She was thinking about how to start that conversation when she walked into Thistles and Stems for her shift one February afternoon. Zoey had started work that morning, and she swooped out of the back room to kiss Mina in greeting.

"Fancy seeing you here," she said.

"I know, it's not like I work here part time," Mina replied. She stuck out her tongue, and Zoey giggled.

"Someone bought three candles this morning," Zoey said, bouncing up and down. "*Three* of them!"

"Congrats, babe," Mina said.

The look on Zoey's face made Mina realize what she'd said. In addition to not talking about their relationship status, they hadn't discussed possible pet names.

Zoey tilted her head, her lips pursed. "You know, I like it. *Babe*. Like David Bowie. I've got the power."

Mina was lost. "What?"

"*Labyrinth*? 'Magic Dance'?"

"I have no idea what you're talking about."

"Oh my god. Okay, tonight, we're watching *Labyrinth*. I can't believe you haven't seen it. It's a classic!"

Mina had been hoping to have the relationship conversation tonight, but maybe they could work it in after the movie. "Okay, sure."

The front door opened with a *whoosh* of cold air, and Eleanor swept in. Her long salt-and-pepper hair was tangled from the wind.

"It's chilly out there today," she said, shivering. Her gaze landed on Mina. "Mina, you're here! Since I've got both you girls today, I wanted to ask you something."

Mina and Zoey exchanged glances as she ran her hands through her hair and unzipped her jacket.

"What's up?" Zoey asked.

"I'd like to update our website and have new material for social media posts, and my dear friend Frankie said she'd be happy to take new photographs. She used to be a wildlife photographer, but she also takes wonderful portraits. She took Minnie's and my wedding photos. I was wondering if you two would like to be in the pictures. We could do it on a Sunday morning when it's slower and have a fun wee photoshoot! What d'you say?"

The idea of a photoshoot made Mina's anxiety flare. But if Zoey was there, it might not be so bad. Mina had found herself stepping out of her shell more recently with Zoey's encouragement.

"Sure, I have no problem with that," Zoey said.

Mina bit her bottom lip. "Can I have veto power over the photos before you post them?" The last thing she needed was to have Eleanor post a photo that irked her and then have one of her family members comment on it.

"Oh, of course, dearie. I would never post something you didn't like."

Mina nodded once. "Then yes, I'll do it too."

Eleanor's eyes sparkled. "Perfect! Are you two available next Sunday? I'll ask Frankie if she can come then."

Both Mina and Zoey were free, so Eleanor went to the back to call Frankie.

"This should be interesting," Mina said, moving behind the counter. "I've never done a photoshoot before." Her brows pinched together.

Zoey rubbed her arm. "I think it'll be fun. I've met Frankie, and she's really sweet. She'll be easy to work with."

"Okay. Cool."

That night, they watched *Labyrinth* as Zoey had requested, although Mina couldn't quite figure out why she loved the movie so much. It was campy, sure, and David Bowie was always a plus. Other than that . . .

"It must be a childhood thing," Mina said with Zoey curled against her side on the couch. The light of the TV glowed over them and the giant half-full bowl of popcorn on the coffee table.

"You wound me," Zoey replied, shaking her head. "I can't believe you didn't like it."

"I didn't say I didn't like it. I said it was fine. I liked parts of it."

"Twist the knife, why don't you."

Mina rolled her eyes but couldn't help her amusement at Zoey's theatrics as she monologued about how great the movie was. She kept up her spiel as they got ready for bed, and she was still going as they slid under the covers.

When Zoey finally stopped talking, she yawned and rolled over. "Spoon me," she said, wiggling her ass.

Mina couldn't say no to that, so she scooched close and pulled Zoey against her, nuzzling her face into Zoey's hair to kiss the back of her neck. She smelled like coconut shampoo.

There hadn't been a good time to talk about their relationship that evening, and it was too late at this point. Zoey seemed to have spent all her remaining energy on defending *Labyrinth*, and Mina couldn't summon the motivation to start a serious conversation. But that didn't mean she wasn't frustrated.

Maybe a label didn't matter that much anyway. They knew they had feelings for each other, and maybe that was enough. Mina knew Zoey wasn't seeing anyone else; she didn't have time to, even if she wanted to—and Mina was pretty sure she didn't.

And yet Mina lay awake that night thinking about it. Wondering how true Zoey's feelings were. Wondering how true her *own* feelings were if she didn't have the courage to bring up the topic.

THIRTY-FOUR

ZOEY

Zoey loved seeing Mina every day. And not only seeing her like before, but *seeing* her in the sense that they knew each other intimately. Mina knew Zoey's favorite foods, how much time she needed to get ready in the morning, what side of the bed she liked to sleep on. She knew how Mina's breathing changed when she was anxious, how to make her tea how she liked it, and how her brows drew together when she was concentrating.

She had lain awake in bed for hours after their dinner date on Valentine's Day, Mina snoring softly beside her, musing about her own stubbornness. She was honestly a bit miffed at herself for refusing to go on dates earlier. Hookups were great, but she could have been missing out on the comfort of knowing someone this well while caring for them so much that her chest sometimes felt like it would explode. Then again, she didn't want to feel this way about anyone other than Mina.

But not having a serious relationship meant she'd avoided the pain of it potentially ending. Now, when she was by herself and her brain gremlins awoke, the thought that she could be dropped like a piece of trash at any moment poked at the back of her mind.

She was pretty sure Mina wouldn't do that to her. Even if she did, it's not like they were officially together. There was nothing to break if nothing existed in the first place. They could go back to being neighbors. Friends, even. Coworkers.

Regardless, she was going to enjoy what they had while they had it.

THE SUNDAY OF THEIR PHOTOSHOOT AT THISTLES AND Stems arrived, and Zoey and Mina got up earlier than usual to prepare. Zoey had run over to her place to get ready, and now she'd returned and sat on Mina's bed wearing navy tights and a burnt-orange dress with Zelda in her lap. She'd have to use a lint roller before they left.

"Is this shirt good enough?" Mina asked, holding her arms out to her sides.

Zoey made a show of scrutinizing her forest-green chinos and her black button-up shirt patterned with tiny cacti. "I think it'll do," she said. At the look of dismay on Mina's face, Zoey nudged Zelda off her lap and stood. She wrapped her arms around Mina's neck and kissed her nose. "I'm kidding. You look great. Very sexy."

Mina laughed and shook her head. "Cactus shirts are sexy?"

"On you they are." Zoey grabbed Mina's collar and pulled her in for a kiss. Mina tasted faintly like rose and cardamom, and her hands were warm on Zoey's lower back as she deepened the kiss. She leaned down further and slid her hands up Zoey's dress, cupping Zoey's butt.

Zoey pulled back, smirking. "Slow down there, babe. We've got a photoshoot to get to, remember? Can't be smudging our lipstick now, can we?"

Mina groaned and glared at her, and Zoey loved it.

"You started it," Mina said.

"And I'll finish it later." She winked.

"I'll hold you to that."

Mina's gaze travelled over Zoey's body, from her pointed brown boots, up the dress's triangle cutout below her breasts, to land on her eyes. If Mina looked at her that way any longer, she'd need to change her underwear.

"We better get going," Zoey said, heading for the front door, very aware that Mina liked how the back of her dress framed her shoulder blades.

They drove to work that day to prevent the late-February wind and rain from compromising their photoshoot-ready looks.

Frankie was already there when they arrived, her camera on a strap around her neck. She looked extra casual in her khakis and vest next to Eleanor, who wore a gorgeous deep blue maxi dress with short sleeves and a V-neck. Ruffles around the neckline and at the waist gave it a boho feel. Eleanor had tucked an anemone into her hair, and she wouldn't have looked out of place at a music festival.

"Good morning," she greeted them. "Mina, this is Frankie. Frankie, Mina."

Mina shook Frankie's hand, and Zoey could tell by the stiffness of her body that her nerves were getting to her.

While Eleanor and Frankie talked about staging, Zoey pulled Mina aside. "Are you okay?"

Mina took a deep breath. "I think so. Just nervous."

Zoey ran her hands up and down Mina's arms. "Let me know if you need a breather at any time. This'll be fun."

The way Mina looked at her, with absolute trust and openness, made Zoey's heart squeeze. "Okay."

"Are we ready?" Frankie asked, her gray eyebrows raised. "I'd like to start in the back room, with the three of you making bouquets. We want to lean candid rather than staged, so forget I'm there. I can prompt you with things to talk about, but don't worry about how you look. Alright?"

"Easier said than done," Mina muttered as they followed Frankie and Eleanor through the swinging door. Zoey put a reassuring hand on her back, wishing she could lift the weight of Mina's anxiety.

The photoshoot felt awkward to start, but Frankie was good

at her job. Before long, she had them all laughing and poking fun at each other. Zoey could tell Mina had relaxed because her shoulders were no longer around her ears.

By the time they moved to take photos in front of the store, the rain had stopped and the sun was peeking through. "The clouds actually make for better lighting," Frankie said, looking at the wispy gray shapes overhead.

She got them all to stand in front of the window with the store's sandwich board placed off to the side. They played around with a few poses there, then they brought out an empty barrel display to work with. The top was full of fresh dirt practically begging for plants.

"Let's get your hands dirty," Frankie said, a spark in her eyes. "People should see how fun it is to work with soil."

"Have I ever told you I like how you think?" Eleanor asked her friend.

"Once or twice," Frankie said, laughing.

Their banter seemed to relax Mina even more. As she and Zoey added a few plants to the planter, dirt working its way under Zoey's nails, Zoey genuinely forgot about the camera. With the smell of rain around them, damp soil against her skin, and Mina laughing across from her, Zoey felt like she could float off the ground at any second.

"Why are you looking at me like that?" Mina asked, her mouth still poised to laugh as she patted dirt around the roots of a white tulip.

"Like what?"

"I don't know. Like you're happy."

Zoey made sure to keep eye contact with Mina when she said, "Because I am happy." She shifted forward and kissed Mina, leaning into the moment until the world narrowed to just the two of them. Mina's lips parted against hers with a sigh of pleasure.

At the click of the camera, Mina jolted away from Zoey as if she'd been stung. Although her hair covered her ears, Zoey knew they'd be as red as a beet.

Frankie grinned. "Don't worry, that one won't go on the website." She turned to Eleanor. "Why didn't you tell me these two are dating?"

Eleanor beamed as if the whole thing was her idea. "They haven't told me, actually. But I see them looking at each other all the time. Sneaking kisses when I'm not around."

Mina went to rub the back of her neck but stopped when she saw the dirt coating her fingers. "We're not hiding it," she said.

"But we're not really dating," Zoey added. "I mean, we're seeing each other, but we're not, like, official or anything."

"Oh." Eleanor looked at Frankie, who shrugged.

When Zoey turned back to Mina, a frown had settled on her face. The joy and embarrassment that had been there moments ago had vanished, and her gaze had gone distant.

"Are you okay?" Zoey asked.

"Um, yeah. Do we have enough photos?" Mina asked Frankie.

Frankie looked at something on her camera, presumably the number of shots or maybe the gallery of photos they had taken in the last hour or so. "I think so."

"Cool. I'm going to go clean up." With that, Mina went back inside.

The atmosphere had shifted so quickly, Zoey felt like she had whiplash. Had she said something wrong?

"I'll clean up too," she said, following Mina.

She found Mina in the back room, washing her hands. She sniffed and turned away from Zoey, almost as if she'd been crying.

"What's wrong?" Zoey asked, taking Mina's place at the sink as Mina dried her hands on a towel.

"Nothing." Mina still wasn't looking at her.

Zoey sighed. "I clearly said or did something wrong. Can you please tell me what it is?"

Mina slowly faced Zoey, as if it took extra effort to move. Tears welled in her eyes, and it made Zoey's heart hurt to think she might have put them there. "I don't want you to get upset at me," Mina whispered. "I don't want you to freak out."

"What? I won't get upset." Zoey grasped Mina's hands in her own. Her skin was cold, so Zoey rubbed her thumbs over Mina's knuckles. "I won't freak out, I promise."

"Maybe we should wait until after work." Mina pulled one hand free and swiped a tear away before it could smudge her eyeliner.

"No. Something is bothering you, and I don't want it to bother you all day. We're not busy right now, and Eleanor will be okay if we take time to talk. I'll even ask her, if you want."

Mina bit her lip, considering, then nodded.

Assuming her crisis-mode persona, Zoey strolled out front and requested that she and Mina have time alone to talk in the back room.

"Of course," Eleanor said, concern in her eyes. "Let me know if I can help."

"If it has to do with that photo of you two kissing, I can delete it," Frankie added. "Just say the word, and it's gone."

"Thanks. I'll let you know."

Zoey didn't want that photo deleted, though. She and Mina had taken a few selfies together, but this was a professional photo of the two of them kissing. She wanted to see it. She had a feeling she'd want to frame it.

But she needed to figure out what was bothering Mina first. Mina was her priority.

THIRTY-FIVE

MINA

Mina couldn't believe she'd broken down like that. At work, of all places. And in front of the professional photographer who'd come to take marketing photos. She hoped Eleanor wouldn't think any less of her for it.

And she hoped Zoey wouldn't bolt once they'd talked.

Over the past few weeks, she'd meant to raise the topic of their relationship status. She'd thought about it often, but it had never seemed like the right time. And she'd managed to convince herself time and again that it didn't really matter, that she was over-thinking everything. People dated all the time without being exclusive, and there was nothing wrong with that.

But when Zoey said *I mean, we're seeing each other, but we're not, like, official or anything,* Mina's heart had broken a little.

"Eleanor said to take our time," Zoey said, re-entering the back room. She pulled out one of the tall stools they used when they were working at the counter, then hooked another one with her foot for Mina.

Mina sat, willing herself not to cry before she even got started explaining what the hell was going on with her. She didn't know if she could express it coherently. But she'd try. She had to try, otherwise this would come up again.

She attempted to channel Vera's no-nonsense energy about relationships. *If you don't talk about it, it gets worse.*

Zoey folded her hands in her lap, her expression open. She wasn't running away from a tough conversation—at least, tough for Mina—and that was a good start.

"I—" Mina stopped then inhaled and exhaled slowly. "I don't know how to begin."

Zoey mirrored her deep breath. "Maybe I can help. Is it . . . Does it have to do with what I said about us? That we're not really dating?"

The words made Mina's throat grow thick. She nodded. Looking at Zoey while she spoke made it harder, so she stared at her hands, at her chipping black nail polish. "Yeah. I know we haven't defined our relationship. We haven't talked about what we're doing." She spoke haltingly, but Zoey didn't interrupt. "Before Christmas, before I went to my parents', when we kissed . . . you said you weren't looking for anything. And what we've been doing has been pretty casual, I guess. But . . . for me, at least, my feelings have gone beyond that."

She looked up at Zoey, but she couldn't read Zoey's expression.

She continued, "I hoped that yours had as well, and I keep meaning to ask you about it. But what you said . . . it's obvious that you still want something casual. It's not fair of me to expect more. I just don't know if I can do that."

Zoey looked down then, her fingers clenched around each other. The tips were turning red.

"I care about you, Zoey. I care about you a lot. If you don't feel the same way, I understand. But we can't continue seeing each other."

Zoey's head snapped up. She grabbed Mina's hands. "Mina, I do. I feel the same way. I care about you so much."

Relief washed through Mina's body so quickly, she almost swayed off the stool.

"You do?"

"Yes, I do." Honesty shone through Zoey's eyes, her gaze intent on Mina's. Every time Mina had thought through this conversation, she'd expected the worst. She hadn't dared to hope for a reaction like this.

"So . . . why did you say we aren't dating then? I mean, I guess we didn't talk about it before. But, can we say that now? That we're dating? Do you . . . do you want to be my girlfriend?"

Zoey opened and closed her mouth without saying anything. She swallowed, seeming to struggle with something. Mina's heart sank.

When Zoey spoke again, her voice was small. "Do we have to put a label on it? Why can't we go on as we've been without calling it anything?"

Mina's brows drew together. "If you care about me enough to make it serious, why not call it something? If you don't like the word *girlfriend*, that's totally cool. We could use *partner* or *significant other* or something instead."

It was Zoey's turn to avoid meeting Mina's eyes. "I don't understand why we need to label it. Labels don't really mean anything, not compared to how we feel."

Zoey wasn't entirely wrong, but she wasn't entirely right either.

"If they don't really mean anything, then why do you have such a problem using them?" Before Zoey could reply, Mina added, "I know some people don't need them, but . . . it feels like you don't want to acknowledge what's between us when you say we're not dating. It feels like you're saying we're nothing to each other." She almost couldn't get the next sentence out, but she needed to say it. "I don't want to be nothing to you."

The truth of that statement rang out even though Mina's words were soft. For her whole life, she'd felt like nothing. Nothing compared to her sisters. Nothing in her relationship with Christian, where his career had quickly outshone her. Nothing in her desired field of work, which her parents wouldn't even recognize as a valid career.

She couldn't do that again. She couldn't be nothing.

Zoey's grip on Mina's hands tightened. "You are not nothing to me, Mina Hasanza. You have never been *nothing*." When she met Mina's gaze again, it was with a spark of determination. "I'm working through my own shit, and I'm not ready for us to be . . . more than we are. But you mean more to me than you probably know. I don't want to lose you. Can we talk about this again later?"

Mina's gaze darted between Zoey's eyes, absorbing the intensity of her pupils against her blue-green irises. Mina couldn't ignore the desperation there. She'd felt that herself. She was feeling it now.

But she didn't want to lose Zoey either.

"Okay," she said. "We can talk about this again later." Even as she said it, the fear arose that *later* would never come. But she wouldn't push Zoey on this. She wouldn't risk it, not right now.

"I care about you, Mina," Zoey said fiercely. "I want you to know that."

She kissed Mina as fiercely as she'd spoken, and Mina melted into it. She wasn't nothing to Zoey, and that reassurance buoyed her.

KNOWING THAT SHE MEANT SOMETHING TO ZOEY— even if that *something* was yet undefined—gave Mina some solace. She couldn't relax all the way, though, wondering when they'd broach the subject of their relationship status again. The potential conversation loomed over her like a bolder perched on the edge of a cliff.

To keep her mind off it, she threw herself into finding a job with a game developer.

She'd already received three rejections, and she hadn't heard anything yet about the four other jobs she'd applied for. Finding a position could take time, but she couldn't quell the increasing urgency she felt about it.

Nowruz, Persian New Year, was approaching on March 20, and Mina wanted to find a job by then. It was the perfect time of year for starting anew—for reflecting on the previous year and setting new goals.

Mina found herself checking her email more frequently as Nowruz approached. She imagined what it would be like to video call her family that day, to wish them "Nowruz Mobarak" and follow it with an announcement of her new job. Her parents would be so proud of her, and for once she could feel like she'd met her responsibility to her family. She'd be the daughter her mother wanted her to be. Even the thought of that filled her with pride.

But by March 4, she still didn't have any promising news. No interviews, not even a positive comment about her portfolio. She was sending off another application one evening when Zoey walked in and kissed her on the cheek.

"Another job opportunity?" Zoey asked.

"Yeah. This one is an unpaid internship, so I don't really want it, but it doesn't hurt to apply." At this point, Mina just wanted someone to accept her. Even though she had the training to work as a video game artist, she didn't have much experience, and she didn't know if her work was truly good enough.

The more time passed with no job offers, the more she feared she didn't have a chance.

"Well, let's hope one of the other *paying* companies gets back to you first." Zoey sat beside her and squeezed her thigh. "Can't pay your rent with exposure or experience."

Mina sighed. "Yeah." But exposure and experience could put her on the right path. She didn't say that, though, knowing Zoey would shoot daggers at that comment.

"So." Zoey's fingers tightened on Mina's thigh again, and Mina could tell by Zoey's tone that she had something important to say. She closed her laptop.

"What's up?" she asked.

Strands of hair had escaped Zoey's ponytail and framed her face. Zoey always looked perfectly put together when she headed out each day, but Mina thought she was just as attractive when her spotless image started to unravel. Even straight out of bed with her hair a tangled mess and her eyes a bit goopy, Zoey was gorgeous.

"My aunt is going to visit a friend in Manitoba next weekend, so I was thinking I might go stay with my mom. If that's okay with you."

"That's totally fine," Mina replied. Zoey worried about her mom enough when her aunt was around; she probably wouldn't be able to focus on much else if her mom was alone. "Do you need me to cover your shifts?"

Zoey pressed her lips softly to Mina's. "No, Eleanor said we're good. But thank you."

"Of course." Mina was slightly baffled that Zoey had even approached her as if she needed permission. It was nice, in some ways, but Mina didn't want Zoey to feel like she needed her approval for stuff like that. "You don't have to ask me to spend time with your mom. I know how much she means to you."

A smile tugged at the corners of Zoey's mouth. "I know. But I want us to make decisions like this together, you know? I'm not going to just announce my actions as if they have no effect on you."

Mina's heart warmed. Yet again, Zoey was highlighting how she was different from Christian. How she was different from Mina's family. Most people in Mina's life seemed to take her for granted. They expected her to drop everything she was doing so she could focus on them, and she caved almost every time. She was worried what would happen if she didn't.

But Zoey never put her in that position.

"And I'll be back by the Sunday night, for sure. So I won't be gone long."

"Okay."

They made dinner together and ate while they watched *Schitt's Creek*. They were watching through the whole series and were currently in Season 4. Mina felt the urge to happy dance every time she realized Zoey genuinely loved the show and wasn't just watching it for her.

Zoey fell asleep quickly that night in Mina's bed, Zelda lying stretched out between them so they couldn't cuddle. Mina didn't have the heart to move her, but she couldn't get comfortable and she wasn't that tired anyway, so she got up.

She went to her office and opened her email, hoping for a response to one of her applications. No one had replied yet, which wasn't surprising. One of her professors had emailed her though, and her heart jumped at the email's subject line: *Potential job for you*.

Biting her lip, she opened the email and scanned it.

It wasn't a direct referral, but it was a job opening with a video game developer called Sawed-Off Entertainment that her prof thought she was a good fit for. She'd heard of the company in passing but didn't know much about them, so she did a quick search and found that they were a small video game house that had made one game in the past two years. Their art style wasn't her favorite, but she could work with it. It was more heavy duty than what she liked, the character models simpler and the games of the shooter variety rather than story-driven like what Mina wanted to work on.

But she wasn't about to turn down the option.

She sent a quick message to Declan, asking if he'd heard of Sawed-Off before. He likely wouldn't be awake at this time of the morning, but she didn't need his response right away.

Back on the application page, Mina read through the job requirements and the starting salary. She had the necessary skills, and she'd never made that much money in one year before, at least not from one job.

With a job like this—a well-paying job for a growing company —Mina could prove to her family that her career choice was valid.

She could show them that art could lead to success, that it was meaningful work. Maybe her mom would actually have something nice to say about and to her at Christmas.

But there was a catch.

There wasn't a remote option for the job. And their office was in Toronto. Mina groaned and sagged in her desk chair, causing it to roll backward.

It wasn't as if she hadn't considered moving to find a job, but she'd pushed the possibility out of her mind. Part of her thought it wouldn't be a problem because there was a good chance she could find a job in Vancouver, which wasn't that far away. She didn't want a long daily commute, but she and Zoey could easily do long-distance if that distance was only a couple of hours.

If Zoey even wanted that.

There hadn't been a point in asking since they were still in limbo about their relationship status.

Without thinking about it too much, Mina filled out the online application and linked her portfolio. Applying for the job didn't mean she *had* to move.

They probably wouldn't even want to hire her.

THIRTY-SIX

ZOEY

Zoey woke alone in bed. Mina was gone, the room oddly quiet. The two of them had been cuddling almost every morning since New Year's, and it felt like part of Zoey was missing.

She rolled out of bed and poked her head in Mina's office, but Mina wasn't there. Zelda was, though, curled up on Mina's desk chair like a fluffy little seat warmer. She raised her head and trilled quietly, then hopped off the chair and followed Zoey downstairs.

"Where's your mama, hmm?" Zoey asked sleepily.

The answer soon revealed itself.

Mina sat at the kitchen table with her laptop open, her hair a mess. She'd changed into sweats and a hoodie at some point, though Zoey hadn't heard a thing.

"Good morning," Zoey said, and Mina blinked owlishly at her.

"Morning." She yawned, sipped from the mug by her elbow, and grimaced.

"What's wrong?" Zoey asked.

Mina pushed the mug away from herself. "It's cold."

"It's cold? How long have you been awake?"

Rubbing the back of her neck sheepishly, Mina said, "I didn't sleep."

"What? Why?" Zoey circled behind Mina and leaned forward, wrapping her arms around Mina's shoulders. She kissed her cheek then pressed her nose gently into Mina's temple.

"I couldn't. I wasn't tired when we went to bed, and then I made the mistake of checking my email."

"What do you mean?" Zoey plugged in the samovar then settled into the chair beside Mina.

"I've been sending out emails to my contacts about jobs, and one of my profs sent me a listing he thought I'd be good for. Zo, it looks like a decent job. Exactly the type of position that could get my foot in the door."

A spark of excitement lit in Zoey's chest. She knew how long Mina had been yearning for a job in the video game industry, how she'd been working hard to hone her skills and make a portfolio she could be proud of. "That's amazing, babe! Did you apply?"

"I did." Mina's voice went quiet. "But I don't know if I should take it, even if they like my application."

"Why? If this could get your foot in the door, why wouldn't you take it? You've been working toward this for years. If it's because of your mom, screw her. You should be able to do what you love for a living, regardless of what anyone else thinks."

Mina smiled, but it didn't reach her eyes. She seemed tired, and not only from a lack of sleep. "It's not because of my mom."

"What is it then?" Zoey's excitement shifted to anxiety, and she put a hand on Mina's forearm, needing the contact.

Mina bit her lip, her eyes wide and slightly red when she looked at Zoey. "It's not a remote position. I'd have to move."

It felt like the air had been sucked from Zoey's lungs, but somehow she managed to ask, "Where?"

"Toronto."

Silence rang out in the room, the name of Mina's home city lingering in the air like a spritz of too-strong perfume.

"Toronto," Zoey repeated eventually.

"Yeah." Mina stared at her feet, her hands limp in her lap.

Zoey swallowed, hard. "Mina . . . If this job is as good as you think it'll be . . . and if they want to hire you . . ." She couldn't finish the sentence.

She wanted Mina to have the job of her dreams. She wanted her to work somewhere she loved, somewhere that recognized her talent and paid her well for it. But Toronto was so far. Too far from Zoey.

But she didn't feel like she had the right to say that. They weren't officially girlfriends. Because of Zoey, they'd been keeping it *casual* even though their feelings for each other were anything but.

"I don't know if it is that good," Mina said. "The art style isn't ideal for me, but I could work with it for a while to get experience. I also don't know much about the company, honestly. I did some googling and all I found was a review from a slighted employee who said the company sucked. But one review doesn't really mean anything. Also, Declan's friend went to school with the CEO and said he's an asshole, but that was years ago. So who knows?"

Zoey hated how that crack in the plan gave her hope. She wanted to be sad if the job wasn't everything Mina wanted, but she also didn't want Mina to leave. To leave her.

"Anyway," Mina continued, "it might not even matter if they don't want to hire me."

"Right. Yeah, okay. Well, I can help with the research if you want." She wanted to add *I'll support your decision, no matter what happens,* but she couldn't get the words out. She didn't know if they were true.

"Thanks. I'll make us tea. I need something to drink that isn't cold."

Zoey tried to enjoy her morning with Mina, but now all she could think about was how Mina might be leaving. How this potential job could change everything.

Zoey didn't do relationships because of this exact scenario.

It was probably best that they hadn't become anything more serious. Yet the thought of Mina leaving made Zoey want to crumple to the floor and hug herself just to keep herself together. She ignored the thought that she was in too deep already.

She wasn't. She'd always held herself up, and she'd be able to do it again. Even if Mina left.

OVER THE NEXT WEEK, ZOEY NOTICED MINA CHECKING her phone so often, she barely paid attention to anything else. She knew Mina was waiting on an acceptance letter from several applications, but that one job kept jumping to Zoey's mind. The one job that would take Mina away from her.

So when Mina burst through the doors of Thistles and Stems the Tuesday before Zoey was leaving to visit her mom, Zoey's heart fell even as excitement sparked in her chest.

"Guess what?" Mina asked, panting and beaming. She must have run there from Juniper Foods.

"What?" Zoey ran to meet her, and the two of them clasped hands.

Mina was practically vibrating. "Sawed-Off replied to my application. They want to do an interview over videocall tomorrow!"

"Babe, that's amazing. Congrats!" She threw her arms around Mina and held her tightly, not sure which emotion was currently winning.

"I'm terrified! But also so happy, I might throw up." Mina stepped back and shook out her hands. "This is the first interview I've gotten. The first developer to show any interest whatsoever in me. I cannot fuck this up."

"You won't," Zoey said with confidence. At least she could be sure of that. "You'll do great. I'm sure they'll love you."

Mina bit her lip. "Toronto, though. That's . . . far. And my parents are there."

She didn't say, "And you're here," but Zoey heard it anyway. Or maybe she just wanted to hear it. Maybe she didn't factor into Mina's decision as much as she wanted to, and that was probably her fault.

She hadn't brought up their relationship status again, even though she knew it was bothering Mina. The two of them had danced around what they were to each other ever since the photoshoot. Zoey could fix it so easily, but she still couldn't bring herself to take that next step.

Every time she tried picturing herself as a *girlfriend*, as someone tied to someone else . . . All she could think about was how her father had walked out, leaving her and her mother to fend for themselves. To build a new life without him. A life where Zoey had learned to take care of herself and her mother, where she'd had to grow up too fast, where she'd learned that giving your heart to someone was a recipe for disaster.

She couldn't do it.

"Okay, I need to go finish my shift," Mina said, pecking Zoey on the cheek. "I just needed to share the news. See you later!"

She was gone before Zoey had even finished saying, "You know where to find me."

THE NEXT DAY, ZOEY MADE PANCAKES FOR MINA TO bolster her before her interview. She had the morning shift at Thistles and Stems, and Mina's interview was at ten. "Did you take your extra meds?" Zoey asked.

Mina nodded. "Yes. But they're not really helping." She'd eaten one pancake and then paced from the front door to the back for the past fifteen minutes.

"Hmm. Maybe listen to Chappell Roan and dance around or something until the interview, okay? Complete that stress cycle. I need to go, and it's probably not good for you to pace for the next two hours."

Mina waved her off. "Yeah, I'll be fine. Declan said he'll be online soon, so we're going to play a game or two to distract me."

"Good. I'm glad you have him."

"Me too." Mina let out a huge sigh. "Okay, I'm calming down. Everything will be fine."

"Everything will be *great*. You'll kick this interview's ass." Zoey pulled Mina toward her and put her hands on either side of Mina's face. "You. Will. Ace. This." She leaned in for a kiss, trying to channel all her faith in Mina through their lips.

"Thank you." Mina looked as if she wanted to say more, but she didn't.

"Call me after, okay?"

"Yeah. I will."

Zoey drove to work instead of walking in case she needed to get home to Mina quickly, depending on how the interview went. She checked the clock every few minutes, waiting for a call. Ten thirty passed, then eleven, then eleven thirty . . . How long was this interview?

Zoey's phone rang at ten after one.

"Finally," she said in greeting. "That was a long fucking interview."

Mina laughed, and the tension in Zoey's body eased. "It was. Way longer than I expected, too."

"So how'd it go?"

A beat passed, and Zoey tapped her toe against the front counter. "They want to hire me," Mina said in a rush.

Zoey's jaw dropped. "They do?"

"Yeah. Seth, the CEO, had me block out something for him live. It was nerve-wracking, but I did it, and he said I'm exactly what he's looking for."

"Wow." Zoey's heart thudded, and she couldn't parse her feelings. This was great for Mina, but . . . it might not be good for the two of them. "That's amazing, Mina. I'm so proud of you." She paused. "Did the CEO—Seth—seem like an asshole?"

"It was hard to tell, honestly. Like, I don't think we'll be best friends, but he was fine."

"Hmm."

"But he loved my work." Excitement infused Mina's voice.

"That's good! Not that you couldn't get a good read on him, but that he liked your work."

"I know." Mina huffed a laugh. "This is so weird. I always hoped for an opportunity like this, but it feels almost fake."

"It's not fake, babe. You are a talented artist! You don't know if you want the job for sure yet, though?"

"I want to think about it a bit more. It's not exactly a small decision."

"No, it's not. And you don't want a disrespectful boss." Zoey felt as if she was staring over the edge of a cliff. "I can talk about it with you later, if you want."

"Okay. Thanks."

"Of course."

Even though Zoey wanted to help Mina work through her decision, she dreaded the conversation. Their relationship hung over Mina's choice, and she knew she'd have to face the topic eventually. She couldn't keep putting it off.

Not if she wanted to keep Mina.

THIRTY-SEVEN

MINA

When Mina got home that night, Zoey ambushed her at the door with a congratulatory hug and kiss. "I made chelo kabob for a late dinner," she said. "I have no idea if I made it right, but I followed an online recipe."

"Oh my god, Zoey!" Mina had mentioned how her dad liked to make chelo kabob on special occasions, how it was one of her favorite foods. "I—" She stopped herself, realizing she was about to blurt the three words she couldn't say to Zoey no matter how much she wanted to. "I can't believe you did that."

"Yeah, well, don't thank me until you try it."

The food wasn't as good as her dad's, but it was still pretty good. Mina let herself enjoy the meal, basking in the joy of getting a job offer even if she hadn't accepted it yet.

"So," Zoey said as they were cleaning up dinner, "have you thought more about what you'll say about the job?"

Of course she had. She'd thought about it all day. She'd made mental pro and con lists, and she'd been so distracted that she'd knocked over an entire stack of cereal boxes. It had taken twenty minutes to restack them.

No matter how many pros or cons she could think of, though, another topic overshadowed them all: her relationship with Zoey. She didn't know what to do with that. She'd put the ball firmly in Zoey's court, and Zoey hadn't said anything about it. Zoey knew exactly where Mina stood when it came to what she wanted, and Mina wasn't about to nag her.

"Sort of. I think I need a few more days to think, though."

A few more days would give Zoey the opportunity to say something.

Zoey nodded. She avoided looking Mina in the eye, and Mina wondered if she knew that her feelings were keeping Mina on tenterhooks. "Yeah, that's not a bad idea. This isn't something you want to walk into lightly."

"Exactly."

They moved on to talking about Zoey's upcoming visit with her mom, a cold fist of anxiety rooting in Mina's stomach.

Having a job offer was great, but trying to figure out what to do with it was not.

The next morning, Mina put together her Haft Seen for Nowruz. It was a bit early, but with everything going on, Mina wanted to set her intentions for the coming year. She thought about everything she wanted to clear out of her life and everything she wanted to bring in. To the sprouts, pudding, dried fruit, garlic, apple, sumac, and vinegar, she added a few coins, a mirror, and a candle. The coins to set her intentions for getting a new job, the mirror to represent her wish for her family to accept her, and the candle . . . The candle represented what she wanted with Zoey. Happiness. Brightness.

Instead of the uncertainty currently scratching the inside of her ribcage.

ZOEY LEFT FOR VANCOUVER ON FRIDAY WHILE MINA was at work. They had said goodbye that morning, and Zoey still hadn't said a word about what she wanted for their relationship. They'd barely talked about the Sawed-Off offer either, likely because they both knew it would lead to a deeper discussion that Zoey apparently wasn't ready to have yet.

Mina didn't know how much longer she could wait.

That night, after Mina was already tucked into bed with Zelda on the pillow beside her, Zoey called her. They didn't chat for long, and something felt off. Maybe it was the physical distance between them since they hadn't been apart for three months. But Mina didn't think that was it.

They hung up, then Mina checked her email, which had become a habit in the past few weeks. An unread email from Sawed-Off sent her pulse into overdrive.

TO: mina.hasanza@gmail.com
FROM: sethceo@sawed-off .com
SUBJECT: Re: Job offer

Hey Mina,

Have you reached a decision about the job? I'm interviewing another candidate on Monday, but I wanted to give you dibs if you're still interested. The project has been delayed enough already, and I'm eager to get you on board. If it sweetens the deal, we'll pay for your flight out, and we can cover whatever's left on your lease. Let me know as soon as you can.

Thanks,
Seth

Mina groaned and stared at her bedroom ceiling. Of course, Seth wanted a decision right away. He was trying to get the new project going, and she'd told him she'd reply to him soon. And his offer to pay for her flight and the rest of her lease . . . She didn't know what to do with that.

She had planned to give herself one more week—until right before Nowruz—to give him an answer, but now she didn't know if she could wait that long. If this was the job that would kickstart her career, she couldn't let it slip away.

She hurled her phone across the room and buried her face in her pillow, knowing she wasn't in a state to reply right now. Maybe the next day, after she'd slept on it.

MINA BARELY GOT ANY SLEEP, AND SHE HAD THE DAY shift at Thistles and Stems so she had to get up early. Rain sluiced down the shop windows, which reflected her mood and explained why she had only a handful of customers. Eleanor came in at two to relieve her. Mina usually would have been excited to get off work early, but she didn't know what to do since Zoey was still in Vancouver and the Sawed-Off offer wouldn't leave her brain.

Instead of heading home, she walked around the pond, not caring about the rain that ran over her jacket and soaked her jeans. Her socks squelched in her shoes with every step, but she barely felt it. She had too much on her mind.

She kept thinking about Seth's reaction to her work. His praise had almost knocked her flat.

She had spent so long on her portfolio making sure everything was perfect, and yet it still hadn't felt good enough. It had seemed like no one wanted to hire her, and when she'd looked at her models, she'd felt like she'd never get a job. She'd thought her parents were probably right in implying that her art was worthless, that it wouldn't amount to anything. That *she* wouldn't amount to anything.

And yet a CEO of a video game developer—a growing company with a lot of potential—was willing to pay thousands of dollars for her to move across the country to work for him.

She hadn't realized how good it would feel to have someone value her work like that. To have an expert in her field acknowledge her talent and offer her a position she never thought she'd get.

It was enough for her to overlook the red-flag comments he'd said in the interview. Stuff like, *You need to have thick skin to work here. We don't coddle anyone.* And, *We're gonna try to play to your strengths, but are you open to doing other assets? We're a small team, so everyone does a bit of everything. Even I work overtime!*

She hadn't told Zoey about those comments, not wanting her to worry.

Part of her was still cautious, though. Returning to her home city wasn't a small thing. She'd be close to her parents again, and she'd gone to Vancouver for university to be away from them. To gain space and figure out who she was on her own terms.

She knew who she was now, though. She knew what she wanted. Her parents still got on her nerves, sure, and she still fought with her mom, but maybe it wouldn't be as bad now. Plus, they'd have to respect her choices if she accepted this job. She could show them what her version of success looked like.

She turned onto a wooden platform that stretched out onto the water, the roof above sheltering her from the rain. Leaning against the railing, she watched the raindrops hit the surface of the pond, creating a pattern that was almost mesmerizing.

If she moved, it wasn't like she'd be totally alone. Her sisters would be there, and she enjoyed spending time with them. She could cook more with her father. And she could see Declan in person regularly again, which would be nice. She could get to know Lila better too.

Maybe she could even begin repairing her relationship with her mother.

But Zoey . . .

Thinking of Zoey made Mina's stomach jump to her throat. She dug her fingernails into the soft wooden railing of the platform.

Zoey had yet to tell her what she wanted their relationship to be, whether that was friends with benefits, or girlfriends, or just friends. Or nothing at all. Maybe just neighbors. She didn't really think Zoey would throw it all away, but she also wasn't sure how much it mattered anymore.

Mina's feelings for Zoey had grown so quickly. More than once recently, she'd had to stop herself from saying *I love you*. She couldn't say it, not with how Zoey had brushed off their relationship during the photoshoot at Thistles and Stems.

It was the first time she'd felt stifled with Zoey, and she hated it. It reminded her of how she'd felt around Christian—afraid to say what she truly thought, walking on eggshells to avoid negative reactions. She knew this wasn't the same, that Zoey wasn't trying to hurt her, but Mina still felt small.

And now, with this job on her horizon . . .

Part of her felt like she should seize the opportunity, no matter what Zoey said. Mina had been hoping for a job like this for years, and she'd been trying to prove herself to her parents for most of her life. Even if the art style wasn't exactly her cup of tea and the boss wasn't the best, this was her chance to join the 3D art community in a significant way, to make a name for herself.

If Zoey didn't want more than what they had, Mina would be able to leave without much fuss. Although the mere thought of that caused her heart to crack.

If Zoey *did* want more . . . Maybe she could go with Mina. Or maybe they could try long distance. Zoey would want the best for Mina if she loved her, right? After all, she'd been the most encouraging person in Mina's life when it came to her art.

The more Mina thought about it, the more she realized she didn't want to make a decision about this job based on her relationship status. This was about her career and her life goals. She had to decide for herself based on what *she* wanted.

She straightened, bringing her attention to her surroundings. A beaver swam alongside the platform with a branch in its mouth, only its head visible. Mina watched it, a newfound confidence running through her.

When the beaver disappeared around the bend, Mina turned

toward home, walking with purpose. She knew what she was going to do.

THIRTY-EIGHT

ZOEY

Zoey and her mom took advantage of their weekend together to visit a few of their favorite haunts from when Zoey still lived in Vancouver. For dinner on Friday, they went to Per Se Social Club so Zoey could satisfy her craving for a good burger, and Mom caught her up on all the school drama that had happened since they last spoke. On Saturday, they slept in then ate lunch at Secret Coffee Co. on Gallant Ave, and after window shopping for the afternoon, they watched the sunset from Jericho Beach.

On Sunday, they planned to walk along the Seawall in Stanley Park before Zoey drove home. Zoey had learned to ride a bike there, and she and her mother used to walk in the park often with Wren. In the summer, they almost always enjoyed ice cream cones as they strolled. Not today, though. Gray clouds threatened rain above them, but they were prepared in their rain jackets and Vessis. Rain couldn't keep many Vancouverites inside, and the path was rife with opportunities for people watching.

Both women were quieter than the day before. Mom had always been prone to listen more than speak unless Zoey prompted her, and Zoey's mind was currently on Mina.

They'd talked on the phone on Friday night, but it had been awkward. Since then, they'd texted a few times, mostly brief check-ins.

Zoey was aware she was pushing Mina away. And she knew it wasn't fair to Mina to keep doing whatever they were doing if Mina didn't feel secure in it. Insecurity had plagued Zoey for enough of her life that she knew how painful it could be. She still felt its effects more than she wanted to.

Mina deserved to be with someone who could provide her with steadiness. With a relationship she didn't question. With a love that was loud and proud, not one that ducked its head at the first sign of a label.

And Mina's potential job only added to the pressure on Zoey's shoulders. She had no idea how her decision about their relationship would affect Mina's choice, if it did at all.

"Penny for your thoughts?" Mom asked, her hands tucked into her jacket pockets. The ocean breeze pulled strands of her graying hair across her forehead.

Zoey bit the inside of her cheek. She hadn't told her mom about Mina yet. She knew Mom would be excited for her, and she had shied away from getting Mom's hopes up. But her mother had gone through heartbreak before—Zoey had firsthand experience of how low it had brought her. Maybe she would have advice.

Zoey took a deep breath. "I'm going to tell you something, and I need you to not freak out, okay?"

Mom's footsteps stuttered and she frowned, but she said, "Okay. I'll do my best."

"For the last few months, I've been seeing someone."

She braced herself for her mother's squeal and when it didn't come, she snapped her head in her mother's direction. Mom's lips were pursed in a smile, her eyes bright. "That's great, sweetie. I'm happy for you."

The enthusiasm in her voice was genuine, but Zoey had expected a much bigger outburst.

"You knew, didn't you?" Zoey asked. "How?"

Mom let out a soft laugh. "I didn't know for sure, but I had a hunch. I could tell by the way you've been talking about Mina. It is Mina, right?"

Zoey pushed down her surprise enough to say, "Yeah, it's Mina."

Her mother nodded. "She's featured much more prominently in our conversations lately. And whenever we've seen each other, you've seemed so much happier. When she hurt her ankle, you two couldn't take your eyes off each other."

She hadn't thought her feelings for Mina were so obvious, but her mom had seen them as if Zoey had projected them in neon letters.

"I was waiting for you to tell me. I'm glad you did." She leaned over and nudged Zoey lightly. "Do you want to talk about her?"

Zoey ignored the question. "How are you so calm about this? How haven't you asked me about it until now? My whole life, you've been pushing me to date, and now it's like you barely care." Her words were snappier than she'd intended.

Mom's expression fell, and Zoey's heart clenched. "I do care, honey. I care so much. But I wanted you to come to me when you were ready. I realized that I had been pushing you, and maybe that's why you weren't saying anything. I don't want to be that kind of mom. I want you to *want* to tell me things."

Those words made Zoey's chest tighten even more. She stopped and pulled her mom into a hug. "Thank you," she said into Mom's shoulder. She broke away and kept walking, needing the rhythm of her feet as a buffer for what she had to say next. "I guess I'm just confused. I never really understood why you wanted me to find someone so badly. Especially after what happened with Dad."

"Ah." Her mother was quiet for a minute. "What happened with your father . . . Our relationship wasn't easy, and it never had been. We married young, before either of us really knew who we were. And he didn't know if he wanted kids, but then after years of just the two of us, we had you. He loved you so much, but I don't think he was prepared. I can't speak for him, and I don't know exactly why he left, but I think he eventually chose himself over us. I think he'd been wrestling with the choice for years."

It took everything in Zoey to stay quiet and let her mom continue. She wanted to interject about how awful it was for her dad to abandon them. To choose himself. How angry she was that he'd left. That he hadn't contacted them since. How what he'd done had influenced her own view of love and had been interfering with her feelings about Mina. But she wanted to hear Mom's side of the story. The two of them had never outright talked about him leaving like this.

Her mother's words wobbled as she continued. "I fell apart, when he left. I knew it was happening, but I couldn't seem to stop it. You were so strong for us both, sweetie. I don't think I've ever thanked you." She laced her fingers through Zoey's, and Zoey held hers tight. "You shouldn't have needed to be that strong. You were a kid. I'm still trying to forgive myself for that." She inhaled deeply through her nose, and her words steadied again. "I don't want the same thing to happen to you. I never want you to feel the despair and helplessness that I felt. I thought that if you could find someone who would support you and make you happy, then you could avoid it."

"But . . . being with Dad in the first place is what did this to us," Zoey said.

Her mom stopped walking and grabbed both of Zoey's hands, pulling her to the side of the pathway to make room for other pedestrians. "No, honey. Your father *leaving* is what did this to us. And that was his choice. I spent some of the happiest years of my life with him, and I don't regret that even with the way he left. Loving him brought me you."

Tears welled in Zoey's eyes, her mother's face blurring before her.

"Loving another person is the best feeling in the world.

Knowing them on the deepest level, and giving them the privilege of knowing you. We need people in our lives to lean on. And it doesn't have to be romantic love. You already have that with Wren. I just want you to have as much love and support as you can."

Zoey sniffed, thinking about Wren now. She'd never been afraid that Wren would leave her. Wren had been there for her in the toughest years of her life, and Zoey didn't even think before asking for help when she needed it, knowing Wren would do her damnedest to be there. They loved each other unconditionally. They'd been best friends for over two decades, and the love they shared was easily one of the best parts of Zoey's life.

Best friends.

Without even realizing it, Zoey had committed to that. She and Wren both had, and she trusted Wren wholeheartedly to not hurt her.

Maybe the label wasn't the sticking point in her relationship with Mina. Maybe it was her own willingness to give a piece of herself to someone else. To commit to something that put her heart at stake. But Mina had expressed that she had already passed that point, and Zoey realized with sudden clarity that she had too. The whole label thing was an excuse, and a flimsy one at that.

She loved Mina.

Mina had been a bright spot in her life since she'd moved to Juniper Creek, and she'd only grown brighter with the passing months. As independent as Zoey viewed herself, she wouldn't have completed her business proposal or have new opportunities on the horizon without Mina. She wouldn't have found *Schitt's Creek* or discovered how fun it was to make scrapbooks.

Her life was leaps and bounds better with Mina in it.

Whether they were girlfriends or partners or whatever didn't really matter to her, but she wanted Mina to know how much she cared about her. How much she loved her.

And she needed Mina to know that before she made a decision about the job in Toronto.

"I need to talk to Mina. Do you mind if we start walking back?"

This was not a phone conversation. She wanted to tell Mina in person, and her pulse raced in anticipation.

She couldn't wait to get back to Juniper Creek.

THIRTY-NINE

ZOEY

Energy thrummed through Zoey's veins as she drove home that evening. She didn't even bother going to her house when she arrived, instead heading straight for Mina's front door.

She knocked, and Mina opened it a few seconds later, her familiar sweatpants-and-T-shirt outfit filling Zoey with warmth. Before even taking off her shoes, she gently grabbed the back of Mina's neck and kissed her.

Mina laughed against her mouth. "Hey."

"Hey," Zoey responded, smiling.

"I take it you had a good time with your mom?"

Zoey slipped off her shoes and hung up her jacket. "I did. We went for a walk today and talked about what happened with my dad. I mean, we'd talked about it before, but we really dug into it this time. It was a bit painful, but I'm glad we had the conversation."

Her mom's words had sunk in on the drive home. *Loving another person is the best feeling in the world. Knowing them on the deepest level, and giving them the privilege of knowing you.*

That's what Zoey wanted with Mina. She wanted to be all in, holding nothing back. She was mad at herself for taking so long to realize it. For guarding her heart so closely that she'd kept Mina at a distance.

"That's good." Mina sat on the couch, a mug of tea on the table beside her. Steam swirled from the surface in soothing curls. "Do you want tea? I just made mine, and the samovar is still plugged in."

"No, it's okay." Zoey sat beside Mina, crossing her legs and facing her. "I have something I want to tell you."

Mina nodded, but she didn't meet Zoey's eyes. Her movements weren't relaxed, putting Zoey on edge. "I have something I want to tell you too."

The layer of tension in Mina's tone piqued Zoey's interest. She wondered what could have happened this weekend that was news-worthy on Mina's end.

"Do you want to go first?"

Zoey's news could wait, especially since she anticipated it leading to a gloriously long night of the two of them tangled with each other in bed, together in a more intimate way as official girlfriends.

Mina shrugged. "If you want."

Zoey linked her fingers with Mina's, loving how they fit together. "I do want. What's up?"

Mina took a deep breath. "So, you know the Sawed-Off offer?"

There was no way Zoey could forget. The idea of Mina moving across the country had chased Zoey all the way home from Vancouver. "Yeah. What about it?"

A beat passed. "I accepted the job."

"You . . . what?" Zoey was sure she'd heard wrong.

"I said yes. I'm taking the job."

For a second, neither of them moved or said anything. Then Zoey pulled her hands out of Mina's. Her feet hit the floor with a *thunk*. She put her hands on her knees, staring at her burnt-orange nail polish.

"You accepted the job," Zoey repeated.

"Yes." Mina scooched closer to her, her leg brushing Zoey's. Zoey didn't react. "Can you say something? Please?"

Zoey rubbed her hands on her thighs, but she barely felt it. She didn't know what she was supposed to say. "So . . . you're moving to Toronto?"

"We haven't worked out the details yet. I need to fill out paperwork, look at the details of my lease, stuff like that. But yeah. I'll be moving to Toronto, probably within the month."

A laugh escaped Zoey's lips, but there was no humor in it. Suddenly, she couldn't sit still anymore. She sprang to her feet and paced to the TV.

"Are you sure this is what you want?" she asked. Mina looked bewildered, as if Zoey was the one who had just sprung unexpected news on her.

"Yeah. I've been waiting for a job like this, and Sawed-Off are the only ones who have gotten back to me. If I don't take the job, I might not get another chance to get into the industry."

"You don't want to wait a bit longer and see if someone else gets back to you? What about Declan's friend who said the CEO was an asshole?" Zoey put her hands on her hips.

"I've been waiting for so long already. And he might be annoying to work for, but this is my chance. This is what I've been working toward for years."

"What about the review from the previous employee who said the job sucked?" Zoey couldn't tell if she was poking holes in this because she didn't like it or because she was genuinely concerned. Probably both.

"We don't even know if that review was real. Like I said, it could have been one person who had a bad experience."

"Don't you think you should find out for sure before you agree to move all the way across the country?"

Mina stood now too, facing Zoey with her arms crossed. "Does it really matter? Lots of people have to take crappy jobs for a couple years before they work their way up. I have to get started somehow, and Seth needed a reply. I wasn't about to let this position go to someone else."

"Mina . . ." Zoey clenched her hands into fists, her nails digging into her palms. "I know working in this industry matters to you, but this doesn't seem like a job you should throw everything at. You even said the art style wasn't your favorite, right? What if you can find something that fits better? I don't think you should commit to this yet."

Mina rolled her eyes. "You're one to talk about commitment."

"What's that supposed to mean?"

Shaking her head, Mina said, "It doesn't matter. I already accepted the job. This isn't up for debate."

Zoey resisted the urge to tug on her hair. "Well, it should be! I think you're making a mistake, Mina. You're jumping into this too quickly."

Mina's eyes flashed. "I am not! I'm finally prioritizing myself and going for what I want. It's not like I said yes without thinking first. I'm not stupid."

"I know you're not stupid." Zoey sliced her hand through the air as tears welled in her eyes. "But I truly don't think you're prioritizing yourself, Mina. You're trying to prove something to yourself and your parents. This isn't the way to do it."

"How the hell do you know what I'm trying to do? You're not in my head, Zoey. You don't know what I'm thinking or what I truly want."

Zoey's lower lip trembled. Her gut told her Mina was making the wrong choice, but Mina was right. Zoey wasn't in her head, and she didn't know what Mina truly wanted. She'd thought she'd had an idea, but maybe she'd been wrong.

"Fine. If this is what you want . . . Go for it. Go back to Toronto to the parents who barely care about you, who don't celebrate your accomplishments, who don't see you for who you are. Go back to the place you left because you felt stifled there. Forget about the options you could have here and the people who care about you. If that's what you want."

Mina glared at her, and Zoey felt the sting of it. "You know that isn't what I'm doing."

"Isn't it, though?" Zoey crossed her arms in a mirror of Mina, anger simmering in her chest.

"No, it's fucking not!" Mina's jaw clenched. "I can't believe you right now."

Zoey couldn't be in this room anymore. She couldn't keep arguing about this with Mina, not when she felt like she was going to explode. She went to the door.

"What are you doing?" Mina asked.

"Leaving." Zoey slipped one shoe on then straightened. "You know, I was going to ask you to be my girlfriend tonight. I realized that I was holding back because I was scared, and I don't want to be scared of loving you. But now I'm glad we didn't become more than *this*"—she gestured between them—"since you're leaving anyway. I want you to be happy, but I think you're making the wrong decision, and I can't support you in that."

Mina said nothing as Zoey put on her other shoe and grabbed her coat.

"I hope the job is everything you want it to be."

She looked at Mina one more time, tears streaming down her face, then she left, closing the door softly behind her.

FORTY

MINA

Mina stared at the door, imagining Zoey walking away from her house and up her own pathway. The past ten minutes had been a whirlwind of emotion, and Mina was furious.

Furious and brokenhearted.

When she'd run through the possibilities of what would happen when she told Zoey about her decision, Zoey saying she couldn't support Mina hadn't been an option. A fight hadn't been on her radar at all.

And Zoey had said she was going to ask Mina to be her girl-friend. The phrase *loving you* echoed in Mina's mind.

She shook her head and threw herself on the couch, staring at her cooling mug of tea.

These past few months, Mina had thought she'd found someone who cared for her for who she was. She didn't feel the need to impress Zoey liked she'd had to with Christian, or like she did with her parents. Zoey saw her and accepted her. Maybe even loved her. All of her.

Except she didn't really, did she? Otherwise she would have supported Mina and her decision to move to Toronto, no matter how painful it would be for the two of them. Even if Zoey didn't want a long-distance relationship, she should have been happy for Mina. Mina could have lived with that.

Instead, Zoey had acted like she knew what was best for Mina. She was no different than Christian or Mina's parents. If Mina didn't follow the path Zoey wanted her on, Zoey left. Her love was as conditional as anyone else's, and Mina felt stupid for thinking otherwise.

For the rest of the evening, she kept herself busy by organizing her house for the move. She ordered a few boxes online so she could start packing, and she googled the rules about taking a cat on a plane.

She tried her best not to think about Zoey. She tried not to wonder what things would have been like if she hadn't accepted the job and had stayed in Juniper Creek with Zoey as her girlfriend. It was too painful to picture how happy the two of them could have been.

But Mina had made her choice, and she wasn't going back. Zoey had revealed the extent of her love, and Mina wasn't about to put herself in another relationship where she wasn't valued.

"We'll be fine," she told Zelda as she wrapped her figurines in tissue paper. She had way more to pack now than she had when she'd moved to Vancouver. She made a mental note to ask Seth if the company would pay to ship her belongings as well. "I'll have a new job, I'll see Declan more often, I'll go to all my favorite restaurants again."

But she'd be leaving her current jobs, she'd be far away from Vera and Eleanor, and she'd miss all of Juniper Creek's festivals. She pushed all of that to the back of her mind, focusing instead on the job itself.

She'd get to make character art that would be in an actual, playable, sellable video game. People would see her work and make fan art of it. She'd get to go to game premieres and network with other artists, designers, and voice actors.

And yet the feeling in her chest wasn't excitement. There were no happy shivers. No joy.

The framed art she was wrapping slipped from her fingers and crashed to the floor, the glass cracking. Mina collapsed to her knees, pressing a fist to her sternum. The panic attack had snuck up on her. She pushed her fist against her chest as hard as she could while she focused on her breathing and counted, trying to re-engage her sympathetic nervous system. Tears blurred her vision. With shaking hands, she pulled out her phone and texted "SOS" to Vera. She'd never used the code before, mostly because she hadn't wanted to bother Vera when she could usually get herself through her panic attacks.

But she didn't think she could get through this one alone.

She had no idea how long she stayed shaking on the floor, trying to breathe but gasping so hard her ribs hurt. She didn't even hear her front door open, but then Vera was there, gathering Mina into her arms.

"It's okay, I've got you," she said, her voice soothing. "I want you to breathe with me, okay?" She shifted so Mina could see her face. "Look at me, Mina. Ready? Let's breathe."

The room slowly came back into focus, and Mina latched on to details to ground herself. Vera's starched white shirt. Her navy-blue Juniper Foods vest. The yellow gold claddagh ring on her middle finger.

Mina sagged sideways with Vera's arm around her. "Thank you," she whispered, wiping tears from her cheeks with the back of her hand.

"There we go. You're okay." Vera rubbed Mina's arm, the friction helping Mina's focus stay in her body. "Do you think you can move to the couch? I can get you a glass of water."

Mina nodded and let Vera help her to her feet.

A glass of water and a banana later, Mina felt much better. Vera offered to return after work with pizza, but Mina told her she was fine now. As soon as Vera left, Mina called Declan. He already knew about the interview, of course, but she hadn't told him about accepting the job yet.

"Congrats!" Declan said, his tone chipper. "Look at you,

becoming a big shot video game artist. We'll have to celebrate when you get here."

Mina laughed softly. "Thank you. You don't think I made the wrong choice?"

Declan hummed thoughtfully. "I think you made the choice you needed to make. I can't tell you if it's the right one because I don't know how it's going to turn out. Even if Seth is an ass, you might love the job. You won't know until you try, right?"

"Right, yeah. Exactly."

"How did Zoey take it?"

Mina took a deep breath and recounted their fight. "Not well. I guess we're broken up. Not that we were ever officially together." Bitterness infused her words.

"Shit. I'm so sorry, Mina. Are you okay?"

A sharp pang in her chest answered for her. "I don't really want to talk about it. Can we play something?"

"Yeah, of course."

Playing video games with Declan took her mind off her breakup that wasn't even really a breakup. Declan knew Mina better than Zoey did, Mina was sure of it. And yet he didn't think Mina was making a mistake.

His encouragement made Mina feel like she was doing the right thing. This was what she needed. What she *wanted*.

She was going to live her dream.

FORTY-ONE

ZOEY

The next day, Zoey called Eleanor and told her she wasn't feeling well, which wasn't a lie. She knew Mina would work her next few shifts before leaving, and Zoey didn't want to see her. For the first time since she'd moved to Juniper Creek, Zoey closed the blinds in her kitchen so she wouldn't catch a glimpse of Mina moving about next door. And when she ran out of groceries, she started ordering in food even though she could barely afford it.

She knew she was being ridiculous. If she truly had her shit together, she would be civil with Mina at work and wouldn't avoid her like this.

But she didn't have her shit together. She was a mess.

Time and time again, she had the urge to go next door to convince Mina she was making a mistake. But that was selfish, and Zoey regretted what she'd said to Mina. She should have been supportive. Instead, she'd put her own feelings first and tore down what they'd had.

Zoey didn't want to hold Mina back. She just didn't want her to get hurt. And she didn't want her to leave.

So she became a recluse, selfishly hoping Mina would change her mind.

As Zoey lay in bed several evenings later, trying to convince herself to at least take out the garbage for the next morning, someone knocked at her front door. She tensed, and the thought flitted through her mind that she had manifested a visit from Mina.

It wasn't Mina, though.

Wren stood on her step with her arms full of groceries, and she breezed past Zoey and into the kitchen.

"How are you holding up?" Wren asked. "Have you eaten any vegetables today? Have you been drinking water?"

Zoey rolled her eyes and helped put away the groceries. Wren had brought all kinds of foods Zoey usually didn't buy, many of them gluten-free.

"You know I'm not actually sick, right?"

Wren shot her a look. "You might as well be. You looked like a ghost on our call yesterday, and you sounded dead inside. When was the last time you left the house?"

"When I visited my mom last weekend," Zoey muttered.

"Exactly. I'm making dinner."

Zoey groaned but let her take over the kitchen. She had to admit she was glad Wren had come to take care of her. Now more than ever, she understood how her mother struggled to take care of herself when she was depressed. It was hard to muster the energy to do anything, including feeding or cleaning yourself, when you didn't feel like you'd ever be happy again.

Wren made stir fry for dinner, and though Zoey found it unappetizing, it did wonders for her mood. She felt more awake after she ate, the world around her clearer and slightly brighter.

She and Wren sat on the couch with a bag of gluten-free cheddar popcorn, *Survivor* playing on the TV.

"How much longer are you going to do this?" Wren asked.

"Hmm?"

"How much longer are you going to play at being a hermit? You can't hide in your house forever. Eleanor is going to want you back at work, and your skin will need to feel the sun again."

"I don't know. Until she leaves, I guess." The fact that she didn't even want to say Mina's name made her feel immensely pathetic.

"And when is she leaving?"

Zoey shrugged.

Wren sighed. "Hon, come on. You can't do this to yourself. I know you love her, but you have to let her go. You can't live her life for her, and I don't think you want to."

"I don't," Zoey said, pretending to be invested in the reward challenge on *Survivor*.

"I'm not saying you need to make up with her, or even talk to her if you don't want to. But you can't put your life on hold until she's gone." When Zoey didn't reply, Wren continued, "Don't make me drive here every night to feed you."

Zoey scoffed. "I won't. Eleanor gave me the rest of this week off, but I have a shift on Monday. I'll go to it." There was a good chance she wouldn't see Mina since Zoey's shift was an evening one. It only took one employee to close the shop.

"Okay, good." Wren squeezed her knee. "Proud of you."

"Thanks for the food."

"Best friends don't let best friends starve."

Zoey didn't see Mina at work on Monday. She wasn't on the schedule anymore, so Zoey assumed she'd resigned. Thistles and Stems wasn't exactly busy right now, so Eleanor had probably told Mina she didn't need to come in anymore.

It was a blessing, but also a curse.

Part of Zoey had hoped the two of them would be forced together so they could talk. Their last conversation hadn't been great, and it felt like they both needed closure before Mina left.

But Zoey still avoided Mina because she'd said some awful things, and she didn't think she could see Mina again without breaking down. She didn't go to Juniper Foods, and she kept her eyes glued to her own front door whenever she came home from work.

One evening, she heard what sounded like a big vehicle out front. She looked out her window to see a truck dropping off boxes at Mina's house. Her heart caught in her throat, and she fled up the stairs to her room. She stuffed her earphones in and turned on a true crime podcast, scrunching her eyes closed.

She'd known Mina was moving, but it hadn't felt real until that moment. The next time Zoey opened her kitchen blinds, Mina might not be on the other side. She might not see Mina ever again.

Tears streamed down her face as she listened to the podcast host tell her how to break out of zip tie handcuffs. She buried her face in her pillow and sobbed until she fell asleep.

FORTY-TWO

MINA

June in Toronto was muggier than Mina had remembered. Her hair stuck to her skin in the heat, and she kept lifting the back of it to fan her neck. It didn't help that the office she worked in had crappy window air conditioning units that only cooled off a three-foot radius. They really needed more than that for how many computers were running in the place. Any day now Mina was sure they would overheat, and Seth would lose his mind.

Mina had learned quickly that it didn't take much for Seth to lose his mind. He'd been nice enough in her orientation week, showing her around the office and outlining her tasks and responsibilities. He'd assigned her a mentor artist, a bald guy named Joel who wore massive glasses, and showed her her very own cubicle. She was free to decorate it as she wanted, so she'd tacked up a photo of herself and Vera, plus one of Zelda stretched out in the sun at her old house in Juniper Creek.

Her heart squeezed whenever she looked at those photos, but it wasn't totally unpleasant.

Seth's true nature had become apparent almost as soon as her orientation was complete. She'd come into work one morning to hear him screaming in his office about something not being up to par.

"What's going on?" she'd asked Joel quietly.

Joel had rolled his eyes. "He does this every few days or so. He finds something he doesn't like, and instead of providing constructive criticism like a normal boss, he does . . . this."

They both stared at Seth's open office door with wide eyes.

"Has he yelled at you like that?" Mina asked, wincing when a *bang* rung out. It sounded like Seth had hit his desk, or maybe thrown something.

"Yeah, a few times. He cools off pretty quick. You just have to let him get it out, and then he'll be fine."

That review Mina had read about working at Sawed-Off rose in her mind. Maybe it hadn't been one upset employee exaggerating things.

"Is there any way I can avoid it?" she asked.

Joel's brow furrowed. "You can try, but unless you get everything perfect on the first go . . . you're SOL."

"Great."

Every day since then, Mina had been terrified of doing something wrong. She did not want to be on the receiving end of one of Seth's tirades, so she stayed overtime and worked her ass off to meet his requests to a T. He hadn't gotten upset at her yet, and she wondered if it was because she was the only woman in the office. Maybe that gave her a strange immunity, at least for the time being. Or maybe he hadn't snapped at her yet because she was new.

But she didn't think that would last.

Combined with how careful she was at home, Mina felt like she was living in a pressure cooker.

She'd intended to find her own apartment when she'd moved, but she didn't want to settle for something she saw online without scouting it out first. Declan had offered his couch to her, but she couldn't bring herself to intrude on his and Lila's privacy, not when they only had one bedroom in their apartment. And she didn't think she could bear living with either of her sisters, seeing their successes up close and personal. So she'd asked her parents if she could live with them until she found her own place, and they'd graciously said yes.

Almost too graciously.

"We'd love to have you home again, joon," her father had said.

"It will be nice to have you under our roof once more. I'm glad we can give you the support you need, Mina," her mom had added. Although the words sounded nice, the tone that accompanied them made it seem as if Ava Hasanza had expected this. As if she'd been waiting for Mina to fail and come begging for shelter with her tail between her legs.

That's not what I'm doing. I'm supporting myself.

Mina had to give herself a pep talk every morning so when she saw her mother before heading out to work, she wouldn't shrink into herself. She often repeated the pep talk after dinner too.

But at least she got to cook with her father again, and Farrah and Yasmin came over once a week for family dinner.

She was also immensely grateful to Declan for keeping her sane. He worked close enough to her office that they often went for lunch together.

Today they were meeting at one of his favorite sandwich shops on the corner.

"Still in one piece?" he greeted her when she walked through the door, a bell tinkling overhead. He looked like a lumberjack with his red-and-black plaid T-shirt, his thick beard, and his blond hair in a bun.

"So far," Mina said, collapsing at the two-person table where he sat. This half-hour lunch each workday allowed her to decompress just enough to get through the afternoon.

"I ordered for you so you can get back with time to spare. Can't upset Boss Man." He slid a sandwich wrapped in checkered deli paper over to her.

"Thank you." She unwrapped it and took a huge bite, the chipotle sauce tangy on her tongue.

Declan dug into his sandwich as well, a piece of shredded lettuce catching in his beard. He narrowed his eyes at her as he chewed.

"What?" Mina asked, subconsciously wiping her chin. Had she spilled sauce somewhere?

Declan finished chewing then set down his sandwich. "Do you like your job?"

Mina took a sip of water to clear her mouth. "Yeah. I mean, I like the art part of it."

"But what about the rest of it? You've been here for two months now, and you seem to be getting increasingly stressed."

"I mean . . . it is a high-stress job. We've got a tight schedule, and we have to get a lot of assets done for this game. Seth has this big launch planned, and he keeps adding stuff with the marketing team. I'm sure it'll calm down after the game is out."

Declan nodded, but he didn't look convinced. "And when is the game coming out?"

"Next summer, hopefully."

He snorted. "You're going to work at this pace for a year?"

Mina crossed her arms. "What else am I going to do? I just started there. I don't really have a choice."

"Right." Without looking at her, Declan picked up his sandwich again.

They ate in silence for a couple minutes, but Mina couldn't ignore what he'd implied.

She popped a pickle into her mouth and chewed. "Okay, fine. Yes, this job is extremely stressful. And it's not quite what I'd expected. But I'm finally making art professionally, and I can't give that up."

"No one said you had to give it up. I'm just wondering if this job is going to burn you out. Maybe you should look for a different one."

He said that last sentence gently, but it was a knife in Mina's chest. She'd only been at this for two months. If she gave up now, her parents would think they were right—that working for a video game developer wasn't a viable career. She hadn't even found a place she could afford yet, and she felt like a failure living in her parents' house after living independently for years. There was no way she could give up this job.

You're trying to prove something to yourself and to your parents, and this isn't the way to do it. Zoey's words ran through her head, and not for the first time. Mina hated how often she thought of them. How often she wondered if Zoey had been right.

The two of them hadn't spoken since that night. Mina had almost gone over to Zoey's plenty of times before she moved, but she hadn't wanted Zoey to influence her decision. To make her change her mind.

And now Declan was also wondering if this job wasn't right for her.

Mina groaned. "Did I make a mistake, moving here?"

"I already told you, I can't answer that," Declan said, balling his empty sandwich paper. "Only you can. I'm just concerned, you know? You worked so hard all through high school to impress your parents, and even then, you didn't seem this stressed."

Mina let her head fall forward in defeat, and the sore muscles all along the back of her neck and shoulders screamed at her. She'd been hunched over at a computer for so long recently that her arms had started seizing. She needed to stretch and go for a nice long massage.

"What do I do?" she asked quietly. Declan leaned forward to hear her better. "I can't quit two months in. How would that look?"

"It might look bad to some people, but to others it would look like you know what you want. And this isn't it. Quitting now wouldn't make you a failure, Mina. There are other video game developers out there. Ones with bosses who don't have anger issues."

"Yeah. Well, we all have issues, don't we?"
And these days, Mina's were threatening to drown her.

255

FORTY-THREE

ZOEY

Zoey didn't want to make a huge deal out of her new candle collection launching at Thistles and Stems, but Eleanor insisted on it. "You've been working on this for months!" she'd said. "And you know there's no better way to get word out in this town than to hold an event. As soon as Elouise Mitchell gets a sniff of the new candles, we'll have people swarming in to buy them." Her eyes sparkled, and Zoey relented.

Which is how she found herself standing at the front counter of Thistles and Stems on a Saturday afternoon with her mom, her aunt, and Wren, each of them with a glass of lemonade in hand. Eleanor had set a rustic drink stand full of freshly squeezed lemonade out front to bring people in, along with a gorgeously drawn graphic on their sandwich board announcing the new Bell Lights candle collection: Botanical Tales.

Zoey was happy she'd managed to put together five new candles for the collection in such a short time. She'd hired a graphic designer to perfect the labels, and she'd even upgraded to wooden wicks because those fit the botanical theme better. She could afford to sell the candles at a higher price too, now that they were in a brick-and-mortar storefront.

And yet she found herself looking around constantly, as if something—or someone—was missing.

"I'm so proud of you, sweetie," Mom said, giving her a side-hug. Her hair was pulled back in a low ponytail today, and she'd donned a floral dress for the occasion.

Aunt Shannon had gone more business-y with navy slacks and a pink blouse. "Me too," she said.

"Me three," Wren added, raising her glass for a toast. Zoey, her mom, and her aunt all clinked their glasses to Wren's.

"Oh, I haven't caught up with Minnie in a while," Zoey's aunt said, gesturing to Eleanor's wife who stood outside chatting with Eleanor. "Mandy, come with me. I'll introduce you."

The two of them headed for the door, and Wren stepped closer to Zoey until their arms touched. In a quieter voice than she'd used before, Wren asked, "How's it going?"

Zoey shrugged. She looked around at the shop, at the new wooden shelf displaying her candles front and center. This was what she'd wanted for years now—to have an expanded audience for her candles. But the joy she thought she'd feel today was achingly absent. "It's going. I hope we sell at least a few today."

"You will. But you keep frowning every time someone isn't looking directly at you. What's up?"

Trust her best friend to see straight through her. She threw the rest of her lemonade back as if it were a shot, placing the empty glass on the counter.

"Mina should be here," she said. It was the first time she'd said Mina's name in ages, and a flood of memories hit her. Mina smiling at her with those cherry-red lips. The two of them curled up with Zelda on Mina's couch, watching *Schitt's Creek* and drinking tea. Mina showing her how to make zoolbia, laughing and saying that her father made them better than she ever could.

"I'm sorry," Wren said, her voice pulling Zoey back to the present. "I know you miss her."

Zoey stared at her feet, wishing she felt as put-together as her brown Oxfords made her look. "This whole collection wouldn't exist without her. She helped me finish the business plan and taught me how to scale up without exhausting myself. She deserves the credit as much as I do."

Wren rubbed her back. "Have you heard from her since she left?"

Zoey shook her head. She'd checked her phone obsessively the first couple of days after Mina had moved, but eventually she'd accepted that Mina wouldn't be messaging her. She had no reason to, after all. Zoey had essentially broken up with her by saying she couldn't support Mina's decision.

Even that morning, she'd checked Mina's Instagram. But there was nothing since that selfie Mina had posted of her and Declan when he'd picked her up from the airport. No sign of how she was doing at all.

Zoey had almost asked Vera for news, but she told herself that if something bad happened, Vera would tell her. Zoey didn't want to look desperate. She wasn't that kind of person.

Or maybe she was, but she didn't want others to know.

She wouldn't let her broken heart take her down. It had already happened once when her father left, and she wouldn't go through that again. Those few days of self-imposed hermithood had been bad enough.

"Do you want to reach out to her?" Wren asked. "It's been a couple of months now. She might be okay with you saying something, even if it's just to thank her for her help."

"I don't know." She would love to talk to Mina again, to apologize and ask how she was doing, but their separation still felt so raw. They hadn't gotten closure. And she didn't think Mina wanted to talk to her since she hadn't reached out. "I'll think about it."

"Okay." Wren grabbed Zoey's empty glass. "Let's get you a refill, and then you can talk to your adoring fans."

Zoey scoffed. "They're customers, not fans. They only know who I am because this is a small town."

"That might be true right now. But you'll be getting fan mail before you know it. People will want you to design custom candle collections for their stores, and Bell Lights will be everywhere." She waved a hand through the air as if picturing Zoey's name on a marquee. "You'll have a commercial on TV, and you'll have to expand into a full corporation to handle all your sales."

"Okay, rein it in," Zoey said, linking arms with her friend as they headed outside. "Let's not get ahead of ourselves."

But Wren's words made her feel better. She was on her way to sustaining herself with her own business, which is what she'd wanted for years. Eleanor had believed in her enough to launch this new candle collection, and there was a sizable crowd outside —larger than their usual Saturday clientele.

Zoey smiled.

She was following the path to achieving her dream, and maybe Mina was too. Zoey hoped she was. She'd never know if she didn't ask, and she didn't want to lose contact with Mina forever. They'd been friends—neighbors—to start with, after all. Maybe they could go back to something like that.

Maybe reaching out to Mina wouldn't be the worst thing.

FORTY-FOUR

MINA

Finally Mina could relax. It was her day off, and she needed it. Seth had lost his temper with her the day before when he came to check on her progress with her current model. Apparently she was a step behind where he thought she should be. "I flew you across the goddamn country with my own money!" he'd yelled, spit flying from his mouth. Mina had flinched. "But I won't blink an eye at firing you if you can't keep up. Don't disappoint me, Mina."

It hadn't been a tirade in his office like the ones she'd witnessed earlier, but it hadn't felt good. And it had happened out on the floor, in front of her three coworkers. Her ears had burned and she'd run to the washroom, splashing her face and tracing the patterns in the washroom tiles to calm herself.

Joel had been waiting for her when she returned to her desk. "You're on track," he said. "Just ignore Seth. He fought with his wife last night, and everyone is suffering because of it. He's all bluster."

It was one thing to know that, and another to have Seth's words ringing in her ears for the rest of the day. *Don't disappoint me, Mina.*

That had hit her hard. The last thing she wanted to do at this job was disappoint her new boss. She'd spent her entire life trying not to disappoint people, wrestling with how to be herself while still making people happy. Somehow, she'd gotten herself a job where she was destined to be unfairly criticized whenever the boss had a bad day. She was starting to think someone had cursed her. Maybe that kid she'd accidentally tripped at Farrah's swimming lesson when she was eleven. She'd apologized profusely, but he'd glared daggers at her.

Now, she lay on the couch in her sweats and a T-shirt, content to do nothing but watch TV and eat her way through a package of Oreos. She hadn't even bothered to shower that morning, sleeping until ten-thirty instead. Her parents were both at work, so she had the house to herself. No one to hover over her or criticize her.

She'd considered playing video games since she hadn't done that in a while, but her laser focus at work had sapped the enjoyment of games from her. Every time she tried to play anything these days, she zoned in on the quality of the models rather than truly playing.

So she went to her other tried-and-true comfort activity: watching *Schitt's Creek*.

The only thing missing from her *Schitt's Creek* marathon day was Zelda and her soothing purrs, but Mina's mother had requested that she keep Zelda in her room because of her black fur. "Everything is white, Mina," her mother had said. "We don't need black cat hair floating around the place."

While Mina didn't love keeping Zelda in her room all the time, she kept telling herself it was only until she found her own place. Her room was large, too, all things considered. Zelda wasn't suffering in there.

Mina had just returned to the couch after adding a bowl of pretzels to her snack pile when the front door opened. She froze, listening for footsteps, trying to figure out who had come home.

The click of heels echoed on the marble tiles. Her mom.

Mina closed her eyes and stifled a groan. So much for relaxing.

She looked at her lounge clothes then to the open pack of Oreos and the full bowl of pretzels on the living room table. There was no time to clean or make herself more presentable before her mother walked in.

Sure enough, her mother rounded the corner a moment later, a stack of folders in her arms. Her hair was pulled into a tight bun at the base of her neck, and her gray skirt suit looked freshly pressed even though she'd been wearing it since early that morning.

"Mina," she said, surprised. "What are you doing home?"

Mina ran a hand through her hair, trying not to cringe at how greasy it was. She hadn't washed it in a few days, too rushed in the mornings and too tired at night to bother.

"It's my day off," she said.

"Oh. I see." She eyed Mina's outfit and the snacks like Mina knew she would. "I'm glad you're enjoying yourself during your time off." She didn't sound glad. "I'll be in my office if you need me."

Her gaze raked over Mina's unkempt appearance once more before she left the room, and Mina didn't relax into the couch cushions again until she heard the office door shut.

She blew out a breath and considered moving to her room. It wasn't as comfortable in there, but at least she'd have less chance of running into her mother again. But no, Mina had nothing to be ashamed of. She'd worked her ass off these past two months, and she was tired. This was her break, and she was going to enjoy it.

Although her mom being home put her on edge, she managed to get back into the show. Her mom stayed in her office for the next few hours, and Mina almost forgot she was there.

At four o'clock, though, the click of heels came again. The fact that her mother hadn't taken her shoes off even to work at home said everything anyone needed to know about Ava Hasanza's work ethic.

Mina heard her mom getting a glass of water in the kitchen.

Then the footsteps approached the living room again, and Mina rushed to grab the cushions she'd kicked to the floor to get comfortable.

"Why don't you get dressed before dinner?" her mother said, more of a demand than a question. Then she turned and walked toward her office.

Mina rolled her eyes and reached for her phone. She needed to vent to someone about how ridiculous her mother could be. She'd already started typing out a message when she realized who it was to.

Zoey.

She'd automatically opened her message thread with Zoey to complain about her mom. It didn't make much sense since the last two people she'd texted were Joel and Declan, and even Vera's text thread had been above Zoey's, yet here she was.

Swallowing hard, Mina closed her phone. She hadn't heard from Zoey since she'd left Juniper Creek, and she hadn't wanted to message her. Until now.

With a sigh, she carried her dirty dishes to the kitchen then headed upstairs to shower and change into something more acceptable for dinner.

DINNER THAT NIGHT WAS QUIET, AS USUAL. HER father had cooked for the three of them, and the food was delicious. But well-spiced lamb couldn't fill the awkward silence.

"So, how was everyone's day?" Mina asked. Almost every night, she felt like she was trying to repair a rift between herself and her parents, but she couldn't see the edges well enough to stitch them together. She much preferred when her sisters were there and could act as a buffer.

"Good," Baba said, smiling. "I'm working with one of my favorite clients. He has the best coffee shop recommendations." At least her dad put in some effort.

"Cool. You'll have to give me a list so I can try them too. What about you, Maman?"

"You know how my day was, Mina. I was in my office all day, going through paperwork." She rubbed her temples, clearly tired. Mina sympathized.

"And you, Mina joon? How was your day?" Baba asked.

Mina opened her mouth to answer, but her mother butted in. "She spent the day lazing on the couch and eating all the junk food in this house. A productive way to spend her time."

Mina's eyes widened. "It's my day off."

"That doesn't mean you have nothing to do," her mother said.

For a second, Mina almost acquiesced and ignored that statement. But something in her had snapped, maybe yesterday when Seth had yelled at her. She was done letting people walk all over her.

"You know what?" she started. "I've been working my ass off at this job. I moved back here and took a chance on a business I knew next to nothing about so I could get my foot in the door and get a *real* job that would make you proud. But nothing makes you proud, does it? Not unless it's saving lives and making people's smiles whiter than white. Even if I did those things, though, I don't think you'd be proud of me. I'm not your perfect angel like Yasmin, and I'm not a do-gooder like Farrah. It's not what I do that you have a problem with, is it? It's *me*."

Her father's face fell. "Mina—"

"No, Baba, let me finish." She turned to glare at her mother. "I don't know what I did to make you so disappointed in me. Maybe I've never worked hard enough or something, I don't know. But I also don't fucking care."

Her mother flinched when she swore, her jaw hanging open.

"I've never been able to be fully myself in this house." Mina turned to her father. "And you never stand up for me, Baba. You take Maman's side every single time. That's not what love looks like."

Her chair got caught on the carpet when she scooched back, and she kicked the leg in frustration. "I want to feel like part of this family, and I can't do that if neither of you support me. I'm going to stay at Declan's. Let me know when you're ready to respect my choices."

She stomped up the stairs and packed her clothes and the few other belongings she'd brought, including Zelda's things. She called an Uber then put Zelda in her carrier. Declan responded right away to her text, saying she could stay with them for as long as she needed.

She should have accepted his offer in the first place instead of thinking she could ever feel at home with her parents again.

Mina had wondered more than once if she should have listened to Zoey and taken more time to research Seth's company and think about the offer. She understood now why Seth's company had such a big turnover, and why their first game was good but they didn't have a huge fan following. Everything on the back end was broken, starting with Seth.

And taking the job clearly hadn't impressed Mina's parents much.

She opened her bedroom door to drag her suitcase down the stairs, and she almost ran over her father.

"Mina." Tears shone in his eyes, and at the sight, Mina just about turned around and unpacked. But she couldn't. She needed to stand up for herself. "I'm not going to stop you. I know you need to go. But I wanted to make sure you got this." He held out a small cardboard box with postage on it.

"Thanks." Mina took the box, wondering who had sent her a package, and Baba opened his arms for a hug. She embraced him, letting him squeeze her tightly.

"I'm sorry I never stood up for you," he whispered into her hair. "I'm sorry. I'll try to do better, I promise. Doostet daram."

Mina could barely get her next words out around her own tears. "I love you too, Baba."

He helped her carry her bags and Zelda down the stairs, and

he hugged her again as she waited out front for her Uber. "Your mother loves you too," he said quietly. "She has a different way of showing it, but she does."

Mina didn't know if she believed that, but she appreciated the sentiment. When her Uber arrived, she kissed her father on the cheek. He waved at her until she couldn't see him anymore, and she fought back another wave of tears.

To distract herself, she looked at the box he had given her. She hadn't examined it in detail before. Now she looked at the shipping address, and her heart skipped a beat.

Zoey had said some hurtful things when Mina had told her about the job, then neither of them had opened a dialogue to talk through everything. They'd both gone quiet, like what used to happen with Christian, and Mina hadn't had the courage to reach out.

If Zoey had meant what she said, maybe Mina was better without her. Although the longer she was away from Zoey, the more she doubted that. Now, with this package in her lap, she doubted it even more.

Using her keys, she broke the tape on the box and opened it.

A candle sat nestled in a pile of orange crinkle paper. Mina carefully pulled it out, and a smile sprang to her face when she saw the candle name: A Journey to Success. Illustrated purple orchids decorated the label. She took the lid off and inhaled deeply, and everything she loved about Zoey came rushing back to her.

Zoey had opened the dialogue.

FORTY-FIVE

MINA

The next morning, Mina woke early. Before she even rose from where she'd slept on Declan's couch, she texted Joel, giving him a heads-up that Seth would likely be in a bad mood today. Then she moved to the kitchen table, drafted a brief resignation email, and sent that to Seth with a sigh of relief. She wasn't sure yet what her next steps were, but she knew Sawed-Off was not for her.

"Tea?" Declan asked, standing at the counter behind her.

"Please." Mina stretched, a smile growing across her face.

Lila padded into the room, dressed but without socks. "Did you do it?"

"I did it." Her grin grew wider.

"You quit?" Declan asked.

"I quit. I'm free!" Lila and Declan both rushed over to her, burying her in congratulatory hugs. She laughed. "Thanks."

Declan returned to the counter and started coffee for himself and Lila. "So now what?"

"I'm not sure yet. But it feels easier to figure out now that I don't have to go into the office today." She'd asked Joel to grab the photos from her desk for her. There was no way she wanted to see Seth again if she could avoid it.

She ate breakfast with Declan and Lila then settled back on the couch in her pajamas. She had no job now. No place to call her own. A few months ago, this level of insecurity would have made her panic. But today, she felt exactly how she'd told Lila and Declan: free.

Before she'd gone to bed the night before, she'd smelled the candle Zoey had sent her and reflected on everything that had happened in the past two months. She'd lost more than she'd bargained for.

But she'd gained one thing for sure by moving across the country: clarity.

It hit her that she didn't regret moving here. Being back in Toronto made her realize that her mom might never approve of her no matter what she did, and that it royally sucked to work for someone who desperately needed therapy. So maybe she needed to learn to live without her mom's approval. And maybe she needed to hold out for a job that, at the very least, wouldn't make her feel inferior.

She missed her little townhouse. She missed her job at Juniper Foods, stocking shelves and making idle chitchat with other townsfolk. She missed the smell of soil and growing things that surrounded her in Thistles and Stems. She missed sleeping in her own bed and having furniture she'd picked out herself.

And she missed Zoey.

Zoey had never torn her down. She'd helped Mina get a new job when she needed one, and they'd celebrated together with ice cream. She'd spent Mina's birthday with her when her parents had cancelled. She'd taken Mina to the hospital when she'd sprained her ankle. She'd made Mina lunch and brought it to her at work more times than Mina could count.

They'd fought, but that didn't mean their relationship wasn't reparable. Zoey had sent that candle, which had to mean something. There was only one way to find out.

MINA

Thank you for the candle. I love it.

Mina's heart pounded, but Zoey didn't reply in the next five minutes. Puffing out her cheeks, Mina grabbed her laptop again. She had a couple more people to email before she could feel secure in the plan she was musing over.

When her phone chimed, she almost jumped right off the couch.

ZOEY

Yay! I'm glad you got it.

I sent the other four too, in a separate package

MINA

Oh! You didn't have to do that

ZOEY

I know, but I wanted to. You helped get me here, and you should at least get something out of it.

Mina smiled at her phone, unsure how to respond. It was sweet of Zoey to send her the entire new collection.

ZOEY

And it's sort of a way of saying I'm sorry.

I was an asshole when you told me about the job

I should have supported you

And I threw the whole "girlfriend" thing in your face

I was awful

Mina bit her lip, her smile growing. Her instinct about Zoey had been right.

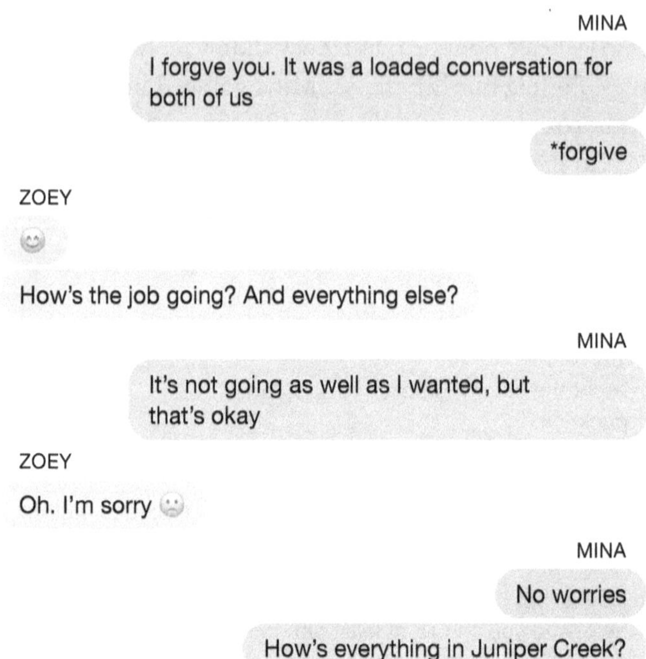

Mina could have given Zoey more information about her job —which she no longer had—but her veins thrummed with new energy and she couldn't sit still. Zoey's apology and check-in had given Mina all the confirmation she'd been looking for.

Without a doubt, Mina knew what she wanted. And it wasn't here in Toronto.

FORTY-SIX

ZOEY

It had been a couple weeks since the launch of the Botanical Tales collection, and the candles had been flying off the shelves. Zoey had also put them in her online store with a link to Thistles and Stems, and she'd sold more than she'd expected. She'd already had to order more labels, and she'd spent the last few evenings pouring candles for the most popular scents.

The success of the collection in such a short period had refilled Zoey's energy reserves. It helped that she'd sent the purple orchid candle to Mina. She hadn't been able to bring herself to send a letter with it, but Mina had reached out anyway. Her heart had ached when she'd read Mina's text, and she'd been able to apologize and express her gratitude. Their conversation hadn't gone much farther than that, but it was something. Maybe it could eventually grow into something more.

Zoey leaned on the front counter in Thistles and Stems, scrolling through the candle orders for the past week to see what she needed to restock next.

Eleanor came out of the cooler where she'd been rearranging their most recent blooms. Minnie's shop had an overflow, so they were storing her extra flowers for her. The whoosh of air from the open door blew Eleanor's salt-and-pepper hair behind her, as if she were a model standing in front of a fan. If they had another photo shoot someday, Zoey would suggest that idea.

"It's chilly in there," Eleanor said, shivering. "I always forget to grab a cardigan. These days my body doesn't hold heat like it used to."

"It's not just you," Zoey replied. "I can't stay in there for more than fifteen minutes without feeling like a popsicle."

Eleanor laughed. "Maybe we should hang a sweater outside the door for whoever needs it."

"Not a bad idea."

They puttered around the store for a while, working on various tasks. It was a quiet day without much traffic coming in or orders to fill. While Zoey enjoyed busy days, she liked these sleepier ones too. It meant she could check smaller tasks off the store's endless to-do list, and she could take her time to appreciate the little things about working at a plant shop.

"Zoey, dearie, can you do me a favor?" Eleanor asked. "This custom order came in, and I feel like it's right in your wheelhouse. It didn't print quite right, but I can pull off the address for you later. It's due this evening."

She handed Zoey a paper she must have recently printed off. The customer's name and address had been cut off, but the bouquet request was there. It was more specific than most of their requests, and more flower-centric than usual. Whoever had ordered this knew their flowers.

"White and apricot roses, marigolds, orange ranunculus, orange snapdragons, white carnations, and eucalyptus." Whoever had ordered this also loved orange. "You're right, this is in my wheelhouse."

If Zoey had to order a bouquet for herself, she'd probably order one much like this. She was more about color than meaning, unlike Eleanor, and orange had always been her favorite. The eucalyptus would complement the orange hues, and the white blooms would add texture while making the orange pop more.

"I thought you'd enjoy it." Eleanor grinned at her, something almost secretive in the smile. "Don't worry about the front. I'll stay out here while you get that done."

"Okay. Cool."

Zoey headed to the cooler to find the flowers she needed, surprised that all of them were in the overflow stock from Minnie's. A joyful trance overtook her as she worked. She always enjoyed arranging bouquets, but this one was special. The colors and textures sang to her.

An hour later, the bouquet was complete. Zoey straightened to admire her work. She was sad to have finished putting it together. Now it would go off to whoever had ordered it, brightening their living space for a week or two. A twinge of jealousy sparked in Zoey's chest. She'd have to make herself one of these soon.

"What do you think?" she asked, bringing the bouquet to the shop area to show Eleanor.

"I've always said you're an artist, and you've proven it yet again," Eleanor said. "That's lovely, Zoey."

"Thank you." She beamed. "When is it getting picked up? Should I put it in the cooler?"

"It needs to be delivered, actually. Would you be able to take it on your way home? Here, I got the printer to work properly." Eleanor handed her a sheet of paper that had been sitting beside the till.

Zoey took it, reading the address. She frowned. "I don't think this is right. The system must have glitched or something."

"No, it's correct. I double checked," Eleanor said.

"But this is *my* address." When Zoey glanced at Eleanor again, Eleanor appeared far too clueless with her wide eyes. "Okay, what's going on here?"

"I don't know what you mean." Eleanor turned and began fiddling with the row of ribbons on the back wall.

Zoey sighed. "I'm not even going to bother. I can smell a scheme from a mile away."

"I don't scheme," Eleanor said in mock offense.

Zoey waved the paper at her. "This is a scheme," she said. "I don't know what kind, but you can't convince me otherwise. I mean, if you wanted to give me a bouquet, you could have just done it."

"Mm-hmm. I suppose I could have." Eleanor looked over her shoulder and winked. "It's almost five anyway. You can take off now, if you'd like."

Zoey had no idea what was going on, but she'd roll with it. "Alright."

She grabbed her bag and the bouquet, sticking her face in it to inhale the fresh, sweet scent. It was too warm out for a jacket, the late June sun bright in the sky. "I'll see you tomorrow then?"

"Bright and early! Have a wonderful evening," Eleanor practically sang.

Rolling her eyes but laughing, Zoey headed out. She mused over the flowers as she walked, confused but in a pleasant way. Eleanor had something up her sleeve, and Zoey would figure it out soon enough.

As she turned the corner onto her street, the bigger picture resolved quickly.

Someone sat on Zoey's front doorstep. Someone with dark hair cut in a shag. Someone wearing a floral button-up shirt and black jeans with ripped knees.

Zoey stopped in her tracks, her heartbeat kicking into a frenzy. Despite the evidence right in front of her, Zoey's first thought was *But she's in Toronto.*

Clearly, she was no longer in Toronto. She was sitting on Zoey's front step, holding a book.

It was a struggle to pace herself when all Zoey wanted to do was run to Mina and hug her tight. Kiss those cherry-red lips again. But she made herself walk at a normal pace, her fingers sweaty around the glass vase of the bouquet.

As Zoey approached, Mina looked up at her. A wide smile grew across her face, and she stood. Zoey didn't want to get her hopes too high, but she had the feeling Mina was trying not to run to her too.

"Hey," Zoey said, trying to play it cool. She walked up her front pathway and stopped a few feet away from Mina, her heart pounding against her ribs. "What are you doing here?"

Mina's grin faltered but ultimately held, and she bit her lip. She took a step forward. "Do you like the bouquet?"

Zoey's gaze flicked to the orange and white flowers. Now it made sense. The bouquet was perfect for her because it was *for* her. "You made me make my own bouquet?"

"I couldn't exactly come into the shop and make it for you. It would ruin the surprise."

A laugh bubbled out of Zoey. "I love it," she said quietly.

"Good. I made this for you too." Mina stepped forward and held out the book.

As soon as she grabbed it, Zoey realized it was a scrapbook. The photo Frankie had taken of her and Mina kissing was on the cover, and it made Zoey's heart flip. She set the bouquet at her feet so she could look through the pages. Selfies of her and Mina appeared on every page beside quotations from a few of Zoey's favorite romance authors: Jacquelynn Lyon, Natalie Naudus, Ashley Herring Blake, Alice Oseman. There were a few *Schitt's Creek* quotes thrown in for good measure, and Zoey found herself laughing, happy tears welling in her eyes.

"This is beautiful," Zoey said, sniffing. "What are you doing here?"

The corners of Mina's mouth ticked up. "Ready for my speech? I practiced it on the plane."

"You have a speech?"

"A short one." Mina made a show of pushing her shoulders back and clearing her throat. "While I was in Toronto, I figured out what I want from life. You may have struggled with labelling what we had, but I was the one who couldn't commit because I didn't think I was worth it. I felt the way you cared about me, and I convinced myself you were just like everyone else who didn't see me. Because I didn't think I deserved that kind of love. But honestly . . . the job sucked. My boss was a dick, and having a steady job in my chosen field did nothing to impress my mother. The only person there who really cared was Declan. I realized that chasing my parents' approval and accepting a mediocre job wouldn't make me happy. *You* make me happy. Living in Juniper Creek with you makes me happy."

Mina stepped closer to Zoey, tentatively grasping Zoey's hands in her own.

Zoey's skin tingled, and her whole body felt like it might float off the ground. She had missed Mina's touch more than she thought possible.

"So, even if you don't want to say it back," Mina continued, "I need you to know that I love you."

The tears Zoey had been holding back overflowed, slipping down her cheeks.

"Zoey Bell, I love you. I love how much you care about other people. I love how you're always willing to help. I love your weird obsession with true crime and that your favorite color is orange. I love how you dress, how you strive to be better every single day. I love your independence and how you cuddle when you sleep."

Zoey let out a watery laugh and pulled Mina closer. She let go of one of Mina's hands so she could run the backs of her fingers along Mina's cheek. Mina leaned into the touch and sighed softly.

"Mina Hasanza, I love you too. And I'm sorry it took me so long to say it."

Mina searched her eyes as if she could hardly dare to believe it, so Zoey leaned in and emphasized her words with a kiss so tender, she felt it in the tips of her toes. She had planned to list the ways she loved Mina, but Mina kissed her so hard, she almost knocked Zoey over.

Zoey laughed as Mina held her up with an arm around her waist. "Whoa there, cowboy."

"I love you, Zoey," Mina murmured against her lips. "And I've missed you so much."

When she leaned in again and explored Zoey's mouth with her tongue, Zoey returned her passion with fervor. "Inside?" she managed to say between kisses.

"Mm-hmm," Mina said. "I'll get the bouquet."

Before Zoey knew it, she was on her back on her couch with Mina hovering over her, showering her in kisses. Zoey giggled and slid her hands under Mina's shirt. She hadn't been able to imagine a reunion between them, much less one like this, but she wasn't at all upset about it.

"Your job was that bad, huh?" Zoey panted as Mina gently raked her teeth over her collarbone.

Mina growled playfully. "It was, and I'll tell you about it later. But right now, there are more important things to do."

"Definitely more important things."

She slid her hand around Zoey's back and undid the clasp of her bra. "Is this okay?"

Zoey arched into her. "More than okay."

As curious as she was about what had happened since they'd been apart, Zoey couldn't deny how her clit throbbed every time Mina touched her. They hadn't seen each other for far too long. She wanted her, and she wanted her *now*.

"More space on the bed," she said, pushing Mina off her. "Come on."

Mina followed her gleefully up the stairs, and for the next three hours, Zoey lost herself in a bliss she'd thought she'd never feel again.

EPILOGUE

MINA

OCTOBER — FOUR MONTHS LATER

Mina hefted the box of candles in her arms, feeling pleasantly tired. "Where do you want this?" she asked Zoey as she stepped through the door into their townhouse.

"The floor. I'll store it later. Right now, I want to veg."

Zoey had already flopped on the couch, the skirt of her orange dress patterned with black cats draped across her legs. She hadn't even taken off her boots.

Pumpkin Days had been extra busy this year—Mina hadn't seen that many people at the festival since she'd first moved to town. She and Zoey had been run off their feet, and Zoey's new fall collection practically flew off the table. Until this market, it had only been available on Granville Island, so the locals were downright vicious to get their hands on the comforting scents.

Mina fell onto the cushion next to Zoey, and Zelda jumped up to join them. She pushed her head into Mina's hand for pets, a purr already rumbling through her fuzzy little body.

"Did you check the numbers?" Mina asked.

"Mm-hmm." Zoey didn't move her body but let her head fall sideways to look at Mina. "They're pretty damn good."

"They are?"

"Yep. We set a record!"

"Oh my god, congrats, babe!" Mina wanted to swing Zoey around, but she couldn't muster the energy. Instead, she leaned down and pressed a gentle kiss to Zoey's forehead. "I'm proud of you. First you're selling candles in multiple shops in Vancouver, and now you've set a record! You're on a roll."

Zoey closed her eyes and hummed in pleasure, her mouth curled in a tiny, satisfied smile. "What about you?" she asked, cracking an eye. "You've got a whole-ass video game coming out next year."

Mina rolled her eyes. "I keep telling you, it's not really *my* game. I'm just working on it." Joel had reached out to her shortly after she moved back to Juniper Creek. He had a friend starting an indie game company in Vancouver and was looking for a character artist. Their first game was a cozy story-driven fantasy story about a mouse adventurer. Much more Mina's style than Sawed-Off had been. Plus, she could do most of her work remotely.

"Yeah, but that's still fucking amazing." Zoey reached over and squeezed Mina's thigh.

"We're *both* fucking amazing," Mina said.

"Okay, fine. We are. I'm also fucking hungry."

"Same. Pizza?"

Zoey's answer was more of a groan than a coherent word. "Please."

Mina dug her phone out of her pocket and ordered a large pizza and breadsticks. By the time she was done, Zoey had already put *Schitt's Creek* on the TV. They cuddled until the food got there then stuffed themselves so full, Mina felt like she might never move again.

Except she wanted tea, and unfortunately it wouldn't make itself. "Tea?" she asked, hauling herself to her feet.

"Have I ever told you how much I love you?" Zoey replied.

Mina raised her eyebrows and looked fondly at her girlfriend. "Once or twice."

"Good, because I do!" Zoey called after her as she walked to the kitchen.

Mina grabbed her samovar from its spot on the counter. As much as Zoey loved her orange mugs, Mina had convinced her to buy a set of clear ones specifically for tea. "It's the true Persian way," she'd said, and Zoey had relented.

While the water boiled, Mina went through the familiar and comforting motions of making tea exactly the way she liked it. Tea leaves, check. Two crushed cardamom pods, check. Three dried rosebuds and a couple of saffron threads, check. Now all she had to do was wait.

She leaned against the counter, and movement through the kitchen window drew her gaze. A family of three from the Philippines lived in the neighboring townhouse now, and all of them sat at the table, eating ice cream. The son, a chubby toddler with the cutest curls, had ice cream smeared all over his face, and his parents were giggling at him.

Mina chuckled too. It had taken her a while to get used to seeing other people living in the place that had been hers for years. For the entire first month that she lived with Zoey, a pang had shot through her whenever she saw strangers walking around through the kitchen window.

But she was okay with it now. That house had been her home for one chapter of her life, but now she was in another chapter. A much better one.

Her phone chimed, interrupting her reflections.

YASMIN

Are we still video calling tomorrow?

FARRAH

Of course! Mina?

MINA

Yeah, I'm still down

YASMIN

Great! I need opinions on a dress for a
company dinner next week.

Another thing Mina preferred about this chapter of her life:
She and her sisters had established weekly video calls, and Baba
and Maman joined them sometimes. Since Mina's outburst at
dinner months ago, her mother had been conspicuously quiet and
careful at these family visits. It was a good start to what would
likely be a long road of shifting the boundaries in their relationship.

Zoey padded into the kitchen, barely picking up her feet.
"What's taking so long?" she asked, pouting adorably.

Mina opened her arms and Zoey stepped into them, resting
her head on Mina's shoulder. The smell of her vanilla perfume
and her coconut shampoo washed over Mina—one of her favorite
scents in the world.

"Sorry, I got distracted by the family chat. Just confirming
we're on for tomorrow."

Zoey kissed her cheek then poured their tea, eyeing the dark-
ness of the drink. "Is this strong enough?"

"I think so. Want to take it to bed?"

"Can we cuddle on the couch a bit longer? Climbing stairs is
so much effort."

"I feel that."

They settled on the couch together with their tea, Mina's legs
on Zoey's lap.

Her phone chimed yet again, this time with a Discord notification from Declan. She glanced at it but ignored it. As much as
she enjoyed video games, she wanted to spend this evening with
the woman she loved.

And to think . . . they'd started out as neighbors.

Now they were each other's everything.

WANT MORE JUNIPER CREEK?

Sign up for Brenna Bailey's newsletter so you'll never miss a new release! You'll also get a free, exclusive short story with your newsletter subscription.

Get your free short story now!

AUTHOR'S NOTE

I hope you enjoyed Zoey and Mina's love story!

No matter what you thought of *And They Were Neighbors*, please help your fellow readers by leaving a review on social media and your favorite reading platforms and stores. Reviews are hugely important for getting books in the hands of the right readers. Cheers!

ACKNOWLEDGMENTS

It takes a community to produce a book, and there are so many people I want to thank for helping me put together Mina and Zoey's story.

As I was writing this book, I attended the When Words Collide 2024 conference and heard the amazing Jessica Johns talk about what it means to be a treaty person and how to bring a mindset of reciprocity to your writing. I'm still learning how to do that, but I know I can start by thanking the land I live on and the Indigenous peoples who have made their homes here since time immemorial and continue to live here. I live in Moh'kinsstis, also known as Calgary, which is on the Treaty 7 territory of Southern Alberta. This is the traditional land of the Blackfoot Confederacy—the Siksika, Kainai, and Piikani; the Tsuut'ina; and the îethka Nakoda Nations—Chiniki, Bearspaw, and Goodstoney. It is also home to the Otipemisiwak Métis Government of the Métis Nation within Alberta Districts 5 and 6. The book itself is set in the fictional town of Juniper Creek in the Fraser Valley, which is on the traditional, ancestral, and unceded territory of the Stó:lō Coast Salish peoples. Most of us don't pay enough attention to where we live and how the land supports us, and it is in all of our best interests to shift to a mindset of bioregionalism—the practice of living in harmony with nature and our local communities.

Now to mention a few specific and significant people who I am incredibly thankful for!

My best friends and alpha readers, Phoebe and Steph, y'all

mean the world to me and I am so grateful that you've stuck by me for this long.

Trisha Jenn Loehr, you pushed through multiple difficult things to do my manuscript evaluation, and I love you to the moon and back.

My beta readers—Molly Rookwood, Todd Aasen, and Jacquelynn Lyon—each of you brought something significant to this book that changed it for the better, and it would not exist in this form without you. I am eternally thankful for your insights and feedback!

Parisa Akhbari, I was starstruck when you said you'd be an authenticity reader for me. You are a shining star, and I highly value every suggestion you gave me. You led me to Sabaa Tahir's *All My Rage*, and you encouraged me to think deeper about Mina's family and their motivations. Your feedback let to a more nuanced story that I hope rings true.

Reader, if you'd like to read Own Voices Iranian stories, I highly recommend looking up the following authors: Parisa Akhbari, Adib Khorram, Kaveh Akbar, Abdi Nazemian, Marjan Kamali, Porochista Khakpour, Annahid Dashtgard, and Marjane Satrapi.

Jessica Renwick, my copyeditor extraordinaire, thank you for pouring your heart into this right before your wedding! Thank you for catching all my new crutch phrases and making me a better writer. You've become a dear friend, and I love you immensely.

Enni from Yummy Book Covers, thank you for creating the most gorgeous and perfect cover! You brought Zoey and Mina to life.

Talena Winters, thank you once again for your blurb expertise. I don't know how you do what you do, but you do it well!

Buckets of gratitude as well to my family and friends, including Jennifer Lindsay and Simone D. Sallé. Every single one of you encouraged me and boosted me in some way, and I can't express how much your support means to me.

That goes for you as well, reader! I write partially for myself, but mostly I write for you. Thank you for picking up *And They Were Neighbors*. Thank you for giving me the time of day and reading something that somehow came from my brain. You are a gem.

Finally, thank you to the love of my life, Orin. You get to see the behind-the-scenes mess of my writing process in all its glory, and you're still happy to be married to me. That's an achievement, truly. I love you.

A huge thank you to my Kickstarter backers for getting the special edition of this book out in the world!

Shout-out to my early-bird backers: Bonnie A. Welch, Jenna Albert, Vara S., Talia Lippke, Sheri Wise, my favourite aunty of all time! (hehe), Sarah S., Naomi B, Jessica Renwick, Molly Rookwood, Deborah, Kel Pendreki, Rachel W, Rachel Simpson, Taylor Riley, Loki Wylde, Kara Frazier, Liesbeth, Simone K., Aerin Caley, Rose Evans, Dr. Andy Lynn, Maddie, Tracy Fox, Trisha Jenn Loehr, Nessa W, Simone D. Sallé, Sam Keir, Chelsea Pennington, Paris J., and Sydney Boles.

I appreciate you all so much!

Image Description: Photo of Brenna smiling at the camera. She is a white woman with curly blond hair and glasses, and she's wearing a blue shirt. End of description.

Brenna Bailey writes queer contemporary romance and owns an editing business called Bookmarten Editorial. If her nose isn't buried in a book, you can probably find her out in the woods somewhere admiring plants or attempting to identify birds. She is a starry-eyed traveler and a home baker, and she lives in Calgary, Alberta, with her game-loving spouse and their cuddly fur-baby.

instagram.com/brennabaileybooks